BANISH THE DRAGON
BY
D.L. ROBINSON

Published by
Mélange Books, LLC
White Bear Lake, MN 55110
www.melange-books.com

Banish The Dragon, D. L. Robinson, Copyright © 2011
ISBN 978-1-61235-008-0

Credits

Editor: Nancy Schumacher
Copy Editor: Taylor Evans
Format Editor: Mae Powers
Cover Artist: Caroline Andrus

BANISH THE DRAGON
D.L. ROBINSON

Forced to choose an English bride, Simon Radcliffe marries the beautiful Katherine Maguire but it's his cousin Jonathan who saves Katherine, time and again, from ravishment. Months later, the marriage annulled, Katherine travels from Seven Oaks Plantation to Carlyle, New York, where she finds love and Jonathan Radcliffe, slayer of dragons.

dandana@shaw.ca

About the Author

Ms. Robinson is married to her high school sweetheart, has two children and two grandchildren. The author feels that what the world needs is to curl up with a cup of tea and a good book. What could be more diverting than a romance, especially in these troubled times – could that be thought of as literary comfort food? She is currently at work on a second book – a Victorian era romance with a twist of suspense.

Website: http://risforromance.net

Blog: http://banishthedragon.blogspot.com/ http://risforromance.net

Chapter One

Two men met in a small village, too distant to be swallowed up by the ever-expanding city of London. The day, cold and gloomy, mirrored the mood of the two as together they approached the beckoning warmth of the alehouse. Pushing the heavy wooden door open, the two eyed those already gathered together for their evening pint and a chance to exchange views on the vagaries of life. An inviting fire crackled in the hearth, the flames dancing wildly as a small gust of wind blew across the room at the opening of the portal.

A momentary lull in a myriad of conversations fell over the smoke-filled room as the shorter of the two strangers stepped hesitantly inside, pausing briefly in the doorway. Good-natured glances containing only mild curiosity were directed at the new arrivals, for the villagers were accustomed to travelers halting temporarily in their quiet hamlet. Finding nothing noteworthy about either, the villagers soon returned to the business of enjoying their ale and the camaraderie of their fellow merrymakers.

Lord Talbot, a portly figure of a man, stepped forward into the dimly lit room, brushing fussily at the droplets of rain on his woolen cloak. A ruddy complexion overpowered his thinning ginger-colored hair and wispy moustache. Pale eyes swept the room, seeking a private corner and, upon spying such a nook, haughtily beckoned the daunting figure who waited, unmoving, behind him. He struck out across the room, weaving his way through the closely packed benches and tables until he reached the corner he sought, hoping the whole distasteful business could be conducted without interruption.

Tall and imposing, the second man lingered in the doorway a moment before following his companion. He absently used his hat to brush away the raindrops that still clung to his cloak, revealing a head of blond curls and an arrogant expression on his handsome face, dominated by cold blue eyes. He surveyed his surroundings and, finding nothing untoward, crossed the room, carrying himself with an air of nonchalant grace. Broad shoulders and long legs completed the picture of a man not to be trifled with.

The remoteness of their scarred table discouraged the rowdier patrons from attempting to join their hushed conversation, should any of them have been so inclined, and both men felt safeguarded from anyone imprudent enough to eavesdrop. A nod to the tavern keeper soon had a bottle of wine delivered to their table by a buxom barmaid who, although long past the age of comeliness, still entertained a distant hope of earning a shilling or two from either of the two richly garbed gentlemen. Coins were paid for the bottle and the disappointed barmaid was curtly dismissed as the two fell into earnest conversation, oblivious to the raucous din of the room.

The older of the two peered apprehensively at the younger man, nervously licking his thin, dry lips before speaking.

"Now sir, I have spoken to my wife and she, well, let me just say only that she went into transports of joy when I explained your dilemma." The blond head nodded slightly but offered no other encouragement. Stuttering nervously, Lord Talbot continued. "I told her only of your urgent need of a wife. I, ah, well, I made no mention of how we came to meet—nor shall I. And I am trusting you, sir, on your word as a gentleman, to return my markers, discretely mind you, once the marriage vows are spoken."

Having finished speaking, Lord Talbot mopped his damp brow with a wrinkled handkerchief. His face had taken on an even pinker hue than the one he normally exhibited, and through thinning strands of hair, beads of perspiration could be seen, despite the relative coolness of their poorly lit corner. His pudgy fingers toyed nervously with wispy strands of his moustache as he waited on the younger man's reply.

The blond head, after slight deliberation, wordlessly nodded his agreement. In the dim light, Lord Talbot could barely discern the younger man's eyes, but as he had already gazed into their icy blue depths in a London gaming room four days prior, he was reluctant to be regarded again in so chilling a manner. Again mopping his brow, he leaned back, satisfied with the precise presentation of his proposal, having rehearsed it repeatedly on the long ride from Marlow Court to the city. He had suffered a sense of panic when at first he couldn't locate the man but as the day progressed, he had chanced upon the Yankee's cousin, who had directed him onward, and now here they were and the deal was all but done.

The younger man spoke, quietly but with the assurance that his words would be heeded.

"You do understand my terms, Lord Talbot? The girl must be unencumbered by kin, no matter how distant the connection. I'll have no long-lost aunt or cousin knocking at my door in either the near or distant future, seeking my financial assistance so they might live out their mundane lives in comfort, with no effort on their part."

"Yes, yes, my dear sir, I do assure you the girl is an orphan—totally alone in the world." He cleared his throat nervously, annoyed at the ominous threat the man seemed to exert over him, and continued, "Why, it was only when I returned home these two days past that I learned my Uncle Hector's widow had died. I arrived just in time to attend the burial and it was lucky I did. My tenants would have held such an affront against me and I need their support if I am to rebuild the fortunes of the estate." He paused as he gathered his thoughts.

"You see, sir, the property was entailed and as the closest male heir, I am now Lord Granville Talbot of Marlow Court." He smiled weakly before continuing, sensing that the Yankee was unimpressed with either his title or his holdings. "I felt I had to show deference to the villagers on the loss of their beloved lady and to ensure them that the future of her great-niece, even though the girl, who is no kin of mine, was being looked after." He paused as he poured the last of the wine into his glass. "It was at that precise moment, sir, standing by her grave, that I recalled your conversation from our previous meeting and knew the sound I was hearing was opportunity knocking." Again he dabbed at the beads of perspiration that had formed on his brow.

"The girl's parents apparently died of some pestilence years ago in Ireland, leaving their only child an orphan. At that point in time, she had only one relative in the world, her great aunt, Maude, my Uncle Hector's wife. The girl's parents had lived in relative obscurity in their crumbling manor, almost penniless and living hand-to-mouth, and what little was left of their estate went toward paying off debts. The village priest, seizing the chance to rid his parish of unwanted baggage, packed the girl off to England posthaste. Hector and Maude, who were childless by the way, cheerfully took her in, raising her as if she were their own beloved daughter."

The man rambled on, his companion listening absently. "Uncle Hector did not appear to begrudge the addition to his household. Since the death of their only child, a son, these many years past, the two of them have simply rattled aimlessly around the manor, taking little interest in the land or the village until this piece of Irish baggage arrived. In his correspondence with my father, Uncle Hector claimed the girl was just the breath of fresh air he and Lady Maude needed. Although my inheritance was secure, the doddering old fool lived years longer than he should have before departing this world.

"Now, as to her lack of dowry, sir. My uncle was not the wisest of managers and consequently nothing was put aside in the way of coin for the girl's future. I might be able to manage a small purse but with all the expenses in recent months, it would be very modest indeed. As I've already made clear, the girl is no kin of mine and I feel no responsibility for her. Truth be told, Mr. Radcliffe, she's been a thorn in my side since our arrival at Marlow Court." Looking up, he hoped he hadn't spoken too freely, giving the man cause to have second thoughts. Hoping to entice him further, he carried on, "I must admit, sir, the girl is a rare beauty. I suspect this is the reason my wife is so eager to be rid of her."

He sighed deeply. "Our union has been blessed with both a son and a daughter, making my wife's worries two-fold. Firstly that our son, who is obviously smitten by the girl, dreams of claiming her for his wife, a disaster not to be borne according to my Hester." He took a long drink, wiping his mouth fastidiously with an already stained corner of his sleeve before resuming his narrative. "And secondly, as long as such a comely maid resides in our village, no suitor from the surrounding countryside will come seeking our daughter's hand, for once a man lays eyes on the Irish lass, no dowry would likely be large enough to attract an offer of marriage for our Fiona."

Admitting such worries to a stranger made Lord Talbot feel disloyal to his family but knew he'd see the truth of things soon enough when he claimed his bride.

"Rest easy, Lord Talbot. The lack of a dowry is of no concern to me. And if she causes me trouble, well, I believe I am capable of managing my as yet unmet young bride."

Lord Talbot leaned back, again pulling at strands of his moustache. He pushed the twinge of conscience he was feeling to the back of his mind, refusing to dwell on what fate he might be sentencing an innocent and defenseless girl to. No matter, it was none of his concern he silently argued with himself. The girl would travel to the Yankee's home, far away from England and his own peaceful hearth; at least it would be peaceful once the chit was gone. And she wouldn't be in need, judging from the quality of the garments this American wore.

Pushing his chair back, the elder of the two stood, swaying ever so slightly, having drained the contents of the bottle almost single-handedly. "I must be away, sir, if I hope to reach Marlow Court this night."

"Lord Talbot?" The Yankee stood, dwarfing the rotund figure, forcing him to look up at him, a necessity Lord Talbot had come to despise. "I have business to attend to in the morning and so will leave London sometime in the afternoon. My cousin, Jonathan Radcliffe, will be accompanying me. I would have the marriage vows spoken the following morning, and the three of us will depart immediately after. I realize it will not be the wedding that a young girl dreams of but to do more would be a travesty, do you not agree, milord?"

The shorter man nodded his head in silent agreement.

The two donned their cloaks and hats, their departure causing as little stir amongst the other patrons as their arrival had. Walking in silence in the misty drizzle toward Lord Talbot's carriage, the younger man touched the brim of his hat in a curt gesture of farewell before continuing on to the stable where his own horse waited. As the softly falling rain turned into a downpour, Simon Radcliffe huddled at the stable entrance. He allowed his thoughts to wander, not to his as yet unknown bride but to the only woman he would ever love and who even now waited patiently for him to return to her side and a lifetime together with none to say them nay.

* * * *

As Simon lingered in the doorway waiting for the deluge to stop, an unbearable wave of longing swept over him as he recalled the last time he had seen Juliana. She had been magnificent that day, furiously pacing the confines of her bedchamber, putting him in mind of some fierce ancient female warrior as she ranted in angry tirades about the unfairness of life, and cursing the unforgiving nature of his grandfather. Her beautiful breasts had bounced with each step taken, her waist curving alluringly inward, full hips tapering into long, shapely legs, satiny skin tempting him to reach out and touch it. Her face was regally, arrogantly beautiful, eyes darkening dangerously. Her unbound flaxen tresses had tumbled carelessly down her back. Her nature was volatile but Simon counted that as part of her charm, knowing he would never be bored by such a woman.

He had watched her hungrily as she strode the length of the room, lace curtains fluttering each time she passed the windows, unconcerned that she hadn't a stitch on. And after all, who would dare enter Juliana's chamber uninvited? No visitor certainly, and there were only a handful of slaves left on what had once been a rich, thriving plantation, yet another reason for her to hate Samuel Langtree. Simon mused that if the old man hadn't been so vindictive over a trifling slur spoken so long ago, real or imagined, Juliana's father might still be alive and managing a successful plantation. Instead, his heart had failed and she had inherited a small plot of land on which stood the home she been born in but was now rapidly turning into a house desperately in need of skilful carpentry and a coat of paint.

She had paused in her rage and gazed down at him, his nudity casually covered by a white cotton sheet. "Simon, while you continue to knuckle under to that old man, I've been planning our future." She fell onto the bed, calculatingly nuzzling his neck in a way that drove him to distraction, knowing that she needed him to be not only compliant but a willing participant in the undertaking she was about to propose. And it was a plan not without risk. As he hungrily reached for her, she slapped his hand playfully, bouncing off the bed and crossed the room, out of his reach. Speaking sharply, she commanded him to sit up and listen, for if this gambit failed, there would be no hope for a future together. Recognizing the threat in her words, he wrapped the sheet modestly around himself and moved to a small chair, warily nodding for her to continue.

"Your grandfather threatens that, if you don't immediately set sail for England in search of a bride, a proper English one, not only will you inherit nothing but he will have succeeded in his desire to thwart our wish to wed, for we would both be penniless, a state neither of us could ever be happy with." She paused, collecting her thoughts before continuing. "Well, what if you follow his decree but change it slightly to suit you? Strike a bargain with him that you will accede to his demands but if the opportunity ever arises for a second marriage, it will be to one of your own choosing, and it will be with his blessing."

At his puzzled look, she perched on the bed, her eyes sparkling with excitement. "What if you indeed seek out such a bride but with a stipulation that he would know nothing about? Find an orphan, a nobody, with no family whatsoever, and no chance of anyone seeking her out, ever!" She paused, trying to gauge his reaction before continuing, her arm thrown dramatically across her forehead. "Wed her, have it witnessed that you bedded her, and then, as you're sailing home, tragedy strikes! She's swept overboard." Breathless, she stopped speaking, anxiously awaiting his reaction.

Blue eyes widened in astonishment as he considered her scheme. Stunned, he could only gape at her, slack-jawed.

"Juliana," he whispered, "What you're proposing is murder!"

Simon, stunned, sat back and crossed his legs, turning his thoughts deeply inward. He wasn't a religious man but he feared the threat an omnipotent god posed, sitting in judgment on him when he had breathed his last. And surely murder would send him to hell! But looking across the room at Juliana, Simon knew he would find hell right here on earth if he couldn't spend his life with her.

She rushed to him, crushing her breasts against his naked chest, smothering his protesting lips with hot, feverish kisses. "No, no, my darling Simon, not murder," she whispered conspiratorially, "consider that this poor waif, alone in the world, would most likely welcome the opportunity to rejoin her parents, who, having sadly departed this world, are awaiting her in the next."

He paused, weighing her words. "How am I to bring about this chance wave sweeping her overboard? I don't relish being a victim of shipboard justice."

"Hire a sailor to do the actual deed, my love. I'm sure that, once aboard, you'll soon find at least one such creature, a man willing to do anything for a coin or two."

With her plan laid out before him, she was suddenly unsure that she could bend him to her will and so she had lured him back to her bed and soon, in the throes of his passion, he had eagerly agreed to all she desired. And now here he was, in England and on his way to fulfilling the first part of Juliana's plan. Shaking his head in wonder that he ever agreed to be a party to such an undertaking, he mounted his horse, ignoring the rain that continued to fall as he made his way back to his room.

* * * *

The clock had just struck the hour when the carriage door creaked open and Lord Talbot sleepily ascended. The heavy door of the manor swung open as he tiredly mounted the steps and the formidable figure of his wife stepped out, holding a candle to light the way. "Well Granville, what news?" Her tone was harsh and demanding. "Were you able to find the Yankee? Has an agreement been reached?"

Motioning toward the driver who continued to stand within earshot, he shook his head warningly. "Not now, my dear. Let us retire to our chamber where we will be assured privacy and I promise to recount all details of my journey. And have some food sent up, for I am much famished. Why, if you can believe it, I haven't eaten since I set out this morning." This last was spoken with some degree of surprise for Lord Talbot never willingly missed a meal.

A hovering servant was dispatched to fetch whatever was readily available from the kitchen while the couple silently climbed the wide, curving staircase.

If Granville Talbot cut a comical figure with his lack of height, balding head atop a portly frame and mottled complexion testifying to his fondness for liquor, his wife was the complete opposite. Hers' was a figure of epic proportions, taller than her husband by several inches and large framed, her bosom enormous but restrained beneath her gown, hips wide and swaying. Unsightly frizzled brown hair streaked generously with grey was pulled back into a tight knot; small close-set dark eyes peered suspiciously out at the world and its inhabitants, her face an unbecoming shade of pink, wearing a perpetually dissatisfied look. Thin lips seemed always to be pursed in an expression of contempt for those beneath her socially and, it was gossiped around the servants' dining table, that since her arrival at Marlow Court, not one of them had received a kind word or witnessed even the most fleeting of smiles across her countenance, unless such a happening was directed at either of her children.

The two entered their bedchamber with few words exchanged between them. Lord Talbot strode to the fireplace and laid another log on the dying embers, chasing the bone-chilling dampness from the chamber. Lady Talbot crossed the room and drew the heavy draperies across the windows, shutting out the gloomy night. A hesitant knock signaled the arrival of the much-anticipated meal and, with a nod from her mistress, the servant set the laden tray on a small table and hastily departed.

With the closing of the door, the tirade began. Lady Talbot paced the confines of the room as she unrelentingly peppered her husband with questions while he tucked into a chunk of roast beef. Tearing hungrily into the meat, he impatiently motioned to a chair opposite his.

"Hester, do sit down!" he snapped. "You weary me with your ceaseless treading about the room and never-ending questions. I'll tell you everything but I beg of you, let me eat."

Taken aback by his sharp tone, she sat down heavily, harrumphing her displeasure but daring to say no more at present. Clasping her hands tightly together lest they reveal the impatience she was suffering, she sipped occasionally from the wine he had poured her as she waited for his appetite to be appeased. Eventually, he pushed his empty plate away and sat back, replete, his wine close to hand. He recited the events of the day as well as he could recall, and the two contemplated the anticipated outcome.

Suddenly Lady Hester shot out of her chair. Shifting impatiently, she fixed her flashing eyes on the drooping lids of her husband's. "The girl! We must see to the girl now, without delay!"

Stunned, her husband raised his tired eyes questioningly at the virago to whom he was wed. "Why must we do anything? The Yankee said he wasn't leaving the city until sometime tomorrow afternoon...and the girl knows nothing of our plan." Folding his arms, he continued to sit contentedly before the fire, unwilling to stir from his cozy nest.

"You fool," she spat out caustically, "Have you forgotten the uncanny ability of the servants to know exactly what is happening in any great household before an announcement is ever made? How long before one of them learns of our little plan and decides to enlighten her?" Casting a last withering glare at her husband whose eyes were now closed in sleep, she stormed from the room. Calling loudly for her cloak and her trusted manservant Larkin, she clattered thunderously down the stairs. Both were waiting by the time she had gained the bottom of the staircase.

Wrapping her cloak snugly about her bulk to ward off the damp evening, Lady Talbot gestured imperiously for her servant to follow her as she swept through the doorway. Larkin, a barrel-chested man followed swiftly on short, muscular legs, adjusting his stride so he followed rather than led. The wind gusted about them, nearly lifting Larkin's stained hat from his head of dark, unkempt hair. Heavy eyebrows hovered above his eyes, merging into one continuous hairy line above a crooked nose and thick lips. Dark eyes glared balefully at the figure ahead of him.

The pair cautiously made their way along the wet, slippery path toward a tiny, dilapidated cottage nestled at the edge of the village. What had once been the gatekeeper's abode in more prosperous times had become a refuge for the former chatelaine of the manor, Lady Maude and her great-niece Katherine, following Lord Hector's death. The newly arrived Lord Granville and Lady Hester Talbot had straight away established a new order. There had been much whispering in the village concerning the callous treatment of Lady Maude but Granville Talbot, to escape his wife's constant badgering, had hastily let it be known that anyone not happy with the way of things could leave his land that very day. The grumbling had gradually stopped but there was no warmth in any greeting extended by the villagers to the new residents of the manor. After all, they reasoned, hadn't Lady Maude been there and taken care of them all these many years, but they were cautious all the same, unwilling to risk the ire of their new lord or his lady.

Upon reaching the doorway, Lady Talbot, panting breathlessly, motioned for Larkin to announce her presence. The burly servant knocked once and, without invitation entered, startling the three women who sat at the rickety wooden table. His deep voice seemed to rattle the very rafters of the cottage as he announced the arrival of his mistress, who swept imperiously into the room. Ignoring the two middle-aged women whom she recognized as wives of her tenant farmers, she fixed her malevolent gaze on the youngest of the cottage's occupants, who sat gawking in open-mouthed disbelief at this uninvited and most unexpected caller, especially at this late hour.

Rising from her chair, Katherine Maguire glared challengingly at the unwelcome intruder. Under gracefully curving eyebrows and thick dark lashes, her eyes flashed icy emerald fire as she faced Lady Talbot. A rich cloud of auburn hair framed her face, tumbling carelessly down her slender back. Her facial bones were delicately carved, her nose daintily up-turned, with a creamy peach-tinted complexion, blending with the dusky glow of her cheekbones.

Lips were full and lush over small white teeth. So exquisite were her features that one observing her for the first time might be forgiven for failing to notice a chin that promised iron determination.

Her figure was willowy slender, and though she was slightly taller than most of the women in the village, she still lacked inches when facing her nemesis, Lady Hester Talbot. Slim arms bent as if ready to do battle with this most evil of dragons, she raised her chin defiantly, desperately assuming all the dignity she could muster.

"Ah, Katherine, do forgive my impromptu visit but it is most imperative that I speak to you at once." Her voice, almost a purr, had an ominous quality to it. Turning to Katherine's guests who continued to stare at the intruders, she motioned for them to depart, a suggestion that did not need repeating as they hastily scrambled for the door, throwing apologetic glances at the girl before fleeing into the black night.

Larkin, stepping aside as they fled the cottage, repositioned himself in front of the door as it closed, folding his thick arms across his chest menacingly. Shifting uncomfortably, he watched as his mistress circled the room, feeling a momentary twinge of sympathy for the lass. He had witnessed many of Lady Talbot's savage attacks on the undefended and helpless over the years but fear of losing his position had always prevented him from interfering.

Katherine, eyes flashing threateningly, stormed up to her unwanted visitor, heedless of the precariousness of her position. "What do you mean, barging into my home, uninvited, and dismissing my guests who were only here to lend what comfort they could on the loss of my beloved aunt?"

Lady Talbot, looking down at the slight girl who faced her so fearlessly, smirked knowingly, causing a shiver of apprehension to course down Katherine's spine. "Tush, my girl, don't bother putting on airs with me." Her tone was chilling. "I come bearing the most welcome tidings to you—an Irish guttersnipe, someone who has no dowry and absolutely no prospects, and this is your way of thanking me."

Startled, Katherine's eyes, still sparkling with barely contained anger, gazed warily at the older woman. "What are you going on about, Lady Talbot?"

"Why, I'm referring to your wedding, of course." A shocked gasp escaped from the girl, making the older woman gloat in satisfaction. The little chit's reaction was so much better than anything she had imagined. Almost trembling with glee, her arms swept the room. "Gather what belongings you have, girl, you're moving back to the manor for the remainder of your time here."

Chapter Two

Katherine stared at the older woman in stunned disbelief. Larkin, noting her sudden pallor and, convinced she was about to faint, stepped forward, rousing Katherine into watchful awareness. Peering up at Lady Talbot's flushed face, she questioned the woman demandingly. "What are you saying? You can't force me to marry anyone—you have no authority over me."

An amused chuckle escaped the pursed lips of the lady of the manor. "Why, Katherine, we are in fact most concerned about your future. Is this your thanks after Lord Talbot has gone to so much trouble to find a suitable husband for you?" Her words were spat out contemptuously. "And, my dear girl, it's my understanding that you have so far refused any offer of marriage that has been made for you. Your aunt and uncle were far, far too indulgent where you were concerned."

The woman's barely concealed sarcasm sparked her anger and, attempting to demonstrate a bravado that she was far from feeling, Katherine spoke in hushed tones. "My aunt and uncle wanted me to love the man I married." Her voice faded to a broken whisper. "I just haven't found him yet."

'Well, search no more girl, for your prince has been found and he arrives tomorrow to claim you," Lady Talbot spoke, her voiced filled with heavy sarcasm. "You will wed the following morning."

Wordlessly Katherine collapsed onto a much mended but still very wobbly chair. Glancing about the poorly lit room, she speculated on her chance of successfully escaping from the clutches of these two odious creatures that stood watching her, her shoulders slumped in temporary defeat.

Taken aback by the ease of her victory, Lady Talbot glanced about the shabby room, her eyes quickly passing over the neatly made narrow bed and the tidiness of the cottage. She had expelled the former chatelaine and her niece from the manor but the two had weathered that particular storm and, until the old woman's death, had emerged seemingly unscathed from their trials and tribulations. As her eyes again swept the room, she spoke in a voice that would brook no further argument.

"Gather your belongings, girl. As I have already stated, you'll spend this night and the next at the manor. Now do try to smile, Katherine, and act the part of a bride eager to wed."

Despondently, Katherine gathered her few possessions. Before she and her aunt had been turned out of the manor, the greedy, grasping fingers of Lady Talbot had confiscated the best of their wardrobes, contending they would be sold to cover the cost of the food and rent for their new lodgings. Despite the fact that the estate was entailed and could only go to the nearest surviving male heir, Lord Hector's will had stipulated that should his beloved Maude survive him, she was to be cared for until the end of her days on this earth. Unfortunately, he had been too trusting and had not explicitly spelled out how this was to be accomplished, a fact the new Lady Talbot had been quick to seize on.

As Katherine moved about the room, she again mused why she and her aunt hadn't fled when they had the opportunity. Katherine could have found employment of some kind and supported them both. But Aunt Maude had been bound to the manor by silken bonds of love and loyalty, and simply could not bear the thought of being buried anywhere but beside her beloved Hector. And so the two had remained, abused and humiliated by the new Lady of the Manor whenever the opportunity presented itself. Who knew that Aunt Maude would follow Uncle Hector so soon—and that on the morrow she would meet the man she was to wed, a man she knew nothing about. Tears coursed unheeded down her pale cheeks as she contemplated her chance of success if she should suddenly bolt but, on eyeing the stolid figure of Lady Hester's manservant planted unyieldingly before the door, she abandoned all thought of flight, at least temporarily.

Larkin shifted his bulk impatiently as he and his mistress watched Katherine's seemingly aimless wandering about the room. Stopping suddenly, she gazed at Lady Talbot who met her eyes unflinchingly. *All right, go with them I must, but should the opportunity to escape present itself, I will seize it.*

Squaring her shoulders, she closed the small trunk which now contained everything in the world that was hers. At a signal from his mistress, Larkin stepped forward, lifting the chest onto his shoulder as if it weighed nothing. Throwing open the flimsy door he stopped abruptly, allowing the two women to precede him into the dismal night. In grim silence the trio made their way cautiously up the slippery path toward the manor. None of them seemed to notice the rain that continued to fall.

As they approached the imposing brick building, the door flew open and two figures stepped out, peering curiously at the entourage as they mounted the stairs. Lady Talbot sighed in exasperation as she motioned them to step aside so she and her small party could gain the welcoming warmth of the hall, ushering her children and her unwilling guest into the sitting room where a fire blazed. Turning in the doorway, she spoke to a servant who nodded in understanding as she hurried off to do her mistress's bidding. Stepping back into the room, she closed the door and Larkin stationed himself in front of it, as much to block any attempt at escape from within as well as to forestall eavesdropping by curious servants.

* * * *

Glancing scornfully at Katherine who stood near the fire to warm her chilled bones, Fiona, cosseted daughter of the house, spoke petulantly, her voice grating on the nerves of her already tense parent.

"Mother, what have I been hearing about this bedraggled Irish chit? Has a husband indeed been found for her?"

Frizzy blond curls hung limply about her sallow-complexioned, homely face as she stared at Katherine, envy burning brightly in her eyes. She moved closer to the girl, unwittingly inviting comparison of her plump, sturdy figure which resembled more of the intimidating stature of her mother, set against that of the slender beauty that stood rigidly beside her—a graceful form with pert, up-tilted breasts, narrow waist and slim hips. A pudgy finger held up a strand of Katherine's rich auburn locks and, wet though it was, still left Fiona's blond curls looking wilted and dull. Pale eyes glared at Katherine, silently begrudging the girl her creamy complexion and stunningly perfect features.

A look of surprise had crossed Lady Talbot's countenance at her daughter's words. She demanded of both offspring how they had come to hear of this matter so quickly, her tone harsh and demanding. She glanced uneasily at her other child, Roland, a man grown but still her son. He stood gazing at Katherine in dismay.

"Fiona overheard the servants talking. You know how she's always creeping about, hoping to hear juicy bits of gossip. This time she definitely was not disappointed. So Mother, I will repeat Fiona's question, is it true?"

Lady Talbot faced her son, wishing once more that he had as robust and hearty a constitution as his sister. His was a slender build with thinning, straight blond hair, pale eyes peering nearsightedly up at her, for he, like his father, lacked the inches that might have given him more self-assurance when dealing with the opposite sex. Unlike his sister, he preferred books and poetry to horses and the sport of hunting. Lady Talbot, towering over him, gently lifted his chin so that she might study his beloved face. Sighing, she wished that she had been the one to break the news herself, for she had been aware for some time that he was besotted with Katherine and hoped to wed her himself. Lady Talbot, a doting and indulgent mother to both her children, smiled but mentally she shrugged. *He'll soon get over this* she thought, drawing both of them onto the deep cushions of the sofa that sat before the warmth of the fire, ignoring Katherine, who stood shivering beside Larkin.

Ignoring his mother's cloying grasp, Roland stood up and, pushing his hands deep into his pockets, began to stride furiously about the room, studiously avoiding Katherine.

"Roland, do sit down," his mother commanded imperiously. The icy tone soon brought about the desired result and he sank into a richly upholstered chair. Lady Talbot settled back onto the soft cushions of the settee. Fiona, unlike her brother, felt only relief knowing that the Irish witch would soon

16

vanish from the manor, the village and her life.

* * * *

Roland could not keep his eyes from resting on the one he coveted. His irritation grew at what he was sure was feigned indifference to him. Did the little fool not realize what her fate might be?

Not wanting to invite the girl into their cozy family circle, Lady Talbot raised her voice so Katherine could fully understand and appreciate what the future held for her.

"Your father, through his business dealings in the city, has met a man, a Yankee in fact, who is seeking a wife. Katherine meets his requirements exactly. A bargain was struck just a few short hours ago. Katherine's intended, a Mr. Simon Radcliffe along with his cousin, will arrive sometime late tomorrow afternoon. The wedding will take place the following morning. Immediately following the ceremony, the three will return to London and, it is my understanding, will set sail for Mr. Radcliffe's home before the month is out."

Roland propelled himself from the handsomely appointed chair and glared menacingly down at his mother. "What about me, Mother? I would marry her. I care nothing about her lack of dowry. Let Fiona marry the Yankee, or even his cousin. Just let me have Katherine for my own."

Flecks of spittle had appeared at the corners of his mouth during his impassioned plea and bright red circles colored his usually pale cheeks. He held his breath as he awaited his mother's reply. He hadn't planned on pleading his case so boldly but it was finally out in the open and he silently rejoiced that it was. He swallowed nervously as his mother arose, towering over him by inches. Despite having attained his twenty-first year two months ago, she could still make him quake inwardly as if he were a misbehaving child.

"Don't be a fool, Roland." Each word was spat out at him in derision. "You're meant for someone far grander than this penniless Irish trash! This little bogtrotter will soon set sail for distant shores, never to trouble our family again, and good riddance, I say."

Pausing for breath, the mother glared at her rebellious son, who stared back defiantly. An almost inaudible gasp was heard by all three and turning, saw that the subject of their conversation now lay in a motionless heap on the floor.

Roland, realizing the girl had fainted, made as if to go to her aid but his mother placed a restraining hand on his arm and forestalled him by motioning to Larkin, who raised an inquiring eyebrow at his mistress as he effortlessly lifted the unconscious girl.

"Take her to the small chamber off the library. I sent Bess to prepare it for our very temporary guest. Both windows in the chamber are too high to climb through, should the little fool take it into her head to try running. And Larkin, you're to guard her door until the vows have been spoken." His face expressionless, the servant nodded and quietly left the room, the burden he carried with such ease now his responsibility.

Frustrated with his failure to win his mother to his point of view, Roland followed the servant from the room and watched, heartbroken, as Larkin lumbered down the dimly lit hallway toward the library. Climbing the staircase to his own chamber, Roland slammed the door in mutinous frustration, the sound reverberating throughout the manor, lending testimony to his mood.

Shrugging her shoulders disdainfully at what she considered an immature and unflattering display of emotion, Lady Talbot met the eyes of her daughter, who had been waiting patiently for her mother's undivided attention.

"And what happens after she is gone, Mother? Will a husband finally be found for me?" Fiona twisted her hands together, a gesture revealing how very concerned she was with her own future.

Chucking her daughter affectionately under the chin, her mother smiled warmly. After all, everything was going so well. Roland would come around and in the end, he would be grateful to her for saving him from the fate he was convinced he desired. And Fiona, poor, plain Fiona, with the dowry they could provide, would find herself married before another year had passed.

"Go to bed, child. This day has been a strain and I would be alone to mull over these matters." With a nod to her mother, Fiona quietly departed, closing the door softly behind her.

Lady Talbot sighed as she poured a glass of wine for herself. *Children,* she thought, staring into the dying fire, *both a blessing and a burden. Roland will come to see the wisdom of my plan, and Fiona's dowry, with no comely maid to distract any offer of marriage, will soon bring eager suitors seeking her hand.* Taking a last sip of her wine, she continued to stare at the glowing embers, and after one last heavy sigh, left the sitting room to seek her own bed.

* * * *

Kicking the door open, Larkin crossed the room, unceremoniously dropping Katherine onto the freshly made bed. He knelt before the fireplace and soon coaxed the smoldering embers into a crackling fire, chasing the chill from the chamber. Looking up from his efforts, he saw Katherine staring wordlessly at him.

"So you be awake, miss. Now, don't ye cause any trouble for old Larkin or me mistress. Soon the whole business will be done with, so long as the groom don't forget to come and claim you." He chortled to himself, marveling at his wit, taking no notice of Katherine's pallor at the crude reminder of her future.

Rising, he brushed ashes from his hands and knees before turning toward the door. "Now, you behave yourself, girl. Lady Talbot is sending Peg to attend you until the time comes to speak your vows. She'll help you prepare for bed, and remember missy, I'll be right outside your door the whole time."

He opened the portal just as the maid, known to all as Peg, bustled in, her quick bird-like movements belying the weight of her many years spent in service to Lady Maude as her personal maid. Katherine, following her arrival from across the Irish Sea, had quickly been taken under her wing. Dismissing the burly Larkin with a brisk nod and disdainful sniff, the maid turned to her charge, temporary as that position might be. Wringing her hands helplessly, she faced the girl who by now had risen rather unsteadily from the bed.

"Oh, Miss Katherine, what misfortune has befallen you since Sir Hector died these many months past? And now you're to marry in two days time." Tears trickled down her wrinkled old cheeks, tears that the old woman dabbed at with a corner of her starched white apron. *And what would Lady Maude be thinking at this turn of events?* Flushing as she realized her remarks were upsetting her charge even more, she pressed her lips together, silently vowing to herself not to broach the subject again.

Katherine crossed the room and hugged the servant warmly. They both knew that no matter how much the maid might care for Katherine, her future, bleak though it might be, was tied to the manor and the Talbot family. She could ill afford to do anything but obey Lady Talbot, no matter how sorely it grieved her to see the lass come to this end.

The younger woman glanced curiously about the starkly furnished chamber. It was a cubbyhole of a room and had rarely been used for anything but storage until Uncle Hector, too ill to climb the stairs to his own bedchamber in his last months, had spent his final days in this room, close to his cherished books, with his beloved Maude nursing him. Katherine had spent many hours reading to him, sharing in his care until the end.

Wordlessly, Peg searched through Katherine's scant possessions until she found a threadbare nightgown and, in companionable silence, the older woman helped Katherine undress. A timid knock at the door announced the arrival of a servant bearing a tray of tea and fresh bread, something Peg had had the foresight to order as she made her way from her own quarters to this cheerless chamber. Katherine obediently sat at the small table, sipping the hot tea but, despite having had little in the way of food for the past two days, could not bring herself to do more than nibble half-heartedly at a crust.

"Ah well, sweeting, if you've no appetite, I won't be pestering you to eat. Come now, Miss Katherine, climb into bed and I'll tuck you in, just as I did when you were but a wee slip of a girl." She held up the covers invitingly and Katherine, exhausted from the day's events, lie down on the crisp white sheet and let the servant fuss over her as she nestled into her temporary bed.

Peg, moving silently about the room, glanced back and saw Katherine's eyes had closed in exhausted slumber. Opening the door and peering out, she spied Larkin snoring softly in a chair nearby, obviously settled in for the night. Whispering a quiet good night to the drowsing girl, she crept out, pulling the door shut before disappearing through the elaborately carved wooden doors of the library. Larkin, through eyes heavy with sleep, studied the old servant's retreating figure before arranging his oversized form in the undersized chair once more, sleeping fitfully through the night.

* * * *

The rattle of crockery roused Katherine from her slumber and, stretching her slender white arms, she slowly opened her eyes. One glance about the room quickly brought back the catastrophic events of the previous evening. Peg, seeing the girl stir, smiled warmly.

"Oh, lovie, I thought you might be feeling more like eating this morning. Now look here, Cook has even boiled you an egg, once I told her that you barely touched anything last night." Concern was reflected in her eyes and wrinkles again furrowed her brow. Not waiting for the girl to reply, she carried the tray over, setting it down on the small table that had once held Lord Hector's many potions and elixirs.

"Now, you stay in bed, Miss Katherine. There's a chill in the air and I've just added a log to the fire. Lady Talbot is taking no chances with your health, and has given her consent that you should be kept warm and cozy." She continued to bustle about the room, tidying and folding, unable to remain idle.

Bemused, Katherine glanced about at what was now her prison and, eyeing the tiny windows high up on the wall, tried to calculate her chance of escape if she could only find some way of reaching one of them. A deep, rumbling voice spoke from the doorway, invading her musings.

"'Tis no good you looking up there, miss. Her Ladyship has taken every precaution to see that no avenue of escape is left open to you and has ordered both windows nailed shut."

"Why Larkin, what makes you think I would contemplate running? After all, where would I run to? I am without coin and know almost no one beyond this village."

Sniffing disparagingly, she turned her back on her reluctant sentry and began to pick at the bread. Peg, determined to maintain the boundaries of propriety, quickly crossed the room and shooed the unwelcome intruder from her charge's boudoir. Giving the old woman a mocking salute, Larkin, having heard the welcome sound of his own breakfast tray being set down in the adjoining library, willingly allowed her to close the door on him.

The hours passed slowly as Katherine waited for the dreaded summons. With time hanging heavily on their hands, the two women set about refurbishing Katherine's meager wardrobe. The servant bustled in and out of the room, each time returning with a bit of lace or ribbon for embellishment of the frayed and shabby gowns. Both she and Peg agreed that the black gown, worn those past months of mourning for Uncle Hector and now for Aunt Maude, was more fitting for this evening and the yellow frock would be set aside for her wedding on the morrow. White lace was stitched around the neck and sleeves of the black gown, giving it a less somber appearance. They busily plied their needles, transforming both dresses into something not quite as threadbare and tattered as when they began. Each time the door swung open from one of Peg's forays, Larkin could be seen in the book-lined room, and Katherine knew he also waited for the summons from Lady Talbot.

A lunch tray was delivered just as the noon hour struck but Katherine took no notice of it, and it was only Peg asking if she wanted to faint from hunger in front of everyone that convinced her to nibble on a morsel of chicken. Her serenity was a fragile shell surrounding her, and she started at the distant sound of doors closing. Peg helped her don her refurbished gown, sighing regretfully that if only the pearls her aunt had worn on special occasions had gone to Katherine, it would enhance their needlework.

It was late afternoon when voices suddenly invaded the tiny chamber, carrying the dreaded summons in the person of Roland who, at his father's insistence, had been sent to escort her, appearing as anxious as Katherine felt. He stood, lost in silent longing and appreciation, as Katherine nervously patted her hair one last time before following him from her temporary prison, both aware that Larkin had fallen in behind them. The trio silently approached the closed doors of the drawing room and, as Roland's fingers reached for the doorknob, she began to quake inwardly. The fearful images she had built in her mind were about to be revealed and she could feel icy ribbons of fear twisting around her heart. The door swung quietly open and conversations ceased as the occupants of the room turned, some out of curiosity and others with ill-concealed malice.

Katherine, standing in the doorway, was unaware of the breathtaking picture she presented to the company assembled within. Lady Talbot strode forward, thus forestalling any further contact between Katherine and her son. The younger woman gasped softly as she beheld Lady Talbot flouncing toward her in a hideous purple gown, accented by the strands of pearls that had always been worn by the chatelaine of the manor, and her highly treasured emerald broach, a pin she was never seen without, testimony to her recently elevated social standing. Her magnificent bosom threatened to escape from the low décolletage of her gown, should she take it into her mind to breathe too deeply. Taking the girl's cold hand in her own, she led her across the room to where two strangers stood, silently contemplating the vision gliding gracefully toward them. The taller of the two stepped forward and bowed his blond head in a courtly gesture.

Lady Talbot spoke in an unfamiliar, simpering voice. "Katherine, may I present Simon Radcliffe, your intended."

Chapter Three

Removing her trembling hand from Lady Talbot's iron grip, Simon brought the slender fingers to his lips before releasing them back to their owner. As the regular patrons in the pub the previous day had noticed, he carried himself with a commanding air of self confidence, and she couldn't help thinking that here was one person Lady Hester Talbot would not be able to push about.

"Ah, Miss Maguire, we meet at last." His cool, impersonal tone broke the stillness, his lips twisting in a cynical smile. Katherine had to look up to meet his blue eyes that studied her most intently. She felt no warmth in his greeting and shivered apprehensively. Turning, Simon signaled the other man forward. "And this is my cousin and travelling companion, Jonathan Radcliffe."

Again Katherine's hand was taken as Jonathan's lips lightly caressed her slender fingers. She noted that there was little family resemblance between the two cousins, other than height, although Simon appeared a shade taller than his cousin. Where Simon had tawny-gold curling hair and blue eyes, Jonathan's hair was as black as the night and unruly, one lock seemed always to be falling forward across his brow. Warm grey eyes met the shifting emerald lights of her own, his arresting good looks totally capturing her attention whereas Simon's handsome face had a forbidding and cold haughtiness about it. Bowing slightly, Jonathan released her hand. Upon hearing his name called, a fleeting scowl crossed his face as he courteously excused himself and strode across the room with a careless grace to where Fiona, dressed in a most unbecoming bright pink creation that highlighted all manner of personal flaws, sat waiting for him at the piano. With an apologetic nod of his head, he turned his back to the assembled company, and stood patiently, turning the pages of her music as she stumbled through the piece she had been attempting to play just as Katherine had entered the room.

Simon and Katherine spoke quietly as they stood together in one corner of the room, much to the chagrin of Roland, who had concealed himself behind a large potted plant, studying them surreptitiously, a plan already forming in his distraught mind. He flushed as he caught his mother regarding him coldly and moved toward her, not wanting her wrath to fall on him before he had time to bring his scheme to fruition.

Lord and Lady Talbot strolled about the room, playing the convivial hosts to their guests until at last dinner was announced. Leading the way, the Talbot's were closely followed by a simpering Fiona, clinging tightly to Jonathan's arm, his mouth set in a thin-lipped grimace. Offering Katherine his arm, Simon followed their hosts into the dining room, leaving Roland, with no one to escort, trailing the newly affianced couple, a murderous scowl darkening his pale features. He took the chair beside his sister, who continued to fawn over Jonathan, completely oblivious to her brother's gloomy presence. Roland, seated opposite Katherine and Simon, glowered malevolently at Simon. Feeling Katherine's eyes fall on him, he cast a look of such yearning she gasped in confusion until, biting her lip nervously, she looked away. A shadow of annoyance fell across Simon's face as he caught the exchange, brief though it was. Leaning forward, he lowered his voice so that only Roland could hear him.

"Is there something amiss, sir? You keep sending me such menacing looks that I fear I have unknowingly done something to offend you."

Taken aback by the man's unexpected forthrightness, Roland meekly lowered his eyes, mumbling an apology for his behavior. After the soup plates had been removed and the meal served, he attacked the food on his plate with such ferocity that he finished before the others had barely begun. Pushing his chair back, he bowed to his mother and begged to be excused, pleading a horse in need of his attention. Glad to be rid of her besotted son before he made a bigger fool of himself, she nodded her consent. A collective sigh of relief was almost audible as the young man fled the room.

Simon, curious about his bride, turned to her. "And how is it that one as exquisite as you, Katherine Maguire, should remain unwed, although I must admit it is my good fortune that no one has captured your heart before this day." Blushing at his extravagant compliments, Katherine could feel the tension as those gathered around the table awaited her reply.

"Ah sir, 'tis no great mystery. My beloved aunt and uncle wanted my marriage to be as blissful as their own and so, although there were suitors, they agreed they would not force me to wed unless my heart was involved. And then there was the small matter of lack of a dowry."

Suddenly frightened that she might have spoken too freely, she glanced at Lady Talbot, who was glowering at her down the length of the table. Studying the others in the room, she could see astonishment at her candor reflected in the faces of the two men and annoyance at her outspokenness written across the Talbots' faces. Struggling to regain control of the evening, Lady Talbot focused her remarks toward the men, hoping to divert their attention back to the mundane topics of horses and politics, anything to steer the conversation down an acceptable path.

Katherine, stomach knotted in nervous tension, merely pushed the food about her plate, having lost what little appetite she had, her misgivings increasing by the minute. At long last Lady Talbot arose from the table, beckoning Katherine and Fiona to follow her to the drawing room, leaving the men to their brandy and cigars.

The door had barely closed behind them before vicious fingers pinched Katherine's arms and Lady Talbot, angry flecks of spittle spraying from her mouth, towered menacingly over her. Afraid of being overheard by the men, she hissed irately at the girl.

"You little fool, what's wrong with you? Do you want this Yankee, this very rich Yankee, to think you a mindless fool?" Strong fingers again pinched at her arms, causing Katherine to retreat as she attempted to escape her tormentor. A shadow of alarm touched her face and she quickly foresaw what her life might become if Simon Radcliffe decided she was too much a simpleton to become his wife.

"Enough, Lady Talbot, enough!" she stammered in surrender, "I'll try harder." Rubbing her aching arms, she moved away, choosing to gaze out into the garden until the men joined them. Lord Talbot, replete after the heavy meal, sank onto the sofa, eyes already heavy with sleep.

"Katherine, I believe it has stopped raining." Lady Talbot spoke in unfamiliar honeyed tones. "Why don't you show Mr. Radcliffe the garden?"

Simon, measuring his hostess with a cool, appraising look, took his intended by the arm and stepped out into the garden. Lady Talbot watched as the couple slowly made their way down the pebbled path. Grudgingly she admitted to herself that they would make a most handsome couple, if only the little trollop didn't ruin things. Facing the two who now watched her, she smiled demurely at the other Yankee, who had also been observing the strolling couple. Discretely signaling Fiona to play again, Lady Talbot led a reluctant Jonathan back to the piano, freeing her thoughts to wander where they would.

As they ambled along, Simon adjusted the stride of his long legs to match her shorter step. Although the rain had stopped, Katherine shivered as a cool breeze played about her hair and gown. Leaning toward her, Simon spoke.

"Miss Maguire—Katherine, you seem to be truly unaware how bewitching you are, a fact I admit, intrigues me enough to wonder why no suitor has claimed your hand. Surely, lack of a dowry would not stop proposals of marriage from any who caught a glimpse of you? Please understand that if we are to marry, I wish to assure myself that no suitor is skulking about, ready to claim you for his own. Also, this young Roland Talbot causes me some concern." His voice was smooth but insistent as he awaited her reply.

Blushing at his words, Katherine barely glanced at the man standing before her. Tears threatened to fall as she remembered the warmth of her aunt and uncle's love for her, and their concern for her happiness, always assuring her that when she married, it would be a love match. And because there had been no pressure to find a husband, she was now faced with marrying a stranger on the morrow, and sailing to his home far across the sea. Sighing, she spoke haltingly.

"It is as I said, sir, without a dowry there were a few offers but none which appealed to me. I foolishly thought there would be time enough to find my own true love. As for Roland, there is nothing between us, although I believe he would have it otherwise. His mother, thankfully, would never allow such a match, no matter what his feelings might be." Shivering again, she turned and wordlessly led the way back to the warmth of the manor where the others awaited their return.

Making her way to Lady Talbot's side, she begged permission to retire for the night. Nodding, Lady Talbot dismissed both Katherine and Fiona whilst pouring wine for herself and her now dozing husband, motioning for her guests to help themselves.

Simon, after the departure of the two younger women, glanced toward his cousin, shrugging at the unspoken question in his eyes. Lord Talbot, his nap interrupted by a subtle poke of his wife's fingers, sat up and proposed a toast, and the four remaining sat before the fire, each lost in their own thoughts, with only snippets of desultory conversation filling the silence.

* * * *

As the door closed behind the two women, the patiently waiting Larkin fell into step behind them, resuming his guardianship once again. Barely glancing at him, Katherine turned in the direction of the library and the small chamber tucked within it, Larkin close on her heels. Unnoticed by either of them, Fiona, having heard her name whispered frantically from the darkened hallway, darted beneath the staircase and furtively made her way toward the agitated presence of her brother, who stood concealed in the shadows.

Peg, awaiting Katherine's return, had a small fire burning to chase the chill from the room but after one glimpse at her unhappy charge, led her to the table where a small repast awaited. "I warrant you ate little enough tonight, pet, and you so thin already. Have a bite of this tasty dish that Cook sent along to tempt your appetite whilst I prepare your bed."

Turning the bedclothes down and laying Katherine's much mended nightgown over a chair close to the fire, she paused as a heavy knock echoed through the room, disturbing both women's reflections on this longest of days. Larkin gingerly edged the door open and peered in.

"Begging your pardon, Miss Katherine, but Lady Talbot has an errand for Peg and me'self to tend to." Turning, his pudgy finger indicated Fiona who stood just outside the door. "Miss Fiona here has volunteered to sit in my place and await our return. We shouldn't be gone long." He backed out of the room, leaving the girl to wonder at the importance of such an errand that two servants were needed to see it to completion.

Peg, bristling at the notion she could be sent hither and yon, expressed her indignation but Fiona, who now stood in the open doorway, assured her that it was her mother's wish she accompany Larkin to Katherine's former lodging in search of her prized emerald pin, thinking that she might have lost it when she was there yesterday.

"Mother says she can trust none but you and Larkin, and prays that you will find it. She insists there be no delay in your search. Hurry along now, both of you."

Katherine, lost in her own abject misery and paying no heed to the whispering at the door, stared distractedly into the fire. Glancing at Larkin, Peg felt a twinge of foreboding. Why could a search not take place tomorrow, when the light of the day would aid them in their quest? Something was not right, she thought, wrapping her shawl tightly about her, and yet she knew she had no choice but to follow Larkin as he lumbered out the door and into the cool night air.

* * * *

As the door was closing behind the two servants, Katherine, spying Fiona, reasoned that she was likely searching for a book to read while she awaited Larkin's return. Refusing to ponder the workings of any of the Talbot minds', she turned back to the welcoming warmth of the fire, staring pensively into the flames. Retrieving her hairbrush, she began brushing her thick hair. Lost in thought, she was unaware of the slow turning of the doorknob until the flames, dancing wildly in the draft, alerted her to the presence of another in her chamber. Turning around, she was startled to see Roland standing just inside the doorway, Fiona leering over his shoulder at her.

"Roland, Fiona! What are you doing here?" The intruders continued to stare at her, offering no explanation for their presence.

Roland, his usually pale complexion flushed with some inner excitement, impatiently brushed away his flaxen hair as it fell across his forehead. Feeling his sister's fingers prodding him further into the room, he hesitantly took a step forward. Beads of perspiration gathered on his brow, rolling down his reddened cheeks. Stepping fearlessly toward the pair, Katherine caught a whiff of liquor. Swaying ever so slightly, Roland leaned toward her and, with an elaborate flourish, bowed.

"Why, my beautiful Irish orphan, I've come to ensure your comfort in this most depressing of chambers, nothing more." He heard his sister's high-pitched giggle behind him.

"Roland, have you been drinking?" In an act of foolish bravado, Katherine turned her back on the pair of them. "Really, I'm too exhausted to chat. You must leave at once, both of you, before someone spies you in my chamber and thinks the worse." Exasperated by their continued silence, she spun back around and began to move toward the door, thinking to usher them out. "Fiona, take your brother to his room before your mother sees him in this state."

Fiona giggled again, drawing a withering glance from her brother as he boldly advanced further into the room. Anticipating that Miss High and Mighty was about to be brought down to the lowest of the low, Fiona again nudged her brother forward. Turning to his plump sister, he curtly ordered her to leave them. Opening her mouth in protest, her brother reminded her that if the deed was to be completed successfully, he required solitude, not an audience. Fiona whined that she had only agreed to help him because he had promised she could listen to the Irish bitch beg for mercy. Through clenched teeth, he ordered his sister from the chamber, reminding her that she was to warn him of any chance passer-by. The slamming door echoed her displeasure but Roland merely shrugged in relief that she was gone.

A flicker of apprehension coursed through Katherine as she nervously bit her lip. Voice trembling, she turned and faced the trespasser.

"Roland, I don't know the purpose of your being here but I think it best if you leave immediately." Her voice was rough with anxiety but she continued on, "Larkin will return shortly and will be most upset to find you in my chamber. And think how your mother would react should she learn that you were here." Her misgivings were increasing by the second.

Even mention of his fierce mother could not stop Roland as he menacingly advanced toward her, his expression suddenly clouding in anger. His words were clipped. "Why, Katherine, surely you're not frightened of me?" He took another step toward her, seizing her wrist in a vice-like grip.

"Release me, you buffoon, or I'll scream." Her breath caught in her throat and she could feel her heart pounding in fear.

A maniacal laugh issued from her attacker. "Scream as loud as you want, my sweet, for there are none to hear you, save for my sister, and I seriously doubt that she will fly to your rescue. Tucked away as you are, not even that pompous Yankee would hear your cries for help, although it will delight Fiona if she could but hear you begging for mercy." He pulled her toward him, imprisoning her in a steely embrace and, struggle as she might, could not free herself as, inflamed with passion, he rained wet kisses on her face and neck.

As she thrashed vainly against his superior strength, he continued his raving, "I've found a way to claim you for my own, my darling Katherine. When I am finished with you, that insufferable Yankee will not be anxious to exchange vows with someone who everyone will know is 'damaged goods'. And Mother won't fight me on this, for what if my seed should find fertile ground this very night and a grandchild were to be already in the making?" Spittle flew from the corners of his mouth and his eyes glittered in wild excitement. A massive wave of stark, cold fear swept through her as she struggled futilely to escape.

Reaching behind him, Roland suddenly brandished a knife, an evil, wicked weapon, causing Katherine to momentarily cease her struggles. He smiled coldly, enjoying the fear he saw in the emerald depths of her eyes. His fingers reached inside the bodice of her gown, holding it away from her pale skin.

"Roland, please", she sobbed, expecting to feel the cold steel plunging into her breast, "you don't have to do this."

He smiled, his eyes feverishly bright as he licked his lips in anticipation. "Oh, my sweet darling, I have no intention of cutting you—as long as you don't struggle overly much. My blade will serve another purpose this night." With those words, the blade made a small cut through the material of the worn gown. Sensing victory, he threw it down and grasping the neck of the gown, ripped the material violently downward. Shuddering in shocked disbelief, she realized only her chemise stood between this slavering beast and his lust.

Slobbering kisses began to rain down once more on her throat while his hands, groping for her breasts, tore the thin material of the chemise, baring her skin to the cool air.

Gasping in astonishment, Katherine's nails raked at his eyes and face, drawing forth thin streaks of blood. His face became a livid mask of rage as he cursed her, his hand shooting out and slapping her, causing her to wonder if her bones could survive another such blow. Screaming as icy fear twisted around her heart she spied Fiona who, having heard a shriek, now hovered in the doorway. Katherine cried out to her for help.

Roland, enraged that his sister had dared to venture back into the chamber, commanded her to leave. Katherine, seeing her attacker distracted, seized the opportunity and, clutching her torn chemise to her, made a desperate dash for the door. Fiona, guessing her intent, stepped back out, slamming the door just as Roland recaptured his prey, dragging her toward the bed. Shock quickly yielded to fury as Katherine struck out at her attacker, her blows falling unheeded on his wiry frame. Realizing that her fate was all but sealed she pleaded sobbingly with her captor, begging him to release her but her entreaties fell on deaf ears.

Fiona, standing outside the chamber once more, leaned against the wall, disappointment washing over her failure to see the much anticipated event unfold. Wrapped in her misery, she failed to notice she was no longer alone in the dimly lit library as a shadowy figure searched the shelves for a book. At the sound of a door closing, the visitor had turned and was now looking questioningly at the plump young woman as she attempted to peer through the keyhole.

"Is all well with you, Miss Talbot?"

Whirling about in alarm, Fiona met the curious gaze of Jonathan Radcliffe. "Jonathan, I mean Mr. Radcliffe, what are you doing here?" Her demeanor became wary, her speech a nervous stammer, so different from the simpering tones heard earlier, rousing the Yankee's curiosity.

"I apologize if I've startled you but my cousin and your mother are discussing the wedding, and my presence was no longer required so I took myself off and am now searching for a book to take to my bed."

Unluckily for Roland, he chose that precise moment to sink his teeth into the tender flesh of Katherine's breast, causing a shrill scream of pain to fill her chamber and carry to those who stood beyond the closed door.

* * * *

With a final, desperate burst of strength, Katherine pushed Roland from her, escaping his clutches momentarily. As Roland fell awkwardly to the floor, he overturned the small table, sending her supper tray crashing down beside him.

Jonathan, hearing the scream and the crash of crockery, strode quickly to the door of the small chamber, throwing it open just as Roland, tearing at what was left of his victim's clothing, forced her backward onto the bed. Seizing

28

Fiona's arm in a savage grip, Jonathan, between angrily clenched teeth, ordered her to run, not walk, to fetch his cousin, her parents and a bottle of brandy, in that order.

Recognizing the folly of her brother's plan and fearing the murderous look in the Yankee's eyes, she ran as she had never run before, panting, down the length of the hallway, toward the parlor and the questionable safe haven of her mother.

Unaware that deliverance was at hand, Katherine, gasping in terror, pummeled helplessly as Roland bowed his head, seeking her pink-tipped breasts once more. She shuddered with revulsion as he left a trail of wet kisses across her skin. So intent was he on the nearness of his prize, Roland had no notion he had been discovered when, pale eyes flying wide in stunned surprise, he was pulled from his helpless victim, his arms twisted cruelly behind his back. Fear crossed his countenance as he faced the wrathful visage of the cousin of the one he perceived as his rival, realizing a pistol was aimed directly at his heart. Shear black fright swept over him.

It was at that moment Larkin, surmising he and Peg had been the victims of a childish hoax for some unfathomable reason, returned to their charge, Peg following closely behind him. Spying the tall American in Katherine's chamber and her state of undress, his hand went for his pistol but stopped as, puzzled, he assessed the situation and realized who the probable villain was. Jonathan, noting the questioning looks on both of their faces, surmised they had played no part in what could have been a tragedy.

Footsteps echoed in the hallway as Lord and Lady Talbot and their American guest, followed by a quaking Fiona, crowded into the room. Katherine shuddered with humiliation as she realized how exposed she was, her chemise hanging in shreds, breasts bared to any lascivious glance cast her way. Peg, seeing her plight, hastened over and wrapped Katherine in her own tattered woolen shawl, murmuring words of comfort.

Roland, attempting to slink out of the room unnoticed, felt the cold steel of the pistol lightly touch his temple. "Were you going somewhere?"

Shaking his head in abject denial, Roland sank back into the corner, reflecting on the muddle he had made of things in his futile effort to claim Katherine as his wife. His hands shook as he contemplated his immediate future, wondering if indeed he had one.

The others studied the shambles of the room and its occupants while Katherine huddled miserably at the foot of the bed, tugging the tattered remnants of her chemise together. Lady Talbot, with a quick glance at her ashen-faced son, sized up the situation. Desperation overcame common sense in a bid to protect her son and she stormed across the room to where Katherine sat, savagely pulling her to her feet.

"What have you been about, you scheming harlot?" she hissed.

Dazed, tears falling unheeded from her eyes and swallowing the sobs that rose in her throat, Katherine haltingly struggled to explain but Lady Talbot's open hand shot out and slapped her, causing the slightly built girl to fall back onto the bed. An angry red mark colored her pale cheek as Lady Talbot advanced forward to strike another blow, before finding her hand suddenly seized in an iron grip as she was spun around to face the angry countenance of Jonathan, who stood closer to the aggressor than his cousin.

"Hold, Lady, you attack the victim. Miss Maguire is the innocent here. It is that cur cringing in the corner that is the villain. And I would advise you, Lady Talbot, that another attack on Miss Maguire will result in severe pain being inflicted on you, and believe me when I say your being a woman will count for nothing." His voice grated harshly in the crowded chamber.

Shrugging in mock resignation, Lady Talbot turned, sending a deeply black look at both her offspring, silently promising retribution for this humiliating turn of events.

Simon now stood next to his betrothed and his cousin, listening wordlessly as Jonathan quickly recounted the events as he had found them. Simon, cocking a questioning eyebrow at both Roland and his sister, spoke quietly to Jonathan and then stepped forward.

"Lady Talbot, as I understand it, no actual harm has been inflicted on my intended by your son. Miss Maguire is badly shaken but I feel she will recover from his cowardly assault. But your son, I fear, must be harboring a death wish. And if it is death he seeks, he need only let me spy him anywhere that my eye falls from this moment until our departure tomorrow. Apparently, as my bride has related to my cousin, young Talbot's plan was to abuse her so all thoughts of marriage would be abandoned and you, with the possibility of his seed having found fertile ground, would forgive him and accept Katherine as his bride."

A deafening screech erupted from Lady Talbot's throat. "What is that you say? Roland, what is this fool going on about?"

Shamefaced, Roland burrowed deeper into his corner. Both Americans almost felt a twinge of pity for him. Lady Talbot, forgetting all else, advanced once more on Katherine.

"You little slattern, did you really think yourself clever enough to trap my boy? Did you honestly believe I would welcome an Irish bogtrotter into this family? Why, if you had succeeded in your devious scheme, I would have pushed you from a cliff."

Rising angrily from the bed, Katherine, wearied by the abuse being heaped upon her, faced Lady Talbot. It was David meeting Goliath. Jonathan made as if to rush to her side but was held back by Simon. Together they witnessed a bravado they would never have suspected existed in such a dainty form, confronting such a formidable foe.

"Madam, if Roland's plan had succeeded, you would not have had to push me—I would have jumped before I would make my home in this nest of vipers!"

An eruption of Yankee laughter filled the room, followed by applause from Jonathan. Even the loyal Larkin had to stare at the floor as he fought to control his mirth. Peg, shocked at the events of the night stood ready to do battle with any other that would dare attack her chick.

Recognizing that she had been bested, Lady Talbot harrumphed loudly. "If it pleases you sirs, Larkin will escort us upstairs to our chambers, ensuring both Roland and Fiona are confined to their rooms and out of harm's way until you have long departed our home. And I sincerely hope they will use their time to reflect on the foolishness of their actions on this night."

So saying, Lady Talbot signaled both her husband and her children who, following in her wake, resembled nothing less than a covey of quail, with the ever faithful Larkin bringing up the rear.

Jonathan hesitantly approached Katherine and gently pulled back the edge of the shawl, exposing the angry red bite mark on the tender flesh of her breast. Glancing about the room, he spied the brandy that Fiona had retrieved from the drawing room. Tenderly he swabbed the wound with alcohol, smiling reassuringly at the two pairs of eyes that followed his every move, for Peg had no intention of allowing harm to befall her charge a second time, not if she could help it. Turning to the servant, he instructed her to find four glasses and Peg, noting the twinkle in his eye, hastened off to do his bidding.

Signaling Simon to take himself off into a corner, he faced the girl. His voice had an infinitely compassionate tone. "Little cousin, we've only known each other a few hours but circumstances are such that, before asking you to disrobe, I assure you that I am a qualified doctor and my only concern is that you might have wounds that need tending."

Stealing a quick look at Simon, who now stood with his back to them in the furthest corner of the room, she reluctantly lowered the protective shawl revealing, in addition to the bite mark, bright red scratches and bruises but nothing more. He swabbed the scratches, knowing that time would heal her wounds. Gently wrapping the shawl around her, he smiled before seeking his cousin's ear to assure him that her wounds were indeed minor.

Both men turned to Katherine who continued to clutch the borrowed shawl tightly around her. Simon gazed at her in consternation. He had assumed he was acquiring a docile and obedient bride but instead seemed to have a woman who would not submit meekly to whatever fate might deal out to her. In a coolly impersonal tone, he broke the silence.

"Will you be all right here, Katherine? Larkin will spend the night outside your door, should there be further need of protection. And remember, Jonathan and I are just up the stairs."

Her voice was just a whisper as she glanced up at both men. "Yes, I'll be fine. Peg has already said she will spend the night with me."

The sound of crystal clinking together heralded Peg's return and Jonathan, taking the tray from her, poured out small libations for the four of them. The women, unused to spirits other than small beer or watered wine, sniffed at the amber liquid with some trepidation but watched as the men tossed the liquor

31

back, both agreeing that Lord Talbot kept a fine brandy in his liquor cabinet. Encouraging them to follow their lead and drink up, Katherine and Peg tilted their glasses back as the men had and drank deeply. There was immediate gasping and sputtering as the fiery liquid burned its way down their throats. Chuckling good naturedly, the men assured them that sleep should come easier now but just in case, they would leave the bottle behind.

Nodding to both women, the men retreated from the chamber, pausing only to caution the now returning Larkin not to desert his post again. Not stopping to listen to his spluttering assurances, they wordlessly climbed the stairs. Jonathan, pausing outside his door, looked inquiringly at his cousin.

"You can tell me it's none of my business but are you sure you're doing the right thing. If you have any doubts, why, we can be away from here before anyone knows we've gone." He paused, unsure whether he should continue. "I always assumed you would marry Juliana—the two of you, even as children were inseparable."

Jonathan's thoughts flew back to summers spent at Seven Oaks. He had always become the outsider whenever Juliana appeared, for even at that tender age, she had only to crook her finger and Simon would abandon his cousin and follow her, prepared to do her bidding no matter what that might give rise to.

Simon's mouth tightened into a thin line. He looked at his cousin, standing there, troubled and concerned. "Have no fear, Jonathan, I do know what I'm about. Grandfather has never forgiven Juliana's family for a wrong done to him, whether imagined or real, years ago. It wasn't important when we were children but once we reached marriageable age, well, he threatened to disinherit me if I chose to marry her. It was at his insistence that I seek a bride on this side of the Atlantic. But I have his assurance that, should I ever find myself a widower, I could marry whomever I chose."

Jonathan, aware that there had been tension between the two men, was shocked that Simon had allowed himself to be dictated to but realized that without his inheritance, his cousin was penniless. And from gossip he had heard, Juliana was close to destitute also. So his cousin had felt he had no choice when he chose this path. But now, having met Katherine, Jonathan hoped she never discovered the truth of her marriage—but, he thought, perhaps with such a beginning, it will be all the stronger for the adversity as they had already suffered. Curiosity somewhat satisfied, Jonathan bade his cousin good night as they retired into their respective bedrooms.

Chapter Four

After a restless night, Katherine awoke just after daybreak by a soft knock on the door. Silently delivering a breakfast tray for Katherine and the faithful Peg, the serving girl looked curiously about her but held her tongue as she left the room, taking the tray of broken crockery with her. The two women broke their fast in companionable silence, nibbling at the fresh bread and cheese. Through the tiny window, the sky appeared sullen and grey, and Katherine silently prayed it was not an omen of her marriage. At last, the breakfast tray was collected and preparations for her wedding were begun.

The previous night, after Katherine had fallen into an exhausted slumber, Peg had boldly gone in search of Lady Talbot, pleading with her to return Katherine's few gowns rather than selling them to pay for her keep, as she had originally intended. The old woman was surprised at how little persuasion the lady of the manor had needed to realize she might be inviting further trouble when the state of the girl's wardrobe became known. Grudgingly, she had allowed Peg to have Katherine's trunk moved to her bedchamber, and it was near midnight before the loyal Peg finally allowed herself the rest her weary bones cried out for.

In the morning, spying the familiar trunk she had thought lost forever, Katherine gave an excited cry and ran to it, searching the contents, holding up gowns and discussing the merits of each with Peg. It was agreed that the yellow gown they had readied for the marriage ceremony would be most becoming, and Katherine sat daydreaming, recalling that she had last worn it at the Christmas festivities, just before Uncle Hector had died and her world, a world in which she had been cherished and safe, was turned upside down.

Plying their needles, the two women companionably settled around the table, refurbishing the rest of her wardrobe wherever needed. Finally, heaving a heavy sigh, Katherine draped the last gown over a chair just as two servants entered, carrying buckets of hot water and a small copper bath, so that she might enjoy that particular luxury once more, another concession Peg had won from the tight-fisted chatelaine of the manor. Smiling in delight, she could hardly contain herself as it was slowly filled. From her pocket, Peg drew out a sliver of scented soap, daringly scooped from her mistress's dressing table.

After the servants had departed, Peg helped Katherine disrobe. Both stared in dismay at Roland's teeth marks, a reminder of the previous evening.

Katherine trembled with the memory of the brutal attack as she viewed the bruises and scratches clearly visible on her wrists and arms. Peg, more practical in her thoughts, silently gave thanks they had chosen a gown with long sleeves. Not wanting the girl to dwell overlong on the previous night, the servant urged her into the bath, and soon the steam and soap helped to push away any lingering memories.

Katherine scrubbed at her skin as if to wash away any trace of Roland, accepting the servant's assistance washing and rinsing her thick auburn hair. As the hours passed, Katherine sat on a stool, drying her hair in front of the fire until finally a talented maid arrived and arranged her hair in artful, curling tresses before weaving a yellow ribbon through it.

At last, Larkin's deep baritone called loudly through the door that the vicar had arrived. Heart beating wildly, Katherine was quickly laced into her gown. Peg cleverly pinned a piece of lace inside the bodice, covering the teeth marks that peeked over the neckline of the dress. Wide green eyes stared fearfully into Peg's watery pink-rimmed ones. 'Oh, my poor wee bairn, I pray that you find happiness.' The two women embraced, parting just as the door opened to reveal Larkin and Lord Talbot standing without.

Both men gawked open-mouthed at the vision before them. Larkin, the first to regain his composure cleared his throat before speaking softly to the bride. "It be time, miss. And here's his Lordship, come to escort you."

Lord Talbot, at last recovering his wits, stepped forward, offering his arm to Katherine. Hesitantly, she slipped her slender arm through his, hoping that no one would notice the ugly blue bruises peeking over the edge of her sleeve.

Wordlessly they walked the length of the hallway toward the parlor where the others were gathered, waiting and, as the door opened, all eyes turned. The clergyman, unaware of the turmoil within the household and the circumstances surrounding the marriage, smiled warmly in greeting.

Lady Talbot, seeing the transformation from ragamuffin to this striking creature before her, was resentful that one person could possess so much beauty and seem so unaware of her effect on those around her. She was grateful that both of her children were locked safely in their chambers. *I doubt Roland could be controlled if he caught a glimpse of her this day.*

Lord Talbot, with Katherine nervously clutching his arm, made his way to where the two Yankees stood. Simon stepped away from his cousin and stood, boldly intimidating, looking down at her. His tawny blond head nodded a wordless greeting and reaching out, caught her slender hand in his large one.

Jonathan stared as if transfixed at the woman before him. He had known Simon's bride was attractive but he was suddenly aware that she was unimaginably superb. Sighing, he met his cousin's blue eyes and flushed guiltily at being caught gawking at another man's chosen, no matter how strange the circumstances leading to this moment were. Unbidden, his mind wandered back to the events of the previous evening and the fleeting glimpse of a rosy-tipped breast. Uncertainty about the wisdom of Simon entering this loveless marriage once again crept into his mind.

The minister cleared his throat and the small group turned toward the makeshift altar. Lady Talbot, not wanting to chance any sort of disturbance from their tenants, had arranged for the ceremony to take place within the manor rather than the tiny church at the far end of the tiny village. As he intoned the marriage vows, Katherine trembled, realizing that she could very well be jumping from the frying pan into the fire, finding little comfort in knowing that none of this was her doing. Simon, sensing her trepidation, gathered both her trembling hands in his own. When at last the vows were exchanged, he slipped a tiny gold band on her finger and bent toward her, lightly brushing her lips with his. The newlyweds signed the marriage papers, studiously ignoring each other. Turning toward his cousin, the two conferred in muted tones, until finally Jonathan nodded and left the room.

Temporarily abandoning Katherine, Simon approached Lord Talbot and, grasping the older man's arm, maneuvered him away from the others before handing him the markers from his gambling debacle when the two had first met. A grateful Granville Talbot hastily stuffed the pieces of papers into his jacket, peering furtively about the room to see if anyone had witnessed the exchange. He paled as he met the piercing eyes of his wife, knowing full well she would have the truth out of him before the day was out. Simon, unconcerned with the Talbot's domestic discord, returned to Katherine's side and, placing her arm through his, silently led her from the room, nodding offhandedly to Lady Talbot.

Larkin met the couple at the entrance, patiently holding both Simon's and Katherine's cloaks. "The baggage is loaded, sir. And Peg has seen to it that you have a small basket of provisions for your journey."

Nodding his thanks, Simon helped Katherine don her cloak before draping his own carelessly across his broad shoulders. Facing Lord and Lady Talbot who now stood by the doorway, impatiently waiting to see the last of them, Simon swept the pair with cold blue eyes. "I doubt we will meet again but I would thank you both for my bride. Farewell." With a brusque nod, he ushered Katherine outside where Jonathan stood waiting beside their hired carriage.

As the carriage drew away, none noticed the forlorn figure watching from a window above, trying to swallow the lump that filled his throat.

* * * *

Katherine, with Simon's assistance, climbed into what had once been a richly appointed coach but time and circumstance had taken its toll and all that remained was a shabby hired conveyance, it's once plush upholstery now faded and stained. She gathered her woolen cloak closely about her in an effort to ward off the chill of the bleak grey day. Simon, broad shoulders filling the small doorway, took the seat opposite, forcing Jonathan to choose between sharing a crowded seat with his cousin or stretching out comfortably beside the much trimmer form of Simon's bride. As he settled beside her, furtively studying Simon's frowning countenance, he was puzzled at the absence of emotion on the face of someone who had just been married, love match or not.

Thinking to relieve the tension he felt, Jonathan claimed Katherine's attention. "Peg spoke to me before we left. She will arrange with her sister, a widow also, living in a nearby village to take up lodgings with her. She had some small savings set aside and I gave her a few coins more. Her plan is to leave when a wagon travelling to market could save her walking the distance." Katherine's eyes filled with tears at his kindness and she murmured her thanks.

Silence filled the carriage as both Katherine and Simon gazed out at the passing countryside, studiously ignoring each other. Jonathan, unable to bear the silence, broke into Katherine's reverie. As he had not been privy to the deal struck between Lord Talbot and his cousin, he knew nothing of her circumstances.

"How did you come to be living at Marlow Court, under the thumb of that odious creature, if that is not too personal a question, little cousin?"

Green eyes narrowing in remembrance, she spoke in a low voice, soft and clear. "My parents, who lived on my father's debt-ridden estate in Ireland, died when I was but a child of eleven years. The village priest, recognizing that there would be no inheritance forthcoming, seized the opportunity to rid his parish of a poverty-stricken orphan and wrote to the only relative he knew of, my great-aunt Maude, telling of my plight. Since I was her only living relative, she quickly arranged my passage to England. Both Uncle Hector and Aunt Maude welcomed me lovingly into their home, where I have happily resided until Uncle Hector died some months ago. You see, the estate was entailed and only the closest male heir could inherit and so the present Lord Granville Talbot took possession of Marlow Court. My uncle's will stipulated that Aunt Maude was to be provided for but sadly he was too trusting. Granville Talbot and his grasping wife interpreted it somewhat differently and soon pushed her from her home into the gatekeeper's cottage, where we have both existed, thanks to the kindness of the villagers. And then she too died, leaving me alone once more."

"You have had a bad time of it, little cousin, but I trust that your new life will treat you differently." Neither man appeared to notice the tremor in her voice as she finished her tale and Jonathan, in a compassionate tone, spoke reassuringly. He paused, observing that Simon continued to appear disinterested and so Jonathan, thinking to distract her from the sadness of her tale, decided a short lesson was needed, should she ever find herself again under attack.

"My dear Katherine, should you, and I earnestly pray that you won't, but should you ever find yourself in the position of hapless victim by some brutish lout, I am about to impart to you advice that you must heed and remember." He knew Simon was watching him, amazed at the turn the conversation had taken. "A man, my dear, has a most vulnerable part of his anatomy that will bring him to his knees if kicked soundly. I am speaking of that area between his legs."

Katherine, blushing, twisted her wedding ring nervously as she grasped his meaning.

Jonathan, unwilling to let modestly deflect the lesson, continued. "You must listen carefully, and remember, I have medical training. I know what I'm talking about. If you are being threatened, kick him as hard as you can. The pain he will suffer will allow you enough time, hopefully, to escape the situation."

Glancing across at his cousin, he sighed in exasperation. Simon appeared to be sleeping, at the very moment that he should have been reassuring his bride that life on the other side of the world would indeed not only be wonderful but she would be protected from ever suffering the lust of any cur who considered her fair game. Seeking to change the subject, his voice had an infinitely tender tone.

"Simon and I have also had our share of sorrows growing up. We are both only sons, our fathers being brothers. My parents married and travelled to Savannah, a city in the state of Georgia, to live. Simon's mother, against her father's wishes, eloped and the pair fled to the city of Charleston, South Carolina. Not so far as the crow flies, and we boys did manage to visit for several weeks at least once every year. Simon's father died when he was a young boy which is when his grandfather stepped in, ending the estrangement with his only child while she was married to a man he didn't approve of. He sold off what property there was and took his daughter and grandson to live at Seven Oaks. Sadly Simon's mother died not two years later and he continued to live with his grandfather on his plantation, which one day he'll inherit, being his grandfather's only kin." His voice trailed off, his mind hearing again Simon confiding that his marriage had to be Samuel Langtree's way or nothing. He studied Katherine's exquisite features as she digested these facts about her new husband, neither of them taking any notice of the English countryside they were passing through.

The rich timbre of his voice broke into her thoughts as he continued the Radcliffe family history. "My own father died when I was much the same age as Simon. He didn't have much to leave, as his career was just beginning, and so my mother struggled on as best she could but it almost proved too much for her. She took in laundry and cleaned homes but with most of Georgia owning slaves, it didn't provide much of a living for a woman with a small child. Just when it seemed blackest, a letter arrived.

"A Mr. Phillip Beauchamp, having somehow been apprised of our plight, invited us to share his home on an island not too far out of Savannah. He explained that my father, who, by the way, was a lawyer, in his first case following graduation, had won a disputed inheritance for him some years ago, and from that beginning and with some astute investments, Phillip Beauchamp provided himself with a very comfortable life. He assured my mother that she wasn't to consider it charity; he really did need her, his wife having recently died in childbirth, leaving him with a young son and an infant daughter. My mother, recognizing Dame Fortune's knock, immediately began packing our belongings. Mr. Beauchamp had prudently enclosed enough money to pay our passage to Belle Isle."

"I was tutored alongside Phillip's children and, when the time came, he arranged for me to study medicine. He ensured my mother wanted for nothing and she in turn became a mother to his children. I owe him more than I can ever hope to repay." His voice trailed off and he smiled warmly at Katherine. Glancing at his cousin, he saw blue eyes watching him intently.

"Cousin, you narrate our history well but I fear you may have bored my bride." Katherine glanced at the faces of the two, unsure of the mood of her new husband.

"Oh no, I was not bored. I was happy to learn something of you and your home. I know so very little and, other than when I crossed the Irish Sea to live with my aunt, I have never travelled anywhere."

She glanced mischievously at the two who sat regarding her. "But truth be told, I was going to travel had I not been taken by surprise by Lady Talbot. I planned to set off for London and make a new life for myself there."

The two men looked first at Katherine and then at each other before bursting into laughter. Simon, recovering first, spoke. "And how, madam, were you going to earn a living? Women on their own, especially beautiful ones, are soon swallowed up by those who would use them for their own wicked purposes."

Indignantly Katherine stiffened her spine before she replied bitingly, "Why sir, I was going to seek a position as a governess or perhaps a teacher in a young ladies' finishing school."

Simon whooped with laughter once more, speaking mockingly when at last he recovered. "I fear, with your physical attributes, the only employment you would have found would have been in a brothel or perhaps as some rich man's plaything. I doubt you would have ever achieved any degree of respectability."

Jonathan, laughter still in his voice, continued. "And I certainly cannot imagine some stout matron allowing a governess who, in reality resembles a goddess, through her doors—not unless her husband was either blind or dead."

Katherine could feel her face flushing at this unexpected humiliation. Avoiding the eyes of both men, she huddled miserably in the corner, drawing her cloak closer about her. Jonathan, ashamed for poking fun at such an innocent dream, felt helpless. Eyes lighting on the wicker basket, he peeked beneath the cover and, gently tugging at a curl that had escaped from Katherine's bonnet, spoke in mock severity.

"Come now, Mrs. Radcliffe, you must forgive us for laughing but the idea of you escaping from the dragon of Marlow Court and making your way to London, unescorted and none to protect you, well, I can think of no other word than foolhardy that would describe such an act." Turning to his cousin, he appealed for his help. "Simon, convince your wife to forgive our rudeness. Come, both of you, let us explore this hamper that the marvelous Peg produced under the malevolent eye of that selfsame dragon."

Katherine at first could offer him only a small shy smile but her lips twitched with the need to giggle light-heartedly at his apt description of Lady Talbot and, setting aside her annoyance, she sat up and helped Jonathan empty the basket.

A small feast of freshly baked bread, cheese and chicken was soon spread between them, and while Katherine poured wine into chipped mugs, Simon and Jonathan tore hunks from the bread and began eating. They munched in companionable silence, each lost in their own thoughts. Katherine, brushing a last crumb from her cloak, tidied away the remains of their small banquet. She relaxed against the threadbare cushions and soon the gentle swaying of the carriage lulled her into a contented slumber. It was some time later that the voices of the cousins talking reminded her of the precariousness of her position, married to Simon or not. Prudently, she feigned sleep but as the men were engrossed in their conversation, they failed to take any notice of her.

"Your grandfather will be well pleased with this particular acquisition to the family, Simon."

"Grandfather is trying to rule me as he once dominated my mother. I doubt my father would ever have let the old man gain such a hold over us but he died too soon and Mother, like all of her sex, was bred to take direction from the men in her life. She was powerless against her father. Yes, he will be pleased, I admit, but Jonathan, do not be misled. Because I appear to have acquiesced to his demands, does not necessarily make it so."

A puzzled frown crossed the face of the darker man. When his cousin's grandfather had written him, beseeching him to travel with his grandson across the ocean, Jonathan had known that Simon was besotted by Juliana, a fact he had been aware of since childhood. He knew that the old man hoped Simon would meet someone much more suitable in England, someone who would make him forget his first love and, when, three short days ago, he had announced to Jonathan that he was marrying someone he had never met, he was doubly perplexed. But now, after meeting her, he hoped for Katherine's sake that she would enchant Simon before they ever reached their destination. Having met the beguiling Juliana many times since childhood, he wondered if such a thing was possible, for she seemed to have cast a spell over Simon, a spell that Jonathan didn't think his cousin wanted broken. And, while he cared for his cousin, he knew Katherine had already crept into a corner of his own heart, and he wouldn't allow her to be used callously.

Noticing finally that Katherine was awake and listening to their conversation, Jonathan's grey eyes looked into the depths of her green ones. Not sure how much she might have overheard, he smiled warmly down at her.

Katherine, realizing she had been unwittingly using her husband's cousin for warmth and comfort, sat stiffly upright, edging into the corner of their shared seat. Again, the conversation dwindled down to nothing and the occupants studied the green countryside they were passing through.

* * * *

After what seemed an eternity, the carriage slowed before turning into the courtyard of an inn. The journey, having taken many hours to complete, with stops only to rest the horses and stretch their own legs, saw the trio alight from the carriage into the cool evening air. The thoroughly chilled driver, handing over the reins to the stable boy, impatiently awaited the departure of his passengers so that he might seek a hot meal and, hopefully, someone to warm his bed. The door of the inn was pushed open and the scrawny frame of the owner emerged, holding a lantern aloft to light the way for the new arrivals.

"This way, sirs and lady, and might I bid you a good evening," he fawned over them in a raspy wheeze. "I see you've returned, as indeed you said you would, sir. And this young lady must be your bride, Mr. Radcliffe," acknowledging Katherine's presence with a slight nod of his head.

In the glow of the lantern, Katherine saw the tavern keeper was angular, with small, dark eyes peering out from under the bushiest eyebrows she had ever seen, beating even Lady Talbot's servant, Larkin. Black stubble covered his lower face, and an apron, spotted with bits of any number of meals the man had either cooked or eaten in the past week, covered his lanky form. The small party followed him into the welcoming warmth of the inn as he assured them that their belongings would be carried upstairs forthwith. The narrow passageway led to the main room of the tavern where only a few old men sat, already too far into their cups to give the new arrivals more than a fleeting look. Retrieving the keys to their rooms, Simon, carrying a candle to light their way up the creaking staircase led the way with Katherine following close on his heels and Jonathan bringing up the rear.

Pausing before a door, key in hand, Simon nodded to Jonathan before guiding Katherine into the room. The door had barely closed before a knock was heard and it was pushed open. The landlord, lantern in hand, entered the room, dragging Katherine's trunk, with Simon's smaller bag resting atop it, all the while apologizing for the chill of the room. Dropping to his bony knees, he threw kindling into the fireplace and skillfully coaxed up tiny flames.

Drawing near to the hearth, Katherine held her cold hands toward the meager fire. Glancing about, she observed peeling wallpaper and faded, dusty velvet curtains which seemed to speak of past glories in a now grimy room. A bed, covered with a dingy white coverlet seemed to loom, large and intruding, filling the room. A flicker of apprehension coursed through her. The innkeeper, finally satisfied with his efforts, withdrew from the chamber, bowing and scraping once more. Simon, closing the door behind his retreating figure, turned to his wife.

"As soon as you are ready, Katherine, we will join Jonathan downstairs for an evening meal." His voice was chillingly emotionless. So saying, he sat at a small wooden table and let his gaze wander out of the dirty, fly-specked window. Katherine, biting anxiously at her bottom lip, opened her trunk, giving silent thanks to the resourceful Peg for recovering her wardrobe from the dragon of Marlow Court.

Unwilling to keep her new husband waiting, she searched until she finally found her hairbrush and quickly brushed the dark tresses. Noticing that Simon was now watching her, she blushed, fussing absently at the skirt of her gown, becoming restive under his scrutiny. Raising an eyebrow inquiringly, she nodded, uncertainty clouding her brow as he rose from the chair and moved toward the door, offering her his arm as they left the room. Simon paused in front of the door next to theirs and knocked softly.

Jonathan, as if he had been waiting on the other side of it, opened the door immediately and stepped out, smiling warmly down at Katherine before nodding to his cousin.

The trio descended the stairway, where the toadying innkeeper stood waiting to usher them to a table near the fire, for the room was filled now with those who, working and living nearby, were stopping for a pint before making their way home to their own fires. Plates of hot food and mugs of beer were quickly placed before them, and the two men made their plans for the following day, a conversation which didn't include Katherine, who sat, absently pushing her barely touched meal around the platter, as her mind wandered over the events of the past week.

Eventually the conversation dwindled and both men unfolded their long frames as they rose from the table and stood waiting for Katherine. Once again, they made their way up the poorly lit staircase and, after bidding each other a good night, Katherine and Simon entered their bridal chamber while Jonathan retreated to his lonely bachelor quarters.

Simon, recognizing his bride's disquiet, watched as she nervously circled the room. "Katherine, I forgot to purchase a bottle of wine that we might toast our union this night. It will only take me a few moments, enough time for you to prepare yourself." With that said, he turned and left the room, leaving her momentarily alone.

Sorting through the contents of her chest once more, she removed the soft cambric nightdress that her Aunt Maude, knowing that her adored niece would one day marry, had lovingly stitched, trimming it with delicate white lace and thin blue ribbon, as part of her trousseau. Katherine, having lived her life in the country, had some inkling of what the night held in store but that small bit of knowledge did little to assuage her fears.

Darting behind the dressing screen, she quickly disrobed, folding each article of clothing carefully, as if willing time to stand still. After she had finally drawn the nightgown over her head, she stepped back into the room. It was at that moment the door opened as Simon returned, carrying a bottle and two glasses. His blue eyes took in the enchanting image of his bride, standing in the centre of the room, silhouetted by the fire burning behind her, face pale and small hands trembling, looking so very vulnerable.

Her breath catching in her throat, she was sure he could hear her heart beating as his bold gaze fell on her. Setting his burden down, he regarded her quizzically for a moment, a look of uncertainty creeping into his eyes before his face closed up tightly, as if he guarded a great secret.

Chapter Five

"Why, Katherine, you're shivering. Not fear of me, I trust?" He crossed to the fireplace and threw a small log on it, causing sparks to fly about. "Get into bed before you catch cold."

Drawing the bedclothes about her, she sat stiffly upright as she watched Simon turn to the task of opening the wine. Keeping his back to her, he stealthily removed a tiny vial of powder from his pocket and sprinkled some of it into one of the goblets. She heard the gentle splash of wine as it was being poured and then Simon turned, offering her a glass, which her hand eagerly reached for, praying this would lend her the courage needed to see her through this night.

He sat on the edge of the bed and looked pensively at her. His voice was calm, his gaze steady, as he raised his glass. "Drink with me, Katherine, for this day we are wed, and so we shall remain—'til death do us part." He drained his upended glass and Katherine, not wanting to displease him, took a sip, shuddering at the faint bitterness of it. Feeling Simon's eyes on her, Katherine drank until her glass too stood empty. Suddenly her eyelids became too heavy to stay open and she sank down into the pillows, blissfully unaware of anything else on this longest of days.

Simon, watching as the wine containing a powerful sleeping potion took effect, sat before the fire, reflecting on this deed. He was certain that any other man, most especially his cousin, would call him mad and have him locked away. But his grandfather had forced him down this path and, in order to protect his inheritance, he had to please the old man. But one day he would marry the woman he loved above all else, silently vowing that Juliana was the only woman he would be faithful to even if he was married to another. It would be just as they had planned and old Samuel's meddling ways would be thwarted. Sighing deeply, he stirred the fire once more before moving to the side of his now deeply sleeping wife. He knew it would require a will of iron if he were to remain true to his own beloved Juliana.

Girding himself with steely resolve, he divested the comely maiden of her delicate nightgown and shakily laid her back against the pillows, her silken hair brushing his hand and throwing him into momentary confusion. After all, he argued silently, Juliana would never know. His eyes boldly raked the lithesome

43

frame of this woman who now called him husband, the pink-tipped breast beckoning so invitingly in the firelight.

Pausing as he noticed the bite mark left by Roland, his fingertips reaching out to touch the angry red scar. *I should have shot the bastard.* His gaze continued traveling hungrily down the melting softness of her body. Determinedly he covered her and, stepping back to the table, poured himself a second glass of wine, regretting the lack of something stronger.

He stared moodily into the fire until he felt once more in control of himself. At last he walked to the other side of the bed, and after slowly undressing, lowered himself onto the lumpy mattress, lying quietly, exercising extraordinary care to not touch the other occupant no matter how innocently, until sleep at last claimed him.

* * * *

Simon, waking just as the sun was rising, crept from the bed and cautiously unlocked the door of the room and, just as quietly, made his way back to where his wife lay, her sleep as yet undisturbed.

The sound of persistent knocking caused Katherine to stir at last. Attempting to raise her head, she realized her hair was caught and, opening her eyes fully, saw it was trapped under the arm of Simon, now her husband in fact. Tugging gently, she finally freed herself only to find Simon's cold and unfathomable eyes staring at her. He raised a questioning eyebrow as the knocking renewed itself. "Are you ready for your first visitor, Mrs. Radcliffe?" Without pause, he shouted for the unseen hand to cease its infernal pounding and enter.

The door opened slowly, as if the unseen intruder was reluctant to disturb the occupant of the room. The morning sun, shining weakly through the dirty window, outlined the figure of a short, portly man, his mouth agape in surprise. He continued standing in the doorway, suddenly unsure of himself when faced with the couple reclining in bed.

"For God's sake, man, step in and shut out those that would gawk at my bride," Simon thundered at the man, embarrassment painting the newcomer's face a deeper pink.

His face had the look of a mischievous elf, a monk-like tonsure of white hair circling a pink scalp, bushy white eyebrows raised in dismay at the scene before him. Startled at the harshness of the man's voice, the visitor glanced behind him, relieved to see the passageway empty. "Ah, Mr. Radcliffe, sir, you did arrange that we would meet here, in your room, at this early hour." He paused, fumbling with his words. "I, ah, I did not expect that I would be intruding as I so obviously am and so will await your pleasure downstairs in the common room, that is if you still wish a meeting." Bowing his head toward them, he made as if to withdraw but another outburst from Simon halted him.

"Featherstone, stop right there. I arranged to meet here so you might bear witness that my wife and I have shared a bed and also to attest to the validity of my marriage papers. But, if you would be more comfortable meeting downstairs, I will join you directly." Saying that, he swung himself, stark naked, out of the bed, managing to lower the blanket that Katherine quickly seized to her bosom in an effort to preserve her modesty.

It was not until that moment she realized she was as naked as her husband, and she clutched the cover even tighter to her. With her sleep-tousled auburn locks and blushing face, she had no idea of the enticing picture she was presenting to the two men who stood, spellbound, watching her.

Once again, Mr. Featherstone bowed in a courtly manner, confusion written across his reddened face. His lawyer's mind puzzled at this young scallywag's behavior as he backed out of the room, eyes averted so as to cause no further embarrassment to the young woman. "Then I will await you downstairs, sir," he spoke with quiet dignity as he shut the door firmly behind him.

Simon, in a seemingly pointless gesture, stepped behind the dressing screen and quickly donned his clothes, stopping only long enough to brush a careless hand through his blond curls. Turning to his wife who sat dazed at the events of the past few moments, he spoke quietly. "Katherine, I have to go downstairs to meet with our visitor. It will only take a few moments and then I will return for you so we might enjoy our first breakfast as a married couple, so be a good girl and get dressed."

She was too surprised to do anything more than nod as he crossed the room in two long strides, closing the door softly behind him. She shook her head in dismayed confusion before flying from the bed, unmindful of her state of undress. Quickly sorting through her wardrobe until she found a gown she hoped would be suitable for whatever the day might bring, she darted behind the screen, fearful that Simon would return and find her unclothed and vulnerable. Her thoughts wandered back to the previous evening but try as she might to recall what ever had transpired between the two of them, she had no memory beyond drinking the wine, which, she reasoned, must have been very strong as she recalled the bitterness of it as Simon urged her to drain the glass.

Long minutes passed before she stepped out, suitably garbed. She performed her ablutions at the tiny basin of water and was just putting the finishing touches to her hair when Simon returned, his expression thunderous.

Somewhat surprised to find her nearly ready, he paced the room, offering no explanation for his agitation, stopping only long enough to peer through the begrimed window before resuming his pacing. Nervously she stood waiting for a brief moment until he noticed her and once again they left their room, pausing only to knock on Jonathan's door.

Jonathan, accustomed to his cousin's moods, smiled down at Katherine before raising a questioning brow at Simon. A brusque nod was all he received in reply and silently the three descended the creakily protesting staircase, making their way to the now deserted common room and the scarred wooden table they had occupied the previous evening.

As breakfast was placed before them, Simon broke his silence. Coldly, he turned to his cousin. "You are aware that, before we left for Marlow Court, I arranged for our return passage on the ship *The Silver Ram* under the command of a Captain Hart, sailing tomorrow evening." Ignoring Katherine's gasp of surprise and expecting no answer from Jonathan, he continued. "Well, that blasted pettifogging lawyer has taken it into his head that he and his wife should see something of the new world and so, knowing the date of our departure, has arranged to sail with us. He says he would like to reminisce about their youthful escapades and days gone by with my grandfather before their advancing years make it impossible."

Jonathan, at a loss to understand his cousin's turmoil, waited patiently but no further explanation appeared to be forthcoming. Glancing at Katherine's pale complexion, he smiled in what he hoped was a reassuring manner.

"Well, cousin, what of it? I am sure Katherine will welcome the company of another woman and Mr. Featherstone will likely prove to be a lively travelling companion. The more the merrier, I say." At this response, Simon merely snorted and retreated into a sullen silence.

Simon quickly stood when Jonathan rose from the table and, turning to his wife, spoke. "Come Katherine, we have some business matters to attend to and, dull as that might be, it will be more entertaining than remaining cooped up in that tiny cubbyhole of a bedroom alone."

Confused at the unexpected invitation, she hesitantly nodded her agreement, falling in between the two men as they made their way outside.

Katherine, seated in the same carriage that had carried her from Marlow Court, stared intently out of the window at the sights and sounds that assailed her senses as they made their way about the city. Clambering in and out of the carriage, it wasn't until she thought she couldn't take another step that the two men agreed their business dealings were complete and they could return to the inn.

Once again, the three met for dinner, an unusually quiet affair as all three seemed lost in thoughts of their own. Katherine, still unable to recall the events of her wedding night, had racked her brain all day to no avail and, other than the dull headache she had awoken with, no memories had been forthcoming. She faced the remainder of the evening with trepidation as Simon escorted her up the creaking staircase but, as they entered their chamber, he mumbled an explanation of sorts and hastily fled the room. Katherine once more made her way behind the dressing screen and prepared herself for bed although, tired as she was, she was convinced she would find it impossible to fall asleep before Simon returned.

Sunlight struggled through the dingy window as Katherine, waking, tried to identify the sound that had aroused her. Simon stepped from behind the dressing screen, looking handsome in his finely tailored jacket and trousers. Seeing his wife awake, he smiled absently as he stepped to the small looking glass, fussing with an already perfectly knotted tie.

"We don't board until late afternoon, Katherine, and Jonathan thought you might have purchases to make, considering that we'll be at sea for several weeks. I'll return for you shortly. We'll have breakfast and then, on to the shops." He shut the door on his last words, leaving Katherine once again bemused with the man she had married.

Climbing out of bed, she saw that, unlike the night before, she was still wearing her nightdress. Blushing, she realized she must have fallen asleep before Simon returned the night before and he had considerately not disturbed her slumber. After selecting a plum colored gown from her trunk, she quickly performed her ablutions and then stepped behind the screen to dress and, as on the previous morning, Simon returned to find her brushing her unruly curls. After pinning the last strands back, she donned her straw bonnet, brushing at the folds of her skirt as she turned to her husband.

With no words exchanged, the two followed their already established pattern and knocked at Jonathan's door. He stepped out and looking at the two of them, Katherine thought they were probably the handsomest men she had ever seen. Jonathan was as impeccably dressed as her husband and the three presented a striking picture as they made their way to what had become their table.

Unlike the previous day where Katherine had followed the men as they conducted the last of their business, the trio were dropped off in front of a shop and Jonathan stood beside her while Simon arranged for the carriage's return. They spent the remainder of the morning wandering in and out of various shops, making few purchases but enjoying what would be their last day on dry land for some weeks.

At last, exhausted, Katherine was handed into the hired carriage where she sank against the cushions, thankful to be sitting at long last. The men followed behind her and seemed just as pleased to have found a place to rest. They decided that they would have a late lunch at the inn and then depart for the ship.

Katherine reflected that, for the second time in her short life, she was about to sail to another country and begin life anew. *Will I find happiness there?* she mused, a slight frown creasing her brow as she pondered the question. Jonathan, happening to glance her way as her thoughts played across her face, guessed at her apprehension but could only offer a warm smile by way of comfort and hopefully, reassurance.

* * * *

Screeching gulls wheeled through the air in their never-ending quest for food as waves lapped playfully against the sides of the ship. The salty smell of the sea assailed Katherine's nostrils, summoning vague memories of her first voyage across the Irish Sea when she was but a child. Shivering in the dampness of the sea breeze, she clutched her woolen cloak tightly about her.

Their feet had no sooner touched down on the wooden deck than they were approached by two men, an anxious Captain Hart and Mr. Featherstone, looking very much like a cat that had just swallowed a canary. The captain, a tall thin man with graying hair and moustache and a stern visage eyed his passengers as if weighing his chances of success once he laid his case before them. His weathered countenance looked upward, as if seeking courage from an unseen source but finding none, cleared his throat as the small group gathered round him, having sensed from his manner that something was amiss.

"Mr. Radcliffe, sir," he began, twisting his hat nervously although it wasn't fear of Simon himself that made the man so apprehensive but rather the thought of losing passage money for three, especially with their sailing time upon them. He cleared his throat once more, squared his shoulders and faced his passengers. "Mr. Radcliffe, an unforeseen problem has arisen regarding your accommodation whilst on board my ship. You and your wife were to occupy one cabin and your cousin the other."

He was definitely ill at ease, tugging at the collar of his shirt, an unfamiliar feeling for a man who was captain of his own vessel. "Well sir, circumstances have forced me to make some drastic changes." With a touch of the theatrical, he hung his head as if to demonstrate to all assembled how truly upsetting he found this.

"First, it was my young niece. She is travelling alone to New York to join her husband and, since we are kin, I felt I could do no less than offer her safe passage. And then Mr. Featherstone here talked his way around me for a place for him and his Mrs. Now I ask you sir, what could I do? Business is business." The captain paused briefly, glancing surreptitiously at his audience in an attempt to gauge their reaction to his plight.

"Now, if you gentlemen are agreeable, there is a solution. I have but two cabins and six passengers but," he paused dramatically before continuing, "there are three ladies and three gentlemen. I wonder if you could see your way clear to separating, just for the length of the voyage." Almost as an afterthought, he added the telling blow. "It's not as if you would be lucky enough to find another ship sailing in the next few days, one that would be willing to take passengers and, as you yourself told me, Mr. Radcliffe, you are in somewhat of a hurry to regain your homeland."

"I know, sir, you and this pretty little thing have just wed but surely you could bear the separation? After all, it's not as if you wouldn't see each other, you'll just not share a bed for a few weeks." His voice trailed off uncertainly-as he began pacing the deck, as if summoning courage for his final argument. Licking his lips, the grizzled captain leered in Katherine's direction. "You won't mind, missy, will you?" He was about to continue his argument when Simon nodded his head in agreement.

"All right, Captain Hart, you've made your point. And, as you have so cleverly pointed out, we're not likely to find a ship willing to carry passengers, and time is of the essence. I must return home as quickly as possible."

Jonathan's jaw dropped in speechless surprise. He had suspected that his cousin was less than happy in his new marriage but it was of his own making, and he certainly never expected him to relinquish his husbandly rights so easily, not when the morsel sharing his bed appeared so tasty. As the captain raised an inquiring eyebrow in his direction, Jonathan merely nodded his acquiescence. After all, if he didn't have a buxom wench to share his bed, it made little difference who he shared sleeping quarters with.

Edmond Featherstone, relief written plainly across his cherubic face, stepped forward, shaking Simon's and Jonathan's hands before executing a courtly bow in Katherine's direction. She blushed again as she recalled their first meeting. Sensing her consternation, he stepped to her side and, capturing her slender fingers between his, he squeezed them reassuringly. Speaking softly so the others might not hear, he uttered words which could not help but gladden her heart. "Let us regard this as our first meeting, my dear, and forget my unfortunate intrusion into your private bedchamber." Smiling her relief, Katherine happily nodded her head.

"It appears that all is settled." Captain Hart stepped forward once more, rubbing his hands smugly. "Your quarters are this way." Turning, he strode confidently toward a small doorway. Glancing back, he cautioned them to mind both their heads and the narrow steps.

Approaching a door, the captain knocked, waiting for the unseen occupant to bid him to enter. As a female voice rang out, the door opened and a head of bright red hair peeked out. Hazel eyes scanned the gathering, quickly landing on Katherine, and a freckled hand was extended out to her, drawing her inside the tiny cabin. Three narrow cots occupied the small, low-ceilinged chamber, leaving scant inches between the beds, two trunks resting at the end of two of the cots.

The redhead, much the same height as Katherine, grinned at her captive before releasing her hand, turning toward the third occupant of the cabin.

"Now, I know you must be the very recently wed, Mrs. Radcliffe. This is Mrs. Mary Featherstone. I believe you have already made the acquaintance of her husband, and I am Margaret McGregor but everyone calls me Maggie." Turning toward the doorway where the men stood, crushed shoulder to shoulder, she smiled at them, her smile warm and infectious.

"Uncle, I think you had better introduce everyone quickly for even now I can hear trunks being dragged across the deck," she admonished the captain breathlessly.

Nodding, Captain Hart introduced the new arrivals and then steered the men across the narrow passageway to their own equally cramped accommodation. Katherine, expecting Simon to speak to her privately, was surprised when he merely nodded before turning his back as he made his way to his own quarters. Head bowed, she remained still for an instant, knowing there was no time to dwell on his callousness for her trunk was being pushed through the doorway.

The three women had to huddle together as a gangly young sailor, straw-colored hair poking out from beneath a wool cap, deposited the trunk at the foot of the third cot, the only free space left. Blushing furiously, he snatched the cap from his head, nodding awkwardly to the occupants of the cabin until his eyes fell on Katherine. Instantly smitten, he bowed deeply before making his way to the doorway, stealing one more glance at the glorious vision before he pulled the door shut behind him.

"I believe you've just made a conquest, Mrs. Radcliffe." Maggie giggled at his hasty departure.

Katherine, disconcerted, crossed her arms and pointedly looked away for a moment. Regaining her composure, she met the eyes of her companions and smiled before stepping back to study the tiny space the three of them would be sharing over the next weeks. Misunderstanding her uneasiness, Maggie again took her hand and gave it a soft squeeze, her words accented by a soft Scottish burr.

"Do not fret, Mrs. Radcliffe, Ned is just a brash boy and means no harm. As for your husband, why, you'll have the whole of your lives to cuddle, laughing over the first days of your marriage being spent apart."

Katherine, suddenly overwhelmed by events of the past few days, felt her eyes fill with unshed tears at these words of kindness. Blinking tearfully, she smiled at the two women. She turned to the older woman and saw a matronly figure, shorter than herself by some inches, with graying hair tucked neatly beneath a small straw bonnet. Friendly blue eyes twinkled warmly at her.

"Yes, my dear," the older woman said, "we're all in this together so we must make the best of it. I have rarely been separated from my Edmond for longer than a night or two when he was away somewhere on business but I know it will make it that much sweeter when we're together again. Bless me, Maggie here has been separated from her man for more than a year. And my dears, let us not stand on formality. I wish to be called by my given name, Mary, and I trust neither of you will be offended if I address you as Katherine and Maggie."

Taken aback by her sweeping away familiar social mores, the two younger women could only nod their agreement but Maggie, after a moment's thought, decided that having been raised to always show respect to those of a higher social standing, declared that her training went too deep and the best she could manage was Miss Mary and Miss Katherine.

Mary, considering this point, agreed in principal but Maggie must relax the formality when it was only the three of them, a concession Maggie happily agreed to. The issue settled, Mary's voice chirped merrily on, eagerly waiting for this adventure to begin. After some spirited conversation, a warm and what would prove to be an enduring friendship was launched between the three.

After a time, a loud knock echoed through the cabin, which on opening revealed Ned. Blushing to the roots of his hair and twisting his cap nervously, he bid the ladies to please accompany him to the captain's quarters for the evening meal. As they stepped into the narrow passageway, Ned told them the men had been summoned earlier and were even now hoisting a glass with the captain.

Mary Featherstone, interested in everyone and everything, soon drew from the lad that he was past his fifteenth birthday and had been cabin boy on Captain Hart's last two voyages. He answered the older woman's questions but, clearly besotted, could not take his eyes from Katherine until a passing sailor, noticing his fascination with one of the passengers, clouted him on the ear and barked at him to mind his manners. Discomfited, the lad flushed before stepping a few paces ahead of his small company, leading them across the main deck toward his captain's quarters, not noticing as another sailor, menacing in appearance, lowered himself onto the deck from above.

Mary gave a startled shriek as a fearsome shape suddenly loomed threateningly before them, a creature smiling vilely from beneath a shaggy black moustache, rotting teeth visible between dry, cracked lips. His face was dotted with faded pockmarks, dark eyes leering wickedly as he studied each of them in turn. Clumps of black hair peeked out from beneath a filthy red scarf, which was tied tightly about his head, a gold earring dangling from one ear. Although lacking any great height, his barrel-shaped chest lent him a formidable bearing, and so the ladies stood, frozen in fear, afraid to shout or even to move.

Chapter Six

Ned, at last realizing he was alone, looked about and, instantly assessing the situation, shouted garbled threats until the man, with a last ferocious glare at the women, stomped away, snarling his opinion of females on board. Katherine and Maggie, assuring themselves that their friend was unharmed, turned to Ned, questions in their frightened eyes.

"That was Spanish Jack—he meant no harm to you ladies, he just smells a little moldy and his thinking is peculiar." Suddenly wanting to be free of this burden, he hurried them along. "Ladies, this way, please. Captain Hart will answer all of your questions."

And so the female passengers burst into, rather than entered, Captain Hart's private quarters. One look at their anxious faces brought the men's conversation to an abrupt halt. Ned quickly stepped forward, explaining that Spanish Jack had frightened the ladies but that he, Ned, had sent him about his business, with no harm done. Mr. Featherstone, assuring himself that his wife was safe, turned to the captain, waiting rather anxiously for the tumult to subside.

"Exactly who is this Spanish Jack, Captain Hart? And do we, especially the ladies, have cause for concern?"

"Now, now, gentlemen," he paused, smiling condescendingly, "and ladies, I do apologize. Firstly, Spanish Jack is not Spanish, but English. His name came about from the years he spent in a Spanish prison. He was in search of passage to America but had no coin so he signed on for this voyage. He seeks to join his wife who settled there some years ago, thinking him lost forever. He's a strange one—my men want no part of him but I believe him to be harmless. He preaches hellfire and brimstone, scaring the b'jesus out of anyone foolish enough to listen. At his own request, he has his sleeping quarters somewhere down in the hold and the crew is happier for that. I keep him up in the rigging as much as I can, away from everyone, or else on night watch but I confess I'll have no regrets when I see the back of him. And now, if you're ready, I'll have our dinner brought in." Poking his head out the door, he barked an order and feet, presumably Ned's, could be heard scurrying off in the direction of the galley.

Simon gained Katherine's side and quietly inquired as to her well being. Jonathan, wishing to give them time alone, even in a crowded cabin, smiled at

Maggie McGregor, much bemused by her bright hair and the generous sprinkling of freckles on her face and arms.

"Mrs. McGregor, how do you do. We met briefly but I feel the introductions were somewhat lacking. I am, by the way, Jonathan Radcliffe, cousin to Simon, who obviously is Mrs. Radcliffe's husband." He indicated his cousin standing apart, talking earnestly to his young bride.

As they all stood chatting, the captain moved toward the small table set for the evening meal, calling for his guests to join him whilst apologizing for it being a trifle crowded. Katherine, standing quietly beside Simon, glanced about the cabin.

It was a richly appointed room, a small table holding instruments of navigation and charts, a chest of drawers and a heavy curtain behind which, Katherine presumed, would be the captain's bed. Pride of ownership was evident in the well polished wood and brass fixtures, testimony of a man who prized the small luxuries his success allowed him.

As her mind wandered, she glanced at Jonathan and Maggie, idly wondering what they had found to talk about. She gazed at the Featherstone's, sitting together, obviously enjoying each other's company in spite of their many years of marriage. Looking at their cheerful faces, she allowed herself once more to speculate on the chance of her future happiness with this cold man she now called husband. Although he sat next to her, she felt very alone.

The door opened and Ned and another sailor slowly advanced into the cabin, arms trembling under the weight of the platters and bowls they carried. Placing their burdens carefully on the lustrous walnut table, they quickly left the room, anxious for their own meal.

As the party chatted merrily over the succulent dishes of meat and flavorful vegetables, Mary Featherstone, her plate heaped as high as any of the men, smilingly inquired of their host, "My goodness Captain Hart, will we dine like this every night?"

Chuckling as he addressed all of them, he spoke. "Oh no, madam, this is just a small celebration to welcome you aboard. We sail with the evening tide and, since the cargo has been loaded and stowed away proper-like, I thought I would take this opportunity to get to know you. Why, on days when the seas are rough, you'll be lucky to get anything other than cheese and bread served in your own quarters. Oh, and ladies, I must not only caution you but humbly beseech you to understand that the main deck belongs to the men in the morning and therefore I must ask you to remain below decks until the noon hour has passed.' The ladies, understanding in their eyes, nodded their accord to his request.

Jonathan raised his glass, toasting the captain and his fellow passengers and soon the conversation and wine flowed easily, with much laughter making it a festive gathering. Eventually, with appetites sated, the ladies stood and announced their intention of retiring. The captain, stepping through the doorway, summoned two sailors to escort them back to their quarters.

"After all," he exclaimed loudly, "with such beauty aboard, I don't want to tempt the men before they have even left port." After the women had departed, he assured the men that he would have a harsh word with Spanish Jack, once again declaring his belief in the harmlessness of the man.

* * * *

The captain, true to his word, kept Spanish Jack away from his passengers, either aloft in the rigging or on night watch, when no one was about. The women had, those first days, felt his eyes boring into them from his perch high above but accepted it as unavoidable and eventually, his unseen presence slipped from their minds.

Mary Featherstone, never one to be idle, had ensured that the tedium of the voyage did not overwhelm them. She had cleverly packed embroidery threads and wool in her trunk, and of a morning while they were confined to their cabin, it helped while away the time. She was soon teaching Maggie the finer points of embroidery and Katherine was learning how to knit, skills neither of them had ever acquired.

It was in these quiet moments that they learned more about one another, hearing tales of Mary's grandchildren who she absolutely doted on, left behind in London, and Maggie's husband Jamie and his dreams of owning his own land to pass down to his sons some day. Katherine shared memories of her childhood and the circumstances that led to her living with her aunt and uncle. The two women felt compassion for her, both having been raised by their own parents, leaving home only when they married, although Maggie had returned to her parents' home when Jamie had set off across the sea, with a promise to send for her as soon as possible.

Katherine, listening to Maggie's happy chatter about the future her beloved Jamie was going to carve out for the two of them, felt a twinge of envy for the certainty of happiness her friend knew would be hers.

I wish I could be as certain of my own future she thought, allowing herself a moment of doubt in those early days of the voyage. Mary and Maggie had chatted on, unaware of the sadness that had descended like a cloud over their young friend. While Katherine had related tales of her childhood, she had been unwilling to reveal the circumstances of her own marriage or of Roland's lecherous attack the night before her wedding. Sharing such close quarters, she knew they had both seen his now fading teeth marks but she had, cowardly and perhaps unfairly, let them assume the wound had come from an over-enthusiastic bridegroom. If they sensed a certain melancholy, they charitably laid the blame on the enforced separation of the newly wedded couple.

But it was during the afternoons that Mary, an aficionado of parlor games, truly excelled. She introduced the others to the game of whist, the loser having to compose and recite a short poem, which was accompanied by much laughter. Simon usually took himself off, refusing to join the others in any of their entertainments. Although both Jonathan and Katherine tried to coax him back, he declared such games were not to his liking and insisted that they continue without him.

In Simon's absence, Jonathan found himself playing escort to Katherine, opening doors, fetching her shawl when the weather turned cool, and a myriad of small favors that he performed in the hopes of glimpsing her shy but beguiling smile. Katherine, in her innocence, secretly lamented that it wasn't Jonathan who she had married. Most evenings before saying good night, the two of them strolled on deck, talking and laughing, exchanging memories of their childhood and dreams of the future, neither of them recognizing that the fondness they felt for each other was blossoming into something forbidden.

And so the long days at sea passed. Simon continued his self-imposed exile, listening to their laughter as it drifted out over the water. Late one afternoon Katherine, hoping he would join them, found him staring moodily out at the water, a look of deep unhappiness on his face. She hesitated to intrude but, sensing her presence, he turned to face her, marveling once more at her uncommon beauty, watching in fascination as an errant breeze tugged a wisp of her rich auburn hair from under her bonnet.

"Madam, were you seeking me?" His words were cold and exact.

Suddenly unsure of herself, Katherine hesitated before answering, her voice trembling. "Simon, wouldn't you consider joining us. Surely passing the time with friends is far better than searching the horizon for land that Captain Hart says won't appear for some days yet."

"Madam, searching for land is all the entertainment I require. And now, if you will excuse me, I have matters to attend to." He turned his blue eyes on her, causing her to recoil from the iciness of his look. He bowed his head and walked past her, unconcerned with the tears that filled her eyes.

Katherine stood at the rail, her emotions in turmoil. *What was the matter with the man? Did he hate her?* The threatened tears finally spilled over, grief and despair tearing at her heart. An arm encircled her, and the heavy lashes that shadowed her cheeks flew up.

"Jonathan!" she gasped. She was glad the fading light hid the flush that colored her face.

"I'm sorry but I couldn't help but overhear." His voice faded but as she looked up, the tenderness of his expression startled her. He continued to keep his arm around her and she leaned against him, grateful for the haven she found there, confused by her unexpected response to his nearness.

Shakily, she drew away from him. "What is to happen to me in this new world? Will I be a wife or some piece of baggage, discarded and ignored?" Suddenly tears were blinding her eyes and choking her voice. "Why did he marry me?"

The ship suddenly listed as a huge wave crashed against it, throwing her against Jonathan. Startled, she felt his arms pull her toward him. He lowered his head, his lips hungrily seeking her, as soft as a whisper, kissing away her tears. Instinctively her lips found their way to his, and she felt herself crushed against him as he smothered her mouth with passionate kisses. Abruptly he released her, leaving her weak-kneed and confused. She searched his face, disappointed that he had stopped.

"I can't. He's my cousin—you're his wife." His voice had become ragged with emotion.

"Jonathan, please, just hold me," she begged.

"For the love of God, Katherine," he whispered hoarsely, "go back to the others, quickly, before I shame both of us."

Startled, she turned and fled back to the safety of her friends, his words echoing in her mind. Neither of them noticed eyes watching them from his perch high above, his maniacal laughter carried away in the wind.

Maggie and the Featherstone's, caught up in their game, smiled as she rejoined them, until they caught a glimpse of her face. Concern rippled through them but she fended their questions off, insisting she was fine. Having observed the couple for some weeks, the three, knowing looks in their eyes, were aware that all was not well between Simon and Katherine. In unspoken agreement, they were certain that this upset could be laid at the door of her husband, a man they were all finding difficult to maintain any degree of civility toward. A short time later, as Katherine recovered herself and was sitting with the others, the door opened to admit Jonathan. He smiled quietly at all of them but his eyes never left Katherine who, with nails digging into the palms of her hands concealed within the folds of her dress, studiously ignored him.

The five were now attempting to stage a play, hoping that might lure Simon into their circle but he turned a cold shoulder on all of them, despite their repeated requests for his company. Mary, shrugging off the rebuff, cast Katherine and Jonathan as the ill-fated lovers in the tragedy they would perform for Captain Hart and any others who cared to watch, in two days time. She was a hard task-master, rehearsing the afternoons away.

Katherine both dreaded and longed for rehearsal of the love scene that would place her in Jonathan's arms, if only briefly. As he spoke his lines, holding her closely to him, he declared his love for her and she for him so convincingly the other members of the cast applauded, unaware of what they were witnessing. But Jonathan, tortured by what he perceived as disloyalty and betrayal, took great pains after the play had been performed to keep Katherine at a distance, ensuring that no chance encounters occurred again.

It was early evening some days later that Simon stood at the railing of the ship, gazing pensively into the water below. So absorbed was he with his thoughts that he was unaware of his cousin's approach until Jonathan stood beside him. The two stared silently at the waves breaking against the side of the ship, the cold spray barely reaching them.

"I fear a storm approaches, Simon. The ladies have declined my invitation for a last stroll above decks, claiming it too cold and rough. I can't blame them for that, I suppose."

He waited in vain for a response, finally glancing at his silent companion. He was taken aback by the misery he glimpsed in Simon's eyes and, misinterpreting the cause, cleared his throat nervously. After all, he argued with himself, he was intruding into a matter that was really none of his business and also trying to right a wrong, for if he couldn't bring about some sense of unity to the newlyweds, he feared he would wrong his cousin and betray Katherine's trusting innocence. Squaring his shoulders, he plunged into the matter that troubled him and damn the consequences of his interference.

"Simon, Featherstone and I have been talking", he hesitated, "and, well, we feel that both you and Katherine are suffering from this most unfortunate separation. What we propose is that the two of you spend time together alone." He paused again. "Shall we say an hour or two before the evening meal? Featherstone and I will keep the other ladies company while you and Katherine become better acquainted, with no fear of intrusion."

Simon, at first astonished at his cousin's proposal, turned it quickly over in his mind. A smile appeared on his lips, one that didn't quite reach the glacial blue of his eyes. Jonathan felt a stab of jealousy, knowing he was throwing Katherine into the arms of her husband instead of where he longed her to be, and then had a momentary twinge of disquiet, wondering if his meddling had indeed been the right thing to do but he found his hand being shaken vigorously while his cousin praised him for his selflessness, not to mention his thoughtfulness.

"What an absolutely wonderful idea. And you and Featherstone are to be commended for both your discretion and concern. Why, if it's all right with both of you, I will take advantage of your offer tomorrow afternoon."

Dazed by the enthusiasm his proposal had received, Jonathan merely nodded, wondering why, if it was the right thing to do, he felt so miserable. As waves sprayed both men, he suggested they would be wise to beat a hasty retreat but Simon merely grunted before asking him to convey his gratitude to Featherstone, assuring his cousin he would stay above decks a few moments longer and savor the bracing wind. He was whistling softly as his cousin went below in search of warmth and shelter.

Turning toward the bow of the ship, Simon cautiously made his way across the slippery deck, seeking the one who would, for a price, solve his present difficulty. An unseen hand laid on his shoulder caused him to start in surprise. The fetid odor of the one he had been seeking assailed his nostrils before he actually glimpsed the features that had so frightened his wife and the others that first night aboard. The scuffed and dusty bible he always carried, quoting from it when prophesying the hellfire his fellow sailors were doomed to suffer, was clutched tightly in his powerful fingers.

Simon had studied the crew for some days after setting sail, quickly determining that Spanish Jack would be the ideal accomplice, cautiously setting out to discover how far the other's willingness to earn a few coins would extend. Over the course of the voyage, they had formed an alliance of sorts and the sailor, coveting the promised purse, was eager to do the other's bidding, giving no thought to legalities. Although he fiercely believed in the hellfire he preached, he deemed that it was reserved for lesser men and he himself could move with impunity through life. He didn't know exactly what he was being recruited for but would risk all to gain an extra coin or two.

The two conspirators moved into the shadows, although with the threat of a storm brewing, there was little chance of being seen or overheard. Coins were exchanged with the promise of more to come when the deed was done.

"Thank 'e, milord, I stands ready to do your bidding." Stumps of rotting teeth were exposed as he smiled in what he believed to be a friendly manner.

"Stop addressing me as milord, you cretin, for I am not a nobleman nor have I the slightest desire to be one." Simon flexed his shoulders as if to shake off the evil he was proposing. The other bobbed his head, fearful of alienating his benefactor. "Tis understood then, that in three days time, you will spirit my wife away as she leaves my cabin, just before the evening meal, keeping her well hidden until all are abed, and, sometime before dawn, toss her over the side. Captain Hart thinks we should reach land before this week has ended so there can be no delay."

Beads of perspiration formed on his forehead despite the coolness of the breeze. He knew his future happiness depended on this venal miscreant's ability to carry out the deed with no one suspecting that he, Simon Radcliffe, was the author of such a dastardly scheme. He felt the tiniest shiver of remorse as he glanced into the glittering blackness of his fellow conspirator's eyes, certain that he could see the gates of hell.

"And you still be certain sure, milord, that this tasty bit of crumpet be mine until I heaves her over the side? To pleasure meself with and none to say me nay?" He examined the face of his benefactor, searching for any possible sign of treachery and, at last satisfied, licked at the spittle that had formed in the corners of his mouth.

Lustful visions filled his head as Simon, feeling unexpected pity for the hapless victim of this scheme, bade him a curt good night.

Chapter Seven

Katherine fussed with her hair and dress, trying to appear as presentable as possible. Mary Featherstone and Maggie smiled fondly at her as she adjusted her bonnet before turning to them for words of encouragement, for encouragement was exactly what Katherine needed.

The past two days should have been the opportune time for her and Simon to talk and become better acquainted but he seemed more than a little reluctant to share any of his thoughts or dreams with her and evinced no interest in anything she might have to say. She hoped that today, instead of reading to her husband as he seemed to want her to do, he would actually converse with her. She fiddled with the bright green ribbons of her bonnet one last time and smiled anxiously at her two companions, wondering if perhaps she and Simon might stroll the decks together.

"Well, I'm off then." She hugged each of them before opening the door, peering down the short, narrow passageway before stepping across to the other cabin. In her innocence, she would have been astonished at the unspoken assumptions her travelling companions had made about the time the newlyweds spent together, who in turn would have been struck speechless if they had but realized Simon and Katherine's time was spent reading, or more accurately, Katherine reading and Simon staring moodily at the ceiling, not snuggling cozily together on Simon's narrow cot.

At the light tap on his cabin door, Simon's deep voice called out, inviting her to enter. He sat on his bunk, gazing at her as she entered. "Ah, here you are, Katherine, and here is but another opportunity to spend more precious time together and make the romantics who are sharing this voyage with us happy." Though his words were courteous, his tone was patronizing.

Confused, she wandered restlessly about the confined space. The silence lengthened between them, making her uncomfortable until Simon gestured wordlessly for her to sit on one of the other bunks, for this cabin was as starkly furnished as her own.

He handed Katherine the dog-eared book she had been reading from the day before and, grateful for the distraction, she searched for the page she had last read, unaware of how sensuous her voice sounded as she continued to narrate the story he had chosen.

There was a faint tremor in his voice as though some emotion had touched him when he finally interrupted her. She had become caught up in the story and had failed to notice the waning light, nor had she heard the door across the passageway closing as the others had made their way to their dinner, although her husband had been listening for that very sound.

He at last rose from his bed, his voice low and smooth as he took the book from her hands and drew her to him. The thick lashes that shadowed her cheeks flew open as she stared wordlessly up at him, her heart racing at what she felt was an alarming rate, although she was unsure whether it was fear or excitement. His expression darkened with an unfathomable expression, throwing Katherine into deeper confusion. Abruptly he released her and bowed his head.

"The hour grows late and soon the evening meal will be served. I had best release you so you might freshen yourself before joining the others. Oh, don't forget your bonnet." He retrieved the bonnet from the bunk it had rested on.

When she tried to speak, her voice trembled. "Of course, the others await." And turning quickly, she stepped into the passageway, pausing only long enough to pull the door firmly shut.

As she released the handle, a rough sack was pulled over her head, falling to below her waist. Arms of steel wrapped themselves about her body. Sheer mind-numbing fright swept through her as she felt herself being hoisted over her captor's shoulder. Sensing she was about to scream, steely fingers encircled one wrist, twisting it viciously. A man's voice chuckled softly.

"Don't scream, me fine beauty, or I'll be forced to throttle ye before we've had time to make each other's acquaintance."

His rasping words chilled her to her very core. She felt him pause as he peered about for unwelcome eyes, taking several more paces and stopping before resuming his furtive gait. Abruptly, she felt herself falling but again those iron-like arms caught and lowered her carelessly to the deck. At the sound of grating being pulled aside, she surmised her destination was below decks. She could not control the violent trembling that had seized her and, just as she began to claw at her covering, she was once more thrown over a hard shoulder as he made his way down a narrow set of steps, pausing only long enough to replace the grating.

He seemed to be traversing the length of the ship when he came to an abrupt halt. Again, Katherine felt herself falling, but this time there were no arms to catch her, only the rough wooden planks to break her fall. Dazed, she scrambled to sit upright, tearing futilely at the dusty, suffocating sacking. Her captor lit a small lantern, its tiny flame flickering weakly in the darkness. A cruel laugh chilled her to her very being as the sack was roughly torn from her. Looking up, Katherine breathed in shallow gasps as she recognized her captor.

"You!" she spat.

Since that night they had first been made aware of Spanish Jack, the three women had rarely ventured out of their cabin alone, fretting that he might be lurking about although he had managed to avoid any confrontation with the male passengers. She struggled to stand but was pushed forcefully back onto the rough, splintered flooring. He rubbed the back of his hand across his mouth, blackened teeth exposed as he smiled, caressing her cheek with filthy fingers. She recoiled at his touch. Seizing her wrists, he quickly snapped them into the manacles he had so painstakingly fastened to the wall and floor. Grasping her slender ankles, he expertly cuffed them.

"What do you mean to do?" she questioned in a voice shrill with anxiety.

"Why, me proud beauty, first I'll be lettin' ye cool yer' heels down here in me cozy little nest." His hands indicated some grimy bedding strewn about. Katherine shuddered uncontrollably, fear, stark and vivid, glittering in her eyes. "And then, as the lord told me," he continued, "when me watch be ended, I'll return to yer' side and we'll snuggle under that there blanket, just the two of us and get better acquainted. By that time, I expects ye'll be most warm and welcoming. And when I'm done with ye, I'll feed ye to the fishes."

He stopped speaking, rubbing at his grizzled whiskers. "And somehow, I thinks ye'll be grateful to old Jack, for I'm not known for my gentle touch with the gentler sex." She paled even more as the significance of his words sank in. "And I be hoping ye'll be as willing with old Spanish Jack as ye was with that other bloke what kissed ye."

Her blood ran cold at his words and, as his fingers squeezed her breasts painfully, she cringed, horror-stricken. He pulled a filthy rag from the depths of his pants and tied it around her mouth, pulling the ends tight enough to cause her to wince painfully. He snatched at her bonnet which somehow still dangled loosely from her neck, smiling coldly as he stuffed it inside his shirt. After covering her with his abhorrent bedding, he extinguished the tiny bit of light the lantern shed, leaving her to listen to his fading footsteps as he abandoned her to the deep terrifying blackness.

Grunting, he hoisted himself onto the deck, replacing the grating carefully to avoid alerting anyone to his movements, unaware of eyes watching furtively from the shadows. Ned, having finished his evening meal, had wandered up on deck when he spotted his shipmate stealthily creeping about, causing him to wonder why Spanish Jack, who he knew should be on watch, would risk leaving his post to go below into the hold.

Alone, Katherine had begun to shake as fearful images built in her mind. Above the creaking of the ship, she could hear footsteps passing above her. Surely she would be missed and a search launched. She struggled to free herself from the cold iron manacles but soon had to admit defeat. Tears of frustration and fear coursed silently down her cheeks as she lay back, contemplating her fate. The raucous sounds of laughter and snatches of song filled the night air mockingly as the crew enjoyed their evening meal and well deserved rest.

* * * *

When Simon entered the tiny dining hall, the conversation petered out as his fellow passengers looked at him, somewhat surprised when they realized he was alone. Maggie was the first to speak. "Why, Mr. Radcliffe, where have you left Miss Katherine? We assumed you would be coming together."

"Why, ladies, I assumed she would be with you. She left me earlier, saying she wanted to take a short stroll on deck before we met again at dinner." A shadow of annoyance touched his eyes as he noted their concern but not yet displaying alarm.

Apprehension touched the faces that surrounded him as they listened to the wind that had begun to howl short minutes before. They all clambered up the stairs, only to be met by fierce waves washing onto the deck, making it treacherously slippery. The ladies stood looking helplessly on as the three men cautiously made their way about the deck of the ship, searching for a slender form. Jonathan paused by the railing and carefully plucked a straw bonnet from a nail poking out of the wooden rail, green ribbons dancing wetly in the wind. Ashen faced, he turned to the other men as they stood, silently staring into the swirling water. The ladies, having spied the bonnet and all it implied, fell into each other's arms sobbing, already mourning the loss of one who had so quickly become a precious friend.

All thoughts of dinner having fled, they trooped wordlessly to the women's quarters, crowding in and sitting closely together in their grief. Words of comfort were directed toward Simon over the loss of his bride but he had turned into himself and they hesitated to intrude.

Abruptly he rose and left the cramped space, refusing Jonathan's gesture offering to accompany him wherever he might be headed. The door closed and the others continued to sit, horror-struck at this turn of events.

* * * *

The distant sound of the grating being moved roused Katherine from the stupor she had fallen into. Icy fingers of terror twisted around her heart. Panic such as she had never known before welled in her throat as she listened to the grating being returned to its position. She peered into the darkness, listening to stealthy footsteps approach, a small lantern lighting the way. Her eyes widened in disbelief as she recognized the cabin boy. Her heart sang with delight as he knelt down beside her, loosening the rag around her numbed lips.

Questions tumbled from her. "How did you find me, Ned? Who else is here?" Fearfully she urged him to free her from her chains but he stopped her words with a cautioning finger.

"I will explain all after I have you free and safe, madam. Spanish Jack could return anytime," he whispered hoarsely. Grasping the cruel manacles that held her, he quickly realized he couldn't affect her release on his own. His expression revealing the wretchedness he felt, Ned glanced around, searching for anything that would help him break her iron bonds.

Frantically, he threw all his weight into wresting the steel shackles from the bolts anchored into the wooden planks but to no avail. Katherine, fearing the return of her captor, silently urged him on but recognized that alone he was powerless. Doubt filled her haunted eyes as he hesitantly explained that he would have to leave her and search out her husband, for he could not free her on his own. Disbelief washed over her as she felt him tie the filthy rag once more across her bruised lips, although his touch was gentler and the knot somewhat more bearable.

Ned cradled her face in his hands and, gazing into her panic stricken eyes, whispered that he would return with the Captain and her husband. Katherine wanted to scream in frenzied protest at the thought of being left alone again but intuitively knew that his plan was sound. She stared imploringly at her would-be rescuer, silently begging him to hurry. He squeezed her slender shoulder reassuringly and turned, taking his lantern and fleeing into the bowels of the ship, plunging her once more into terrifying blackness. Again, the muffled sound of the grate being moved reached her and, tears flowing unheeded down her cheeks, she prayed for his speedy return.

It seemed only minutes before Katherine heard the metal grate once again. Peering fearfully into the darkness that enveloped her, she realized only a single set of footsteps approached. She gasped, panting in terror as Spanish Jack's unshaven face leered down at her, seeming more ghastly in the pale glow of the lantern he carried.

"So, me pet, ye didn't run off. Have ye been missing me?" He chuckled, amused by his own drollness, his voice rasping as it cut into the silence.

Reaching down, he tore the rag from her mouth, unmindful of the pain he caused. Whistling tunelessly, he searched his pockets for the key to the detested manacles that held her prisoner. Revulsion like nothing she had ever experienced before welled deep inside her. He crouched over her as he turned the key, almost suffocating her with the foul stench that filled the air. He backed away from her slightly, enough so she could massage her wrists and ankles, scraped raw in her futile struggle to free herself. Looking up at her jailer, she found herself shrinking away from his cold twisted smile. Without warning, he seized the neck of her dress and ripped both it and her chemise, exposing her pale breasts to the damp night air. Licking his lips in anticipation, a thread of drool hung suspended from his slack mouth. Shock and anger lit up her eyes as she felt his fingers roughly caressing and then brutally squeezing her exposed flesh. Her slender fingers turned into talons as her nails scratched his face, leaving deep welts on either cheek. Her hands were seized in his steely grasp, curses falling from his mouth.

"So the kitten has claws." His anger turned to a scalding fury as he slapped her with such force she thought her jaw must surely be broken. Katherine opened her mouth to scream, her only thought that Simon and the others might be close enough to hear but he shook her into a gasping, sobbing silence. He once more seized the material of her gown and ripped it from her. Her hands attempted to cover what this monster had exposed, unheeded circles of scarlet coloring her cheeks.

Her attacker's satisfied smirk mocked her as he leaned forward. She shuddered, struggling hopelessly in his arms as she realized he was about to kiss her. Nausea rose in her throat, threatening to choke her. Grief and despair tore at her heart as she twisted her head in a futile effort to escape his rank breath. Just as his lips met hers, there was a scraping sound as the metal grate was once more shoved aside.

Her attacker's head lifted, peering warily into the darkness just as Katherine had done earlier. The sound of voices and many footsteps echoed in the hold, the wicks of lanterns lighting the way. Spanish Jack snarled in frustration and hatred as he was yanked off his helpless victim. A cry of relief escaped her lips as she hastily attempted to cover herself with the tattered remnants of her dress.

Jonathan stepped forward and, removing his cloak, shielded her from curious eyes. She started, realizing it was not her husband who sought to protect her but his cousin and she smiled gratefully up at him. Voices were asking if she had been hurt but she could only shake her head mutely. Glancing around, she saw Simon holding a pistol on the miscreant, as Captain Hart and Ned looked on. An anguished howl startled both the rescuers and the rescued as Spanish Jack made an attempt to catch hold of her as Jonathan guided her toward the stairs. 'No, she be mine. The lord…'

A shot rang out and lifeless, he fell to the floor. Simon, holding his pistol loosely, smiled wanly at the others. "I couldn't bear the thought of him threatening my wife again." As he finished speaking, he met his cousin's grey eyes, reading curiosity in them as Jonathan tried to puzzle out why Simon suddenly couldn't bear the thought of his wife being threatened by anyone.

A tense silence filled the hold until Captain Hart laid a comforting hand on Simon's shoulder, murmuring a few conciliatory words. All eyes then turned to Katherine who became increasingly uncomfortable under their scrutiny. Trembling as she remembered Spanish Jack's promise to throw her overboard after he had finished with her, she could feel no remorse that the man was now dead, a threat no more.

Hugging the heavy cloak tightly about her, she wordlessly made her way to her quarters, Jonathan and Simon providing a silent, brooding escort. She abruptly turned, facing her husband and his cousin, tears trickling down her pale cheeks.

"I did remember your advice, Jonathan, about delivering a hard kick but my ankles were bound before I recovered my wits after he had seized me, and there was no further opportunity."

Smiling into her emerald eyes, Jonathan reassured her that he knew her chance for defense hadn't presented itself, and she drew comfort from his words, knowing he wasn't disappointed with her.

At the sound of voices, the door of her tiny cabin flew open. The tearful and frightened faces of Mary Featherstone and Maggie soon blended with Katherine's own teary visage, the three hugging each other as if they had no intention of every being separated again. Eventually, tears dried, the two surreptitiously observed their young friend, curious as to what had happened. The cloak that she had wrapped herself in gaped open and both women spied her state of undress.

Mary, horrified, looked questioningly at the men. "Has she...was she...?" She was unable to put her fears into words.

Jonathan shook his head, reassuring both women. Ned, who had been released from duty by the captain, had been standing off from the passengers, ready to carry out any job he was bidden to do. He was quickly enlisted by the two women to boil as much water as could be spared and fetch it to their cabin, with a hip bath or as near to one as he could manage. As he rushed off to do their bidding, the other men, unsure of their roles, muttered to each other and maneuvered themselves beyond the reach of the bustling Mary and her able assistant, Maggie, closing the door softly behind them.

At the sound of the door closing, Katherine collapsed onto the nearest bed, fresh sobs shaking her. Maggie grasped her hand, murmuring soothing words of comfort while the older woman patted her shoulder. Slowly, as her tears subsided, the task of undressing her began. The elder of the two stopped abruptly and, with a hasty excuse, left the room, returning minutes later brandishing a bottle of liquor.

"There's no reason why men should be the only ones to seek comfort in a glass of brandy. And this night, comfort is sorely needed."

She poured three tiny glasses of the brew and, smiling tremulously, they swallowed the fiery liquid, gasping at the burning in their throats. A quick knock at the door heralded the arrival of Jonathan.

"I saw you take the brandy, Mary."

The older woman blushed but stood defiantly beside Katherine, causing him to chuckle softly.

"I'm not here to confiscate it but to use it to clean any wounds she might have."

As he bent to the task, Katherine felt his fingers tremble as he dabbed softly at her abused flesh. Smiling, he questioned her softly as to what had transpired between her and Spanish Jack but she quickly assured him that, other than ruining a dress she could ill afford to lose, and the scratches and bruises he had already seen, there was no other damage. She was thankful he made no reference to the other time he had tended her after Roland's attack, for she surely couldn't have faced unspoken questions from her friends

In a quavering voice, she repeated Spanish Jack's threat. "He said he was going to feed me to the fishes, after he was finished with me," she gulped in remembered terror. "He said I would welcome it once he was done." Fresh sobs wracked her body.

The doctor continued with his ministrations until at last a soft knock at the door announced the arrival of Ned and two other sailors who, having been apprised of the situation, kept their eyes respectfully down while they carried in buckets of steaming water, emptying them into the brass tub that Ned had set down. Smiling, he produced a small sliver of soap, presenting it with a flourish.

Concern crossed his face as he stole a glance at the woman whose face had rarely left his thoughts since she had boarded the ship. Removing his cap respectfully after the sailors had departed he shuffled his feet in dismay at her distress.

"Begging your pardon, Mrs. Radcliffe, but here be your bath. I know it's not the way of things that folks has a bath regular-like but me own ma always swore how a good soak could make all her troubles disappear, and she never failed to have one every Sunday if she could get one of us kids to fetch her water, until winter would freeze the river over. I hope you'll feel the same." Not waiting for a response, he nodded his head, turned and fled through the door.

After Jonathan had satisfied himself that there was no permanent damage, he excused himself and left. Both women gasped in surprise as they saw the extent of the bruises and scratches on her face and breasts, Mary shocking them both as she muttered that she was thankful such a beast was now on his way to hell. Maggie, opening Katherine's trunk, soon laid out a nightgown and mended undergarments.

Mary Featherstone continued to fuss at her but Katherine could not bring herself to dismiss her. As the two washed bits and pieces of debris from her auburn hair, a knock was once again heard. Opening it just a crack to preserve Katherine's modesty, the elder of her two guardians faced Ned, who was once more a messenger.

"Begging your pardon, Mrs. Featherstone, but Captain Hart wants to know if you ladies would feel up to coming to dinner or should he send it here?"

Turning, she sent the others an inquiring look. Katherine merely shook her head, declaring in a voice fragile and shaking, that she had no appetite and only wanted her bed.

Ned, hearing her reply, shouted through the door. "If Mrs. Radcliffe is not up to it, Captain Hart told me to stand guard outside the door until you ladies returned.'

Katherine, having related Ned's part in her rescue, assured them she would feel quite safe if he was nearby and, so saying, she donned the nightdress Maggie now held, before climbing into her narrow cot. As Maggie bent to extinguish the tiny candle, Katherine begged her to leave it burn.

Chapter Eight

The six travelers stood at the rail of the ship, as eager to disembark as they had once been to board. Land had been sighted the day before and at breakfast, the captain had promised to have them on dry land sometime in the afternoon. Katherine, curious about her new homeland, gazed at the buildings and the people that bustled about on shore as the ship entered the harbor, the sun shining welcomingly on the new arrivals. Trunks had been packed and stood waiting to be carried ashore. Simon, standing at Katherine's side, scanned the shore as tiny figures became people and faces became familiar friends and acquaintances. The anchor was dropped and soon their feet felt solid ground once more.

The ladies, clinging to each other amid the hustle and bustle of the busy port, stayed just behind their escorts as they surveyed the flurry of movement all about them. A shout penetrated the din and Simon, turning slowly, was soon waving his hat in greeting as a familiar carriage approached.

The door was thrown open and an elegantly attired man appeared in the doorway, waving a carved walking stick at them. The driver of the conveyance hastily alit and assisted his elderly passenger down. A man, although slightly stooped with age but still a handsome figure approached the small company. He was an older version of Simon although he sported a very impressive moustache, his hair, probably as thick as his grandson's, was wavy rather than curly, the same silvery hue as his moustache. His blue eyes, faded with age, fell on each of them before alighting on his beloved grandson.

"Grandfather, how did you learn of our arrival?" He spoke coldly, almost reluctantly extending a hand to the elderly man who cautiously stepped forward, leaning heavily on his cane.

"Hmpff," he snorted, "as if I had nothing better to do than meet every ship that called here." The old man smiled, obviously anxious to make amends to his grandson after their stormy parting so many months ago. "No, my boy, as luck would have it, I was in town on business but, upon hearing a ship was docking, decided to wait on the chance you might be aboard. And here you are." He patted his grandson's shoulder awkwardly, uncertain how an embrace would be received after their last bitter exchange.

Wheeling around, he grasped Jonathan's hand in greeting. "My boy, how are you? I see you somehow managed to keep this scallywag out of trouble. For that I am in your debt. And who are all these people?" He paused, his tired blue eyes widening in disbelief. "Featherstone, is that you? Did your angel of a wife finally convince you to put away your law books and visit the colonies?" The two men thumped each other's back in their delight at meeting once more. Removing his hat, he made a courtly bow before gallantly taking Mary Featherstone's hand and pressing his lips to her fingers. "And Mary, you were brave enough to accompany him! I am not only overjoyed to see you both but completely flabbergasted." He took out a handkerchief and dabbed at his eyes, discomfited to be displaying such sentimentality.

Turning his attention to the other newcomers he paused as he glanced at both young women. "Well, Simon, I'm waiting for an introduction to these two beautiful young things."

Simon and Jonathan stood attentively on each side of the women. Nudging Maggie forward, Jonathan faced the old man and spoke. "Samuel Langtree, may I present Mrs. Margaret McGregor, who much prefers to be called Maggie. She left her native Scotland to join her husband in New York, sailing on her uncle's ship and has become a treasured friend to all of us."

Maggie, never one to hang back, extended her hand, obviously expecting the same courtly treatment as Mrs. Featherstone, and she was not disappointed. Samuel Langtree made much of her as Jonathan explained that she had proven to be an invaluable companion during the crossing.

He continued, "Maggie's uncle, Robert Hart, the captain of our ship, will be in port for some days. As his niece is to continue on with him to New York where her husband awaits, I have taken the liberty of inviting her to stay at Seven Oaks, a much appreciated solution when one considers the alternative would be to have her stay at an inn, where all manner of harm might befall her."

Samuel's blue eyes twinkled as he gazed at Maggie. "Why, it would be no trouble at all. There are too many bedrooms standing empty at Seven Oaks. Please let Captain Hart know we shall be only too pleased to entertain Mrs. McGregor." He turned to his grandson. "And now Simon, who do we have here?"

Katherine felt Simon's apprehension as he anxiously cleared his throat before clasping Katherine's hand and stepping forward. "Grandfather, may I present my wife, Katherine Maguire Radcliffe. We were wed just days before sailing."

Katherine smiled nervously at him. "How do you do, Mr. Langtree? I am so very happy to meet you." There was a gentle softness in her voice.

Samuel, sensing her unease, tilted her chin upward until their eyes met. She became increasingly uneasy under such intense scrutiny. A faint tremor could be heard in his voice as though some deeper emotion had touched him.

"Well, my dear Mrs. Katherine Maguire Radcliffe, I believe you have just made me the happiest man in South Carolina." He smiled at her and then at his grandson, taking Simon's hand and shaking it vigorously. "Simon, you rascal, you've kept me waiting for this moment for so long. And if your mother were here, I know she would rejoice with me."

Chuckling, he turned and surveyed the crowd that had been gathering, curious to know the identities of all these newcomers. Turning his back to them, he carried Katherine's hand to his lips but stopped abruptly as he spied her scraped and bruised wrist. He grasped her other wrist and, after assuring himself that it was in a like condition, cast a cold eye on his grandson. "Did you find it necessary to keep her in shackles, Simon?"

Ignoring his wife, he stared defiantly into the old man's eyes. "Grandfather, it's nothing to be concerned about. A small disturbance on board that could have turned into a disaster but by the grace of God and a sharp-eyed cabin boy by the name of Ned, tragedy was averted at the eleventh hour." Katherine paled as she heard him offer such a casual explanation of her scrapes and bruises.

Samuel, remembering the crowd still gathered around them, smiled and, with a promise to discuss the matter further at home, gestured toward his carriage.

"Simon, since I wasn't expecting you and your party, I can only provide the comfort of my carriage to two or three of you. I propose that I return to Seven Oaks with the Featherstone's so we may reminisce without fear of boring you young people, whilst you young men hire a carriage for the four of you and the baggage." Without waiting for an answer, his arms encircled his old friends as he led them toward his waiting carriage.

Simon tersely delegated Jonathan to stay with the ladies as he strode off to hire a driver and carriage from the livery and it seemed no time until they were travelling down a dusty road.

Maggie, eager to see all she could of her new homeland, gazed out at the passing countryside, unaware of Katherine's brooding silence. Jonathan had missed the exchange between Simon and his grandfather but sensed that his cousin had said something that Katherine was having trouble coming to terms with. Simon and Katherine, sitting stiffly side by side, gazed out at the scenery but saw nothing.

Katherine again pondered what manner of man she had wed. *How dare he refer to the threat of Spanish Jack as 'a small matter'?* Bristling with unspoken anger, she edged as far from him as was possible in such a confined space. She knew Jonathan was watching her but couldn't bring herself to meet his eyes. If anyone showed her the least kindness right now, she knew she would burst into tears and that would be a humiliation she could not bear. They rode along in strained silence, even the effervescent Maggie finally sensing the tension between the newlyweds, until Simon abruptly called for the carriage to halt. As it slowed, he tipped his hat to his wife and Maggie, gave a quick nod to his cousin before climbing down. Katherine looked about but other than a tree-lined lane, she could see nothing to attract her husband's attention.

"Simon, for God's sake, consider what you're doing!" Jonathan, recognizing the lane and his anger barely contained, looked down at his cousin, taken aback at the animated expression on the other man's face.

"Please extend my apologies to everyone, especially my grandfather but explain to them I had to stop to visit an old friend." Saying this, he carelessly bowed to the carriage and its occupants, whistling a merry tune as he strode light-heartedly down the narrow road.

Katherine and Maggie, speechless at his abrupt departure, looked inquiringly at Jonathan as he, with a thunderous expression playing across his handsome features, instructed the driver to continue on to Seven Oaks. Not wishing to incur his wrath with questions, both women sat silent as the carriage continued on its dusty journey.

At last, the carriage turned onto a narrow tree-lined lane similar to the one Simon had disappeared down, and short moments later a large white house came into view.

"May I welcome you to Seven Oaks, Katherine." Jonathan spoke in an odd yet gentle tone.

She stared open-mouthed at her new home as he pushed open the carriage door and stepped down. He had just finished helping the two women alight when the door of the plantation house opened and Samuel stepped out, smiling broadly in welcome until he realized that his grandson was not among the arrivals. A questioning expression appeared on his face as he confronted Jonathan, who could only shrug to indicate he had been powerless in the matter.

Katherine and Maggie, aware that there was something hugely wrong, stood back, uncertainty clouding their faces until Samuel, intent on welcoming Katherine to her new home, put all thoughts of his errant grandson behind him and smiled the smile of a genial host, happy to greet his guests. Grasping their elbows, he gently guided them inside where a handful of black house slaves awaited them.

Samuel lightly nudged Katherine forward and then spoke in a voice that had depth and authority to those assembled. "This is my newly arrived granddaughter-in-law, Master Simon's wife, Katherine Radcliffe. You are to see to her every need for she is your new mistress. And this young lady is her friend and travelling companion, Mrs. McGregor, who will be staying with us for a few days. Clover, I know you have already settled the Featherstone's' chamber but now I need you to prepare rooms for Mr. Jonathan and Mrs. McGregor.

A plump, middle-aged black woman nodded her head and quickly dispatched two young girls up the stairs to prepare the rooms. The rest of the servants, after a final curious glance at Mr. Simon's new wife, returned to whatever duties from which they had been pulled.

"Should either of you ladies require anything, just ask Clover. She runs both me and this house. She has already settled the Featherstone's in their chamber and by the look of their tired faces we'll not see them before dinner."

Clover, a brightly colored scarf tied around her hair, looked at both women as if measuring their worth. Turning to her master, she spoke, a jubilant smile lighting her face.

"Well, Master Sam, if Mr. Simon and this pretty young thing has a baby, you can bet it will be uncommon beautiful. I declare I ain't never seen such a fine looking lady."

Katherine, blushing at the servant's words, smiled shyly at the compliment. "Now child, you just come with me and we'll get you all rested up. And when you're ready, I'll take you around this big old house so you don't never get lost in it." Saying this, she grasped Katherine's hand and steered her toward the staircase before pausing as she remembered the other guests. "Now, Mr. Jonathan, you done know where your room is at. But the other lady, Mrs. McGregor, I just plain forgot about you, I'se so excited to know Mr. Simon got hisself a bride at last. So come on now, you follow us up and I'll get you both settled and your trunks sent to you just as soon as I can find a man with a strong back to carry them."

The two young women, astonished at the ease with which the black woman had sorted everything out, followed her up the stairs. Had Katherine glanced back, she would have seen Samuel lost in thought as he contemplated the new mistress of Seven Oaks.

After Maggie had been shown to her room, Clover led her new mistress down the hall to her bedchamber. Katherine was delighted with its cozy warmth for a small fire had been lit, chasing away any chill in the air. The walls had been painted a soft violet and the bed covered with a white quilt embroidered with tiny purple violets. A few small tables were scattered about, one of which was beside the bed and on which a crystal lamp rested, casting a welcoming glow in the dimly lit room before Clover threw open the heavy velvet drapes.

The black woman bustled about the room, brushing away imaginary specks of dust from a tabletop. A tap at the door heralded the arrival of her trunk as a servant entered and, at a signal from Clover, laid it in a corner. Undoing the leather straps, the big woman opened it before casting a troubled look in Katherine's direction, uncertain whether she should speak. "Miss Katherine, you be expecting another trunk?"

"No, Clover, I only have one trunk and all of my belonging were packed in it. Why do you ask? Is something amiss?" She felt a moment of panic at the thought of any further mishaps to the meager wardrobe contained within.

"No, no, Miss Katherine, nothing is wrong, nothing at all." Her voice faded as she became lost in thought. Straightening up, she glanced about the room. "I done unpacked everything and was just wondering if there was more to come, that's all. I'll have that laundry gal freshen your things up after being stored in a trunk all these weeks past."

Katherine continued to inspect her new bedroom, barely hearing the servant's comments. Even when she had lived at Marlow Court with her aunt and uncle, her bedchamber had not been anywhere near as fine and elegant as this one.

"Is there anything else you be needing, child? Would you like a nice hot bath? I can get some hot water fetched up here in no time."

"Oh, Clover, is that possible? I would dearly love to soak the salt from my skin."

The servant, summoning a young maid, gave orders for buckets of hot water, and leading her new mistress into a small room off the bedroom, soon had a brass tub filled with hot soapy water. When it became obvious Clover wasn't going to leave her side while there was any task left to perform, she shyly undressed and stepped into the bath. The servant's sharp eyes quickly took note of the collection of fading scrapes and bruises on her white skin but prudently said nothing.

As Katherine lay luxuriating in the soothing water, Clover ordered a light supper for her new mistress and also for Mrs. McGregor, explaining to Katherine that Master Sam and Mister Jonathan would be shut away in the library, most likely drinking and smoking those smelly cigars, and lord knew when anyone would see them next.

Sometime later, as the girl sat brushing her hair, the tray arrived and the housekeeper directed the maid to set it on a small table near the fire. The housekeeper looked askance at the threadbare nightgown as Katherine moved hungrily toward the tantalizing aromas wafting from the tray.

"Child, you may not have many gowns but why you be wearing that old rag when there's a pretty nightgown right here?" She held up the nightdress Katherine had worn on her first night as Simon's wife.

Blushing, Katherine took the gown from the servant and folded it carefully before putting it into a dresser drawer. "I'm saving that for a special occasion, Clover." Her tone, which had been so soft, suddenly had a firm ring to it, one that brooked no argument, and the servant realized that to pursue the subject would be folly indeed.

Clover soon had Katherine tucked into the huge bed, nestled between crisp white sheets, her eyes already heavy with sleep, sighing deeply as Morpheus claimed her. The housekeeper, glancing at her charge, silently left the chamber, vowing to talk to Master Sam as soon as he was free.

* * * *

After watching the ladies ascend the wide staircase, Samuel motioned for Jonathan to follow him into the library, closing the door against any chance eavesdroppers. He crossed the carpeted floor and poured a liberal splash of whiskey in two glasses. Handing Jonathan one, he raised a bushy grey eyebrow inquiringly.

"Well, why did he abandon the lot of you, instead of returning here to his home? And to leave his bride to face all of us, with everyone aware of what was going on!" He stopped his angry pacing. "Does the girl know anything?" His voice, always loud, became brusque and demanding.

Uncomfortable with the questioning, Jonathan stared into his glass as if seeking an answer. "I can't say for sure what she knows, Samuel. They've had precious few private moments until the last days of the voyage but I somehow doubt if Simon told her anything about Juliana. And if you're wondering how I know that, well, let's just say, having had time to observe her on that voyage, I doubt she would be here now, no matter what inducement might be offered."

"Damnation, I thought if the lad married elsewhere, that wanton hussy would lose her hold on him." He sat down abruptly, looking directly into Jonathan's clear grey eyes. "And the woman he married! How could he possibly choose that harlot over such an enchantress?" He paused in his tirade before continuing. "But I might be misjudging him. Perhaps he stopped merely to tell her of his marriage and to end the affair."

His voice was coolly disapproving as he splashed more whiskey into their glasses before his questions took another tack. "Now what could have caused such wounds on the girl's wrists, not to mention the marks on her neck and jaw?" He stared at the younger man, impatiently awaiting a reply. "The Featherstone's, especially dear Mary, made mention of some near disaster a scant few days ago but when I attempted to question them, they said I should get the whole story from Simon or Katherine. Well, my boy, will you enlighten me?"

Discomfited, Jonathan hesitated, and when he spoke there was an edge to his voice. "Sam, I don't think it's my place to tell you anything about Simon or Katherine."

Just as he spoke, the library door opened and the errant grandson entered the book-lined room, a cynical smile playing about his mouth. "Am I intruding on a private conversation or was that not my wife's and my name being bandied about?"

Samuel slowly rose from his cushioned chair. "Simon, at last you're home." His greeting contained a strong suggestion of reproach but he held his tongue. The two men seemed to wordlessly call a truce to their endless wrangling as he stepped forward and embraced his grandson.

Jonathan, still annoyed at his cousin's sudden departure from the carriage, was barely able to nod a greeting. "Your grandfather has heard whisperings of our crossing and has asked for enlightenment but I have declined as I knew you would want to tell him all that has happened since meeting Katherine."

Irritated by his derisive tone, Simon, his expression a mask of stone, turned once more to his grandfather. "Perhaps I could have some of whatever you two are drinking, Grandfather."

The old man started to rise once more but Jonathan forestalled him and poured a drink for his cousin, scowling as he handed him the glass.

"Well, that Irish wench, beautiful as she is, seems to invite trouble, Grandfather. Already I'm asking myself if perhaps I wed too hastily."

Jonathan, his face a study in contempt, cleared his throat, ready to right the wrong that was being done to an innocent. "Simon, I believe you're painting a picture that is entirely undeserved. Anything we have been witness to was never of her doing. She is entirely without blame!"

His words hung heavily over the other occupants of the room.

"All right Jonathan, perhaps I was harsh but even you, with that soft spot you seem to have for her, must admit wherever she goes, trouble soon follows. Correct?"

The old man, having followed this heated exchange, stood and demanded silence.

"Jonathan, you were offered a chance to relate what has befallen since Simon and Katherine met but you chose not to, quite rightly, of course. And now, here is my grandson, attempting to enlighten me and you keep interrupting. Please sir, hold your tongue! If you have anything to add when the telling is done, you will be given the opportunity."

Chastened, Jonathan sat back in a gesture of compliance.

"Well, Grandfather, I met Katherine through what was her guardian of sorts, Lord Granville Talbot. It seems his uncle, Lord Hector Talbot, had died childless and so his estate, which was entailed, went to the nearest male relative. Katherine herself had been orphaned in Ireland some years earlier with her only relative being Hector's wife, the Lady Maude. Hector and Maude took her in and raised her. Sadly the estate had been badly mismanaged over the years and consequently there was no dowry and few suitors, until I happened along." He paused, taking a long swallow from his glass before continuing.

"It was arranged that our wedding would take place in the morning, Jonathan and I having arrived the day before. We were to spend the night at Marlow Court, planning to be away as soon as the ceremony was over, although truth to tell, we desired nothing more than an escape from Lady Talbot, an absolute harridan. After Katherine had left the table the evening before the nuptials, retiring to her temporary quarters in a small chamber off the library, she foolishly allowed Lord Talbot's son, Roland by name, into her room. Some noise attracted Jonathan, who fortunately had gone into the library in search of a book and he surprised the two of them. The girl of course denied complicity. I could have called off the ceremony but she was so irresistible that I, perhaps foolishly, allowed things to proceed. The lad Roland had labored under the misconception that if he dishonored the girl, I would retract my offer of marriage, as she would then be damaged goods. He also foolishly thought that his mother, who absolutely loathed Katherine, would not allow her to leave if there was any possibility of a grandchild forthcoming."

As his discourse ended, there was an audible gasp from Jonathan. About to spring to Katherine's defense, he was stopped by a gesture from Samuel, whose countenance held a look of disbelief.

"As I said before, Jonathan, you will have your turn, should you want to further explain the events that led to this moment. Continue, Simon."

"We had a brief honeymoon in London where I had arranged for Featherstone to witness our bliss, planning to send you word with the first ship that sailed. But as events transpired, that wasn't necessary. Ours was the first ship leaving for America and Featherstone and his good wife, unbeknownst to me, had booked passage on it. Mrs. McGregor, who you have met, also had passage on the ship, and so we were left in something of a quandary, three men, three women, two cabins. We split up according to gender and crossed the Atlantic until, just days from port, Jonathan and Featherstone generously offered to vacate the 'gentlemen's quarters' every afternoon so that Katherine and I might become better acquainted. I naturally took them up on it and for two days, we happily whiled away the hours in seclusion. But sadly, on the third day, just as she left my quarters, she was seized and spirited below decks to the furthest corner of the hold. The miscreant, a deluded sailor by the name of Spanish Jack, had taken the notion that the Lord had promised her to him. He must have been planning it for some time for he had salvaged some rusty manacles and fastened them to the wall—hence the marks on her wrists and ankles. She was gagged and so couldn't scream for help, not that anyone would likely have heard her, concealed as she was. Spanish Jack had been fiendishly clever for he left her bonnet dangling conspicuously on a nail, making it appear she had been swept overboard."

Simon paused, after so long a narration, to take a generous swallow of his drink. Jonathan wordlessly arose and refilled the three glasses, refusing to meet his cousin's eyes as Simon resumed his tale.

"Fortunately for Katherine, Ned, the cabin boy, spotted Spanish Jack disappearing below decks when he should have been on watch. Curious, he awaited his chance and soon discovered the sailor's lair and the prey within it. He couldn't free her alone so he fetched Captain Hart, Jonathan and me. We arrived just as the brute was about to ravish her. I shot him right between the eyes. Katherine told us later that his plan was to throw her overboard, after he had his way with her."

The ticking of a clock could be heard in the silence that ensued. Samuel, an expression of doubt on his face, arose once more. "Simon, I find it difficult to believe that one that looks like an angel could be the author of such misfortune. Perhaps it is her innocence that has landed her in these situations but whatever, I intend to give her the benefit of any doubt. And Jonathan, I know I promised you the opportunity to defend the young lady but I fear that would be an affront to my grandson. I'm exhausted by the happenings of the day and would seek my bed before I collapse. I trust I will see both of you at breakfast. Good night." Both young men watched him wearily leave the room.

As the door closed behind him, Simon took one look at his cousin's seething face and arrogantly moved toward the door. "Well, good night Jonathan. I trust you will take care not to expose my wife to any further scandal."

Fury almost choked Jonathan as he seized his cousin by his sleeve. "How could you be so despicable? You know both attacks were none of Katherine's doing. How could you deliberately mislead the old man?"

Freeing his sleeve from the other's grasp, Simon stood steps away from his cousin, his eyes dark and contemptuous. Nodding his head in an insolent gesture, he walked stiffly to the staircase. Stopping suddenly, he turned toward his cousin. "And will you admit to my grandfather that you're in love with my wife, Jonathan? Have you told her yet," he laughed mockingly, "or have you even admitted it to yourself?"

Chapter Nine

Sunlight streamed through the bedroom window as Katherine opened her eyes. She glanced about the room, at first unsure of her surroundings but then memory came flooding back. Wondering briefly where Simon was, she threw the covers from her just as a door she hadn't noticed earlier opened and her husband appeared.

"Good morning, Katherine. Did you sleep well? I got in late so, rather than disturbing you, I slept in the adjoining bedroom. I think for the present time at least, I'll continue to use that bedroom. I quite often return after everyone is already asleep, and I'm gone again before they're awake. Until you become accustomed to my habits and there's little chance of being disturbed by my comings and goings, we'll keep this arrangement." His words were once more as cool and clear as ice water.

Surprised, Katherine shrugged to hide her confusion in a future that continued to seem vague and uncertain. "If that's what you want, Simon," she spoke in a broken whisper. She rose from the bed and wandered restlessly about the room, feeling his eyes boring into her. His cool voice broke into her reverie.

"I am leaving shortly but if you wish, I'll wait and have breakfast on your first day in your new home." His voice, when he spoke again, was friendlier.

"Yes, that would be nice, Simon." Her words were stifled and unnatural. Turning from him, she began to rummage through her wardrobe, barely noticing the door closing softly behind him.

Short minutes later, there was a heavy knock at the door and unbidden, Clover entered, a young girl in tow.

"Miss Katherine, this girl be your new maid, Daisy. She been trained to dress a lady's hair like nobody's business and she can keep all your clothes clean and pressed."

Clover stood, waiting for a sign of approval. Moving toward the bed, she beckoned Daisy to follow.

"She also be keeping your room neat as a pin." Signaling to the girl, she turned to the bed, straightening the sheets and quilt.

Katherine saw how her sharp eyes had settled on the bed, guessing the maid knew Simon hadn't joined her there, yet she likely knew he'd returned to the house sometime last night. Mortified, Katherine's gaze slid away from Clover. Katherine saw Daisy studying her and smiled slightly at the girl.

Banish The Dragon ~ D. L. Robinson

Clover, followed by Daisy, bustled about the room, preparing to choose a gown from her mistress's skimpy wardrobe. She snorted her disapproval at the poor selection but maintained her silence until finally she selected a faded grey gown, deciding that this would have to do for today.

Leaving the maid dressing Katherine's luxurious auburn locks, Clover made her way down to the kitchen, peering into the dining room as she passed. Master Sam was there but he wasn't alone. The Featherstone's, Simon and Jonathan, sat waiting for the new mistress of the house and the other young lady to join them.

Clover muttered under her breath, "Later, I give him an earful of what that young lady needs." Satisfied with her plan, she continued into the kitchen to supervise preparations that were already underway for breakfast.

Katherine and Maggie, meeting by chance in the hallway, entered the dining room together. Maggie greeted everyone as the old friends she felt they were but Katherine, after her earlier interview with her husband, was unsure of her position and so remained quiet and somewhat withdrawn. Samuel beckoned her to the chair beside him.

"I trust you slept well, my dear." He looked into her green eyes and smiled.

The two seemed to form a bond of mutual affection, chatting to each other as they ate, leaving a reluctant Simon to entertain the others. Samuel hoped that Jonathan knew that at least after he left, she would have a champion, even if that champion was an old man. *But I hold the purse strings, even if it is a struggle to control my willful grandson.*

Simon was the first to leave the table, ignoring the look of annoyance that crossed his grandfather's face. The rest of the party continued to sit and chat, as if the black cloud that was Simon had passed and the sun now shone brightly upon them. Eventually they took their leave of each other, promising to meet at lunch if not before.

Clover magically appeared in the doorway, reminding Katherine that she was ready to show her the house that would now be her domain. Maggie and the Featherstone's wandered outside to enjoy the crisp autumn air and Jonathan followed Samuel as he made his way painfully to the library to enjoy a cigar together, and again the doors were closed against listening ears.

The two sank into the deep leather of the chairs, smoking companionably for a few moments before Jonathan, thanking him for his hospitality, reminded him of his own upcoming marriage in a few months and the need to return to Savannah and take up his medical practice. Samuel bowed his head in understanding.

"I expected that you would leave shortly, my boy, I just didn't think it would happen this quickly. I must tell you, while we have this time alone, that I tossed and turned most of the night, digesting what Simon disclosed about his bride."

Jonathan, ready to renew his argument against his cousin's implied insinuations about Katherine's possible lack of morals was cut short by Samuel before a word could leave his mouth.

"Please son, I'm not a fool. I don't know what Simon's game is but so far I find that young woman completely charming. The Featherstone's, albeit unwittingly, also testified as to her character this morning before you joined us." He paused, lost in thought for a moment. He cleared his throat and began speaking again. "Maggie's uncle, Captain Hart, and the cabin boy, Ned, have been invited to join us for dinner in two days time. I trust, lad, you will delay your departure, at least until then?" His voice trailed off expectantly.

Jonathan, recognizing that the old man had outmaneuvered him, bowed his head in silent acceptance. "I will be pleased to join such a fine company but Sam, I will leave the following morning."

"One thing more." Samuel hesitated before he spoke again. The old man's face seemed to sag as he continued. "I don't quite know how to say this, and I do pray you will not think too harshly of me." He paused as if searching for the right words. "As I said, I don't know what Simon is playing at but having met Katherine, I fear for her well being." Jonathan was too surprised to do more than nod at the old man's words and what he thought he was implying.

"My health is failing. Hell man, you're a doctor. You probably guessed as much." He looked at the younger man's face and read the truth of his statement. "The sawbones that attends me says I probably have less than a year. If Simon and Katherine have not worked out their differences before I'm gone, what will become of her?"

Jonathan, out of a long ingrained habit, started to defend his cousin but hesitated as he reflected on the other's behavior since Katherine had entered his life, especially his despicable performance last night.

"Sam, I hope and pray that you are misreading the situation but I imagine that you, tossing and turning in your bed last night, have already forged a plan of sorts. Will you share it with me or am I being intrusive?"

"You're right, my boy. I do have a plan but it's still in the rough stages. I need time to work things out. Fortunately, Edmond Featherstone, as well as being a friend from my youth, is also an extremely competent lawyer. He can advise me on the legalities. But I'm still worried." He paused, an expression of despair on his lined old face. "Jonathan, if things are not going well, or even if I sense my end is near, will you return to Seven Oaks?"

"You have only to summon me, Sam, and I'll be here as fast as is humanly possible." The two men clasped hands, mutual respect and fondness evident in both their faces.

* * * *

The house was a flurry of bustling slaves for, under the sharp eye of Clover, no dust was allowed to settle anywhere. The polished oak floors gleamed as they wandered from room to room, passing the morning away. She led Katherine out to the cooking shed where all manner of pots and pans hung from the low ceiling, the room a beehive of activity as preparations for lunch and dinner were well underway.

Clover rattled off the names of the cook and her helpers but Katherine laughingly apologized to all, begging their forgiveness if she got their names wrong in the beginning. As the kitchen door swung shut behind them, Clover knew her mistress had charmed them all, even that prickly cook, Marigold. As they slowly made their way upstairs, she pleaded exhaustion, whereupon a contrite Clover immediately led her into her bedroom, fussing at her until she was lying down with a promise of being awakened for lunch.

The smile on Clover's face faded as she made her way to the door of Master Sam's library. As she rapped on the door, it swung open to reveal a somber-faced Jonathan, who merely nodded to her as he strode toward the front entrance, shouting over his shoulder that he was going riding but would return in time for lunch. Peering into the room, the generously proportioned woman met the eyes of her master and was suddenly unsure of herself but he beckoned her in, cutting off any thought of postponing her plea for her new mistress.

Clover studied her old master's face, sadly realizing that his days were numbered. *And what will become of us all then,* she thought. *Master Simon won't care for us like Master Sam.*

Samuel's deep voice rang out, interrupting her reflections. "Well, Clover, what is it?"

Unused to pleading anyone's case, let alone a white woman's, even if she was the new mistress, Clover squared her shoulders and straightened her spine, preparing to do battle. Wondering one last time if she was doing the right thing, she plunged right into her observations and laid the problem in old Sam's lap.

"It's Miss Katherine's wardrobe that I come about, master. It be in one sorry state. I knows you wouldn't want people to think you was too poor to have her dress as anything but a Radcliffe. Her gowns, what there are of them, are threadbare and downright shabby. And her nightgowns and undergarments, well sir, they're little more than rags. There's just no end to what that child needs. Breathless, she halted her plea, wondering if she had perhaps gone too far.

Samuel, an expression of bewilderment and disbelief on his face, mulled over what his housekeeper had just revealed. His first impulse was to blame Simon for being parsimonious with his bride but then recalled that they had wed just short days before sailing. There would have been no time to attend to dressmakers and the like. Simon had told him Katherine was almost a pauper, living on the largesse of people who had no blood ties to her. He'd talk to his grandson as soon as he returned home and, if he was agreeable, Samuel would take the girl into town tomorrow and purchase everything she could possibly need or want.

Suddenly aware that his housekeeper still hovered in the doorway, he looked at her troubled face. "Thank you, Clover, for bringing this matter to my attention. Most likely Mr. Simon never gave his bride's wardrobe a thought but then he never had you looking out for his interests while he was abroad." He chuckled softly as he pictured Simon, with Clover in tow, making his way around England. "And Clover, perhaps we'll have reason to decorate the nursery before too much time passes. You would certainly have your hands full then."

Clover, turning to leave the room, muttered loudly that it had always been her understanding that two people had to occupy the same bed if they hoped to fill a nursery. Samuel's head jerked up in consternation as the door closed behind her. "*What the devil is going on?*" he wondered aloud. *How can he resist playing husband to such an alluring creature?* He mulled over these troubling thoughts, wondering if he dare approach his grandson on his duty to his family. *No, I think just tackling him about her wardrobe will be enough to contend with for the time being* he thought as his faded blue eyes closed tiredly.

It was some time later that Katherine made her way down the stairs, once again meeting up with Maggie. They linked arms fondly as they descended, both determined to treasure what time was left to them to enjoy each other's company. Maggie's uncle had sent his acceptance of the invitation but added that his ship would be sailing the following morning, much sooner than he had expected, and could Maggie be prepared to return to the ship with him.

Maggie suggested that they find pen and paper so they might exchange addresses, so no matter what life handed them, they would always stay in touch. They tapped softly at the closed study door and a muffled grunt bade them enter. Samuel beamed his pleasure when he saw it was Katherine, nodding politely as he spied Maggie. As the two advanced into the room, Katherine became concerned when she saw his tired face, almost grey with exhaustion. She made as if to leave but he gently urged her to sit and visit with him, kindly including Maggie in the invitation.

"Now what errand could you two lovely ladies be about?"

"Mr. Langtree, sir," Katherine stammered, unsure as to just what form of address she should be using to her husband's grandfather.

"Katherine," he spoke with mock severity, "I thought I had made it clear you would call me Samuel. It makes me feel far too advanced in years to have such a sweet young thing like you call me grandfather. And you, Mrs. McGregor, must also call me Samuel."

Taken aback by his warmth, Maggie stuttered her acceptance of his offer, on the condition that he address her as Maggie, as indeed she had already invited him to do so, as a friend would do. He nodded in dignified agreement and turned to Katherine.

"And now, young lady, I doubt you came in here seeking the company of an old man. What were you hoping to find?"

"Well, Samuel," she smiled shyly as she used his name, her voice soft and clear, "we are searching out a scrap of paper and something to write with so that I might have Maggie's address and she mine. We thought we might exchange letters, telling how our lives are, and perhaps, one day in the future, I might travel to New York or she might return here to Seven Oaks."

He directed Katherine to his large oak desk where she quickly found paper and ink. Maggie, sitting beside Samuel, called out the address her husband had sent her so many months ago and which Katherine now wrote on the paper. Samuel instructed Katherine to make him a copy of Maggie's address also, explaining to them that he tried to stay in touch with all who had visited Seven Oaks over the years. Finished at last, Katherine handed Maggie her address and Samuel, with a young woman on each arm, led them to the dining room where the others awaited.

As the three entered the room, Samuel drew Katherine aside. "My dear, you shouldn't have to go searching for something as simple as a piece of paper. There's a pretty little writing desk in Simon's mother's old room that would take up no more than a small corner of your chamber. I'll have it moved in immediately. And," he continued conspiratorially, "there will also be a small purse with a few coins in the drawer. No lady should be without pin money."

As the last of the meal was being removed, Samuel cleared his throat as a means of gaining everyone's attention. "I just wanted to let you all know that Maggie's uncle and the cabin boy Ned will be dining with us in two days time. I trust you will all join us." He paused and looked pointedly at his grandson who had made a surprise entrance just as they began to eat. "It will be Maggie's last evening with us as Captain Hart's ship will sail with the tide. Jonathan will also be leaving us at the same time. He is anxious to return to the business of setting up his medical practice in Savannah, and where a certain young lady is waiting to become his wife a few months from now." A flurry of conversation sprang up as the Featherstone's and Maggie extended their congratulations.

With a steely-eyed glare at his grandson, he requested his company in the library. As the two withdrew, the others slowly made their way out of the dining room also. The older couple mounted the stairs, declaring the need of a short nap after such a delicious meal. Maggie followed in their wake, declared her intention of examining her wardrobe before continuing on her journey to meet her Jamie.

Katherine, unfamiliar feelings surging through her, rose from her chair and, murmuring her need of fresh air, opened the door that led to the garden and stepped outside. Welcoming the cool breeze that played gently about her face and hair, she made her way down the meandering path. Lost in thought, she slowly became aware of another walking beside her, his long legs matching her shorter step.

"Jonathan," she gasped in surprise. Looking up into his darkly handsome face, she saw how sure he was of himself and his rightful place in the universe. *How must that feel? To know you are in charge of your own fate?*

Searching for the right words, he hesitated before speaking. " I feel I owe you an explanation."

Vowing to show how unconcerned she was with anything he might have to say, she waited for him to continue. "An explanation, Jonathan? What explanation could you possibly owe me?" Struggling to maintain an even tone, she knew her voice was becoming shrill with the effort.

A hint of annoyance flashed in his grey eyes. "I'm speaking of Sam's unexpected announcement that not only am I leaving shortly but also that I'm to be married."

"Oh, that," she sniffed scornfully, "well yes, I did wonder, just for an instant mind you, why, in all the many weeks we've known each other and been in each other's company, that fact was never mentioned." Her green eyes stared contemptuously up at him.

He paced about, at a loss to explain such an omission. Scuffling his feet as if he was a small boy caught raiding the cookie jar, he answered her. "For some reason, it never seemed important enough to mention."

From beneath lowered lids, she shot him a look of disbelief. "I find that almost impossible to believe. You never thought your impending marriage important enough to mention? I can only hope your bride never comes to know of your cavalier attitude toward her and your future together."

She stood motionless for an instant before angrily increasing her pace, hoping to leave him well and truly behind her, vowing to show him how unconcerned she was. *We shared a kiss, nothing more.* Trying to ignore his nearness, she turned toward the house, thoughts tumbling wildly about in her mind. Biting her lips to smother her sobs, she ran inside, wanting only to reach the safe comforting haven of her bedroom. Flinging herself onto the bed, sobbing uncontrollably, she agonized over his reluctance to share such an important happening with her, especially after that night he had kissed her. And he had rescued her not once, but twice from ravishment and probable death.

As Katherine made her hasty exit, Jonathan glanced at the window of the library and, flushing, saw Simon staring out at him, smirking. Realizing that, although he couldn't possibly have overheard the conversation, her sudden flight might have provoked his husbandly curiosity. *Damn* he thought, striding angrily toward the stable, intent on freeing his mind of this most vexing of women.

Chapter Ten

Immediately following breakfast the next morning, Katherine, Samuel and Jonathan climbed into the carriage and headed into Charleston. Simon, again being the first to leave the table, wished them all a good day. She was irked by his cool, aloof manner but, with the others watching, straightened her spine in what she hoped was a gesture of dignity. An invitation to join them had been declined by all but Jonathan, who claimed he had business to attend to. Katherine, on learning that he was joining them, promised herself she would show him that he meant less than nothing to her.

When Samuel had approached Simon the previous day about the state of Katherine's wardrobe, he had seemed willing enough to let his grandfather take her into Charleston and make whatever purchases were needed. He said he had no personal desire to stand about, hands in pockets as the hours ticked away, watching the process of choosing a gown or two ruin his day. Katherine, when told of the shopping expedition, roused herself from her pique over Jonathan's lapse of memory concerning his forthcoming marriage and decided to look forward, burying any girlish dreams she might have had.

As the carriage bearing the threesome travelled along the dusty road, Samuel proved to be a veritable fountain of knowledge, pointing out various mansions that were visible from the main road and relating small verbal sketches of the families who lived within. Jonathan, unsure of Katherine's temper where he was concerned, remained uncharacteristically quiet. Both were content to let Samuel ramble on.

He revealed that the dressmaker they were going to call on had studied under the best in Paris before following her ne'er-do-well husband across the ocean to America many years previous. The man had died shortly after their arrival, shot in a duel over a game of chance, leaving Marie alone and almost penniless. Samuel had met her as she struggled to keep body and soul together. His wife had died many years before, his daughter married and living elsewhere. He was lonely and so was Marie. They had spent many pleasant hours together over the years but then his daughter had been widowed, and he had moved both her and his grandson to Seven Oaks, leaving him unable to visit Marie as often as before. Sadly, his daughter, Simon's mother, had sickened and died within a year of her return to Seven Oaks.

A hint of regret for what might have been washed over his face, leaving

Katherine to wonder how deep his attachment to the lady in question was. As the carriage slowed, she was surprised to see they had arrived in Charleston, so enthralled had she been with his narrative.

Samuel directed Noah, his driver, to the dressmaker's shop. Noah, familiar with Samuel's growing infirmities, assisted him from the carriage before handing Katherine down beside him. After arranging a meeting time with Jonathan, Samuel, leaning heavily on his cane, guided Katherine through the door, a tiny silver bell over the door announcing their arrival.

A face, framed by dark curling hair tucked into a pink lace cap, appeared from behind bolts of material, peering inquisitively at the two who stood waiting. A smile lit up her face when she recognized Samuel. As Marie St. Pierre stepped into their view, Katherine observed a petite, tidy woman, somewhat shorter than herself, with a gap-toothed smile, dimples and warm brown eyes that settled a welcome on Samuel before moving curiously to Katherine.

"Samuel, it's been far too long." The two embraced warmly and then drew apart as Samuel introduced his granddaughter-in-law.

"Simon has finally wed, Marie, and just look at the bewitching creature he somehow coaxed into becoming his wife."

The warmth of his voice assured Marie that this young lady must be very special indeed.

"I heard some gossip that Simon had returned to our shores with a bride. And I was also told she was very pretty. What I didn't hear, Samuel, was that she is absolutely enchanting." The diminutive seamstress paused as she smiled cheekily up at the old man, her dimples charmingly displayed. "And I suppose you're here because she must have the perfect gown for the Christmas celebrations, is that not so, cherie?" Her words were lightly accented by her French roots.

Samuel glanced about him as if to ensure no chance listeners were about and he lowered his voice, forcing Marie to move even closer to him, as he whispered into her ear. Katherine, sensing that he was about to reveal her lack of wardrobe to the dressmaker, moved away, a blush suffusing her cheeks.

"Marie", Samuel spoke softly, "the girl is in dire need of absolutely everything. And not only must it be done discretely, it must also be done as speedily as possible. If you have to hire more seamstresses, do so. Due to a series of unfortunate events, none of which were her doing, she has been left with almost nothing to wear, decent or otherwise. I simply will not have her take her place as the mistress of Seven Oaks or enter Charleston society, in such a pitiful state. And Marie, money is not important but the girl's happiness is. She will need several frocks just to serve the curious ladies of Charleston and the neighboring plantations tea and cake when they come calling and, of course, at least two gowns for the coming Christmas festivities. God willing, we'll both return in the spring to replenish her wardrobe."

Marie winked conspiratorially at her old friend. Their shared passion had faded with Samuel's advancing years and ill health but she still cared deeply for him and was pleased that he was seeking her assistance.

"But of course, cherie, I will dress this exquisite child in finery that would dazzle the European courts." She patted his hand softly before tracing his lined cheeks in an intimate gesture from days gone by. She steered Samuel into a softly cushioned chair so he might enjoy what she was about to create. Pulling Katherine into the centre of the room, she called for her apprentice and together they measured her from top to bottom, hastily making notes as they turned Katherine this way and that. The assistant pulled bolts of cloth from the shelves, draping them against Katherine, all the while watching her mistress's face for a nod of approval or a frown signaling rejection.

Sketches were produced of gowns for various occasions, with the three women laughingly debating styles and complimentary fabrics and color. Eventually, all three were satisfied, having planned everything from cloaks and gowns to the most delicate of undergarments and nightwear. A cobbler was sent for to measure her feet for slippers to match the gowns and a pair of leather riding boots to complete her wardrobe.

The dressmaker eventually instructed her assistant to fetch tea for her visitors and led them to a secluded alcove, pulling a chair up for Samuel and patting another in an invitation, which a weary Katherine accepted in quiet gratitude. The three sat chatting pleasantly over cups of steaming tea and Katherine, still numbed by the events of the morning, let her thoughts wander as the other two engaged in a most intimate conversation, forgetting her presence in their enjoyment of each other's company. Setting the delicate cup down, she rose from her chair. At Samuel's inquiring look, she told him that she just wanted to poke about the shop, never having visited such an establishment in her life. Smiling fondly at her, he squeezed her slender hand in his oversized ones, a gesture Marie's sharp eyes didn't miss.

"Browse through the shop, my dear, and should you discover some finery that you feel essential to your wellbeing, let Marie know, and it's yours."

Overwhelmed at his generosity, Katherine, her smile alive with growing affection and delight, protested that he had already showered her with more today than she had had in her entire life. She wandered off down the aisles, pausing at the beaded reticules displayed in the shop window. The tinkle of the silvery bell announced the arrival of a new customer but Katherine, captivated by the tiny bags, paid no attention until she felt the presence of someone standing immediately behind her. Thinking it to be either Samuel or Marie, she turned to greet them, only then realizing it was a total stranger.

A woman, taller by several inches, stood before her, an odd look in her dark eyes. Katherine was taken aback by the attractiveness of the stranger; her artfully arranged blond hair curled into beguiling ringlets, tied with a black velvet ribbon, her ivory complexion accentuating a thin, shapely nose and generous red lips. Deep sapphire blue eyes, emphasized by dark brows and lashes, gazed speculatively down at Katherine.

The gown she wore was a becoming shade of azure with delicate lace stitched into the neckline and sleeves. Her figure, much fuller than Katherine's slim one, blocked the aisle. Katherine, suddenly unsure of herself, murmured politely as she attempted to step past the beautiful stranger but the other refused to move. Tilting her face slightly upward, Katherine saw the woman's smile was faintly scornful.

Neither woman, standing in full view of the window, saw Jonathan, an alarmed expression on his handsome face as he spied them, rush into the shop. Katherine experienced what was becoming a familiar sense of relief as she saw him approach.

The entrancing stranger, still unaware of his presence, nodded her head regally. "Well I declare, you must be the recently married Mrs. Simon Radcliffe, although I certainly never expected Simon's wife to be such a drab little creature."

Stung by her words, Katherine could only nod her head in bewilderment, wondering how anyone could possibly know who she was.

A fixed and decidedly unwelcoming smile appeared on the taller woman's face. She spun around, startled, as she felt someone touch her arm, her eyes falling on Jonathan. She smiled provocatively at the one man who had never fallen under her spell.

"Jonathan," she said softly, her eyes narrowing. "Fancy meeting you in a dress shop."

Her words were crisp and cool as she moved toward him and, in a particularly intimate gesture, plucked a piece of lint from his jacket. Katherine, both relieved at his timely arrival and annoyed at the woman's audacity, looked questioningly at him.

'Why, Juliana, I might ask the same question of you. Whatever are you doing here?' The rich timbre of his voice seemed to Katherine to have a challenge to it.

"I was passing the shop window and spied a stranger wandering about." Fluttering her lashes coquettishly, Juliana Taylor laughed softly, seeming to take a perverse pleasure in his challenge. "Naturally I wondered if this could be the new mistress of Seven Oaks that everyone is talking about and decided to make her acquaintance. But so far, this timid little mouse has yet to utter a word."

Katherine, blushing at the hurtful criticism, suddenly became aware of the dowdiness of her clothes. It was at that moment that both Samuel and Marie, having heard voices, made their way toward them, looking at the young people curiously. Samuel, recognizing the intruder, flushed a deep, angry red.

"Miss Taylor, I might have guessed." His tone was coolly disapproving. Marie, anxious for the well-being of her former lover as he leaned heavily on his cane, was also concerned about a woman who loved to dress well, giving her much business over the years, was at a loss for the right words to soothe the situation.

Jonathan, seeing the effect this unexpected meeting was having on Katherine, stepped forward.

"Sam, you hush now and mind your manners," he chided gently. "Miss Taylor happened to be walking by and saw Katherine through the window, correctly surmising that it must be Simon's bride. She merely stopped to wish her well and welcome her to her new home. Isn't that correct, Juliana?"

Juliana, somewhat embarrassed by the old man's volatile reaction to her presence, was relieved that Jonathan had stepped into the breach and headed off what could have been a mortifying scene. Nodding her head in grateful agreement, she again turned to Katherine, ignoring the others. Taking the hands of the smaller woman, she smiled down at her.

"Until we meet again, Mrs. Radcliffe."

Katherine nodded in confusion, smiling hesitantly, unaware of the delightful picture she made as she gently squeezed the other's hands.

"I am sure we will, Miss Taylor." Under any other circumstances, Katherine would have extended an invitation for her to call at Seven Oaks but glancing in Samuel's direction, she sensed the disfavor in which he regarded the blond woman and certainly did not want to distress him in any way.

With a graceful nod and a swirl of her skirts, Juliana wordlessly made her way to the door, the bell tinkling at her exit. Only when it closed behind her did everyone seem to breathe a sigh of relief. Her curiosity aroused, Katherine turned to Jonathan and Samuel but they were already making their way to the front of the shop and Marie, not wanting to be faced with awkward questions, bustled after them.

Katherine took a moment to compose herself. '"*What a rude woman*," she mused, "*and how does she come to have such an effect, especially on the likes of Samuel and Jonathan?*" Sensing that there was more to Juliana Taylor than met the eye, Katherine slowly followed the others to the front of the shop.

Chapter Eleven

Katherine, together with the Featherstone's and Maggie, had gathered in the parlor after another delectable meal, chatting amiably about Maggie's imminent departure. Samuel had made his excuses to the company and withdrawn, gesturing to both Jonathan and Simon, who had once again surprised everyone by joining them for lunch.

An hour and more had passed when Mary, blue eyes smiling at the chattering girls, spoke.

"My dears, Edmund, and I have decided it's time for a stroll. Would you care to join us?"

Maggie stood, brushing at the folds of her dress. "Oh, that sounds lovely. Are you coming, Katherine?"

"Thank you but I'm feeling somewhat tired. I think I'll visit Samuel's library and find a book to read me to sleep." The young mistress of Seven Oaks didn't see the sympathetic looks her friends sent her, thinking sadly that a new bride shouldn't be seeking a book to take to her bed.

Linking arms, the two girls followed the older couple into the hallway. As they paused outside the door of the library, the raised voices of Simon and his grandfather intruded on their pleasantries. They stood, stunned, as bitter words drifted through the polished oak door that, unnoticed by the room's occupants, stood slightly ajar. At first, the words were indistinguishable but the rancor was instantly discernible.

"Damn it, Grandfather, I have done as you wanted. I married in England, a nobody, a penniless Irish nobody, someone who, as I have already pointed out, trouble follows. Since meeting her, two men have tried to wrest her virtue, despite knowing I was nearby, not to mention that she has somehow twisted you around her little finger and Jonathan, well, both he and I know his feelings where it concerns Katherine. And so, if I continue to see Juliana, as a solace to the shambles of my so-called marriage, you will have to remember she is the woman I love, the woman I should have married and to hell with my inheritance and to hell with the woman who now bears my name."

The reluctant eavesdroppers flinched as the door flew open to reveal a flushed Simon, who now stared open-mouthed at his unwilling audience before pushing roughly past them. An almost inaudible gasp was torn from her throat, as Katherine stumbled back fearfully, not wanting his wrath to be visited on her. Seeking only to escape the pitying faces of her friends, Katherine spun around toward the staircase just as Samuel and Jonathan reached the doorway and realized that Simon's words had been heard by more than just the two of them. Samuel's already flushed face reddened a deeper hue at the laundering of his family's dirty linen in so public a manner, gazing at the door closing as Simon stormed from the house.

Jonathan, seeing Katherine's pale face, caught her as she slowly crumpled to the floor. He carried her back into the parlor, laying her gently on the sofa. Mary Featherstone perched on the edge of one cushion, worry wrinkling her brow, tenderly stroked Katherine's hands. Concern for her welfare was reflected in all of their faces as Katherine slowly opened her eyes and saw them looking down at her. The painfully humiliating memory of her husband declaring he loved another and had only married her to placate his grandfather in order to remain in his will, came flooding back. Her mind reeled with confusion. She struggled to sit upright, ignoring the proffered array of hands. Standing, she brushed at the folds of her gown, unwilling to meet the eye of anyone, her misery so acute it was a physical pain.

"I'm fine, thank you." She was filled with humiliation. Jonathan moved toward her but she held him off. "Please, let me go to my room. I want to be alone." Her voice was fragile and shaking as she stepped toward the hallway and, head held high, regally climbed the staircase.

A sudden groan caught Jonathan's attention and from the corner of his eye, he caught Samuel's brief look of pain as he massaged his chest, his face grey. Rushing to his side, he led the old man into the library where he gave him a brief examination.

"Sam, this has all been too much for you. I know you won't listen to my advice as a friend but you must heed me as a doctor. Your heart is weak Sam, and the strain of these past days is taking its toll. As your doctor, temporary as that position might be, I'm ordering a bed be moved in here. Absolutely no more stairs or physical exertion, for the time being at least! And Sam, the cigars, the whiskey, I think you should cut back, just a little." An eyebrow shot up at the list of his favorite things being taken away and, as he opened his mouth to argue, Jonathan gave the final, most telling argument. "Katherine needs you, Sam. You have to take care of yourself so that you can take care of her." The old man nodded his head weakly, his eyes already closing in exhaustion.

* * * *

As the door closed behind her, Katherine leaned against it briefly. A raw, primitive grief overwhelmed her as she closed her eyes, her heart aching with pain. Tears slowly found their way down her cheeks as she made her way to the bed, collapsing on it in an agonized heap. Time passed, slowly, painfully, distant sounds drifting up the stairs to her room. Occasionally, a soft knock at her door was heard but, with no response from within, the unseen caller soon went away. And Katherine slept.

The sound of a tray being set down on the small table by the fire roused Katherine from her fitful slumber. Opening her eyes, she saw it was Clover, peering down at her.

"Well, at last you is awake. I done brought you some supper since you didn't come down. Master Sam is worrying himself into fits about you, Miss Katherine. And Master Jonathan ain't done nothing but pace back and forth, muttering about the things he gonna' do to Master Simon. And the others just sit, waiting for you to make an appearance."

"Stop, Clover, that's enough." Her voice rang out sharply in unaccustomed command. Sitting up, she turned her back to the servant and stared into the small fire that had been lit. She felt a hand touch her shoulder in solace before the black woman moved toward the tray.

"All right, Miss Katherine, I won't keep on at you. But I did bring this here tray up, knowing you must be powerful starved by now. And the Lord knows you're too thin already. So you come over here now, and set yourself down." She held out the chair invitingly, waiting for her mistress.

"Please Clover, I couldn't eat anything, just tea."

The servant poured a cup of the steaming liquid and carried it over to the bed. Setting it down on the bedside table, she shook her kerchiefed head disapprovingly.

"All right, missy. But Master Sam is going to be some upset if he hears you not eating. I'll just leave the tray here and maybe you'll feel like picking at something a little later."

Katherine stood as the door shut behind the worried housekeeper and began to pace the confines of the room. It was then she noticed the tiny writing desk, just as Samuel had promised. Curiously, she opened the middle drawer and saw the purse he had wanted her to have, pin money he had called it.

As Katherine held the purse, a plan slowly began to form in her mind. She recalled how she and her aunt had been treated when the new Lord Talbot and his appalling family took possession of Marlow Court. She had begged her aunt to flee with her to London but her pleas had fallen on deaf ears as the old woman implored Katherine to understand she wanted nothing more than to be buried beside her beloved Hector.

Well, there was no one but herself to be concerned about now. And what had seemed like a good plan in England would serve her just as well in this country, in spite of Simon and Jonathan's earlier warning about young women, alone, and what might befall them. She counted the coins, hoping the contents would be enough for her to establish a new life somewhere, anywhere, as long as it was far away from Seven Oaks.

Moving determinedly about the room, Katherine lifted the lid of her trunk, pulling out the few items left inside and tossing them onto the bed. Opening the wardrobe, she drew out the shabby gowns that hung there. Thinking regretfully of the lovely frocks that had been ordered only this morning, she shrugged her shoulders.

Laying the gowns onto the growing pile, she spread out a shawl and bundled everything she would be taking with her into the centre of it, knotting the ends together. It would be unwieldy but not impossible to manage, she thought. And now, the hardest part of all, saying good bye. She knew instinctively that if she were to announce her departure, she would be stopped by Samuel and perhaps even Jonathan, in spite of his desire to return to the side of the woman he was going to marry. A letter would have to suffice. She crossed the room slowly, thinking how ironic that the first letter she would write at the desk would also be her last. Sitting down, she drew out a sheet of paper, addressing it to Samuel. Unnoticed tears fell as, finally finished, she folded the note, propping it against her pillow where Clover would find it in the morning.

In the solitude of her chamber, the ticking of the miniature clock told her it was much too early to consider leaving. As she sipped the now tepid tea, she turned her attention to the tray of food. Not knowing when her next meal might be, she picked daintily at some tasty bits of chicken. At last, she heard footsteps as the other occupants of the house climbed the stairs, murmuring quietly to each other lest they disturb the slumber of the one that occupied all their thoughts.

Katherine crossed to the window but this time it was not to admire the grounds of the plantation. Glancing upward, she saw the moon was bright enough to light her way, which surely would help as she made her way to a new life. Studying the tree nearest her window, she decided it was not close enough—she didn't want her plans thwarted by a broken bone. No, there was no help for it. She would have to leave by the front door. And so she perched on the edge of her bed and listened as silence descended on the house and its occupants.

At last judging it time, she opened her door quietly and poked her head out, deeming it safe to make her escape. Taking a deep unsteady breath, she clutched her cumbersome bundle closely to her and began her descent, certain the thunderous beating of her heart would wake everyone. She held her breath, stomach churning with anxiety, fearing a chance squeaking of a stair or floorboard, which would alert anyone still awake to the fact that someone was up and about.

Listening to the steady ticking of the hallway clock, she moved stealthily downward. A flicker of apprehension swept through her as she struggled to open the heavy door but at last, she stepped out into the cool night air, closing the door firmly and decisively behind her. Clutching her cloak tightly to her, she flew down the steps, wanting only to reach the shadowy cover of the trees that lined the road. At last, in the welcoming darkness, she felt she could pause long enough to look back to see if her flight had been discovered but the house, glowing ghost-like in the moonlight, appeared to be slumbering as peacefully as its occupants. She brushed away the tears that trembled on her eyelashes and swallowing determinedly, lifted her chin and boldly strode forward.

A flicker of apprehension coursed through her as she marched down the carriage path that led to the public road. The tall trees she had once considered stately and majestic now seemed only menacing. She trembled as fearful images grew in her mind. A soft breeze rustled the leaves, causing Katherine to anxiously question the wisdom of her flight until she recalled Simon's angry, hurtful words. Yes, she reassured herself, she was doing the right thing.

She quickened her pace, wanting nothing more than to be free of Seven Oaks. Reaching the main road, she turned in the direction of Charleston, pausing to shift her bundle over her shoulder before setting off, determined to look behind no more.

Wearily Katherine pulled her cloak tightly about her as the moon disappeared behind dark clouds and a soft rain began to fall. Her steps became mired in soft mud but she continued to trudge tiredly along, trying to ignore the unfamiliar noises of the night and its creatures that seemed to surround her, until at last the clouds passed and the moon once more lit her way.

Countless steps later Katherine paused, listening. The distinctive rumbling sound of a horse and wagon were coming up from behind. Panic seized her at the thought of a search beginning so soon. In desperation, she ducked behind a small thicket that offered a hiding place of sorts until whoever shared the road with her had passed. Scrunching down, she waited until at last a horse and cart lumbered into view, driven by a male slave, a woman of the same dark complexion sharing the seat with him. Relief coursed through her as she judged the couple was no threat to her and, recognizing opportunity, stepped out from behind the covering brush as they drove by. Startled, both occupants clutched at each other for courage as the apparition moved toward them, holding out her hands in a supplicating gesture.

"Please, I'm so tired." Her voice, little more than a choked whisper, was full of entreaty as she met their astonished eyes, fading to a hushed stillness as the chirping of crickets now filled the night. The woman perched on the seat reached a decision quickly.

"Virgil, help her before she falls down in the mud."

Virgil, accustomed to obeying orders, jumped from the cart, looking to his companion for further instructions, lending a hand as she descended from the wagon, bewilderment obvious in both their dark faces.

Katherine saw the man that the woman had called Virgil look around, wide eyed, his fear palpable until his woman, Tilly, spoke sharply, distracting him from the terror he was so obviously feeling.

"Quick Virgil, clear a space in back. This little lady done gonna faint dead away if we don't get to hurrying faster." She put a protective arm around Katherine and led her to the back of the wagon where Virgil's muscled arms quickly pushed sacks of vegetables aside to make room for her on the rough floor of the wagon.

"Where you be headed, missus?" Virgil asked, already regretting getting mixed up in white folks' business.

"Please," Katherine spoke with a pleading intensity, "can you take me anywhere near the railroad station in Charleston?" She held her breath as the two considered her request. It would barely take them out of their way, as the market, which was where they had been heading with produce to sell for their master, was just a mile past.

The woman, with a shy smile, nodded. "Course we can takes you there, child. But you look tired enough to drop where you're standing. You crawl into that little nest my Virgil done fixed for you and rest your weary bones. We'll wake you when we gets there."

With Virgil's assistance, Katherine crept into the small space created for her. The last words she heard were Virgil's as he badgered the woman as to why they was helping white folk and then she heard no more.

The sun had already risen when Katherine felt Tilly shake her gently, urging her to wake herself cause they was at the train station. Startled, she opened her eyes and saw the back of the depot. Taking Tilly's arm as she clambered down, she experienced a moment of apprehension, wondering once again if she had done the right thing by leaving the safe haven of Seven Oaks. Squaring her slender shoulders defiantly, she faced her benefactors, thanking them for the ride. As the wagon rumbled off, Katherine made her way to the front of the whitewashed building.

Dismayed at finding the shutters of the ticket window closed, Katherine settled herself on one of the sun bleached wooden benches that lined the station platform, unshakable in her determination to strike out on her own. The warm sun beat down on her, lulling her back to sleep until the sound of a window opening roused her. Gazing about as she got her bearings, she glanced up at the railway agent who was regarding her with undisguised curiosity, unused as he was to lone females sleeping on railway property, and unsure what exactly he should do about it.

Looking down his bulbous nose as she approached the window, he quite openly studied her. Katherine, daintily licking her dry lips, smiled nervously. Making inquiries as to train schedules and the price of a ticket, she kept glancing at the road that led to Seven Oaks. If there was to be a search for her, would anyone think to look for her here? Deciding that someone might, she realized it would be wise to stay out of sight for as long as possible, at least until the train arrived which, according to the monosyllabic ticket agent, would be in less than two hours.

Katherine, with the agent's help, carefully counted the unfamiliar coins, having decided she would go to New York and find employment there. And best of all, she had Maggie's address. By the time she reached her destination, Maggie would already be there, reunited with her Jamie and hopefully in a position to help Katherine find lodgings and a position of some sort. Clutching her ticket, she sat on a bench that was tucked neatly into a corner, hoping her disheveled appearance would discourage any of her fellow passengers from taking too much of an interest in her.

As the minutes ticked slowly by, a smattering of people began to gather. All glanced inquisitively at the dusty, bedraggled woman, taking in her shabby, mud spattered appearance and the fact that she was unaccompanied by anyone. Drawing their own conclusions, she was left in solitude whilst they crowded together on the other benches. Katherine brushed self-consciously at her cloak and gown, wondering why she wished to form a more favorable impression on those who glanced askance at her.

At last, she heard the distant chugging of a train. Excited voices called for children to return to the sides of their parents, and boxes and bags were gathered up. Katherine, anxious to blend in with the milling crowd, gathered her belongings and began to stroll in what she hoped was a casual fashion toward the train when she was abruptly caught by the elbow and spun around. A shudder passed through her as she stared into the glacially cold, angry eyes of her husband.

"Simon," she gasped. For a brief second he studied her face intently. She swallowed nervously before lifting her chin, defiantly meeting his gaze. Those about to board the train, sensing there might be a drama unfolding before their very eyes, nudged their fellow passengers, and all stood silent, watching, wondering. His voice was absolutely chillingly emotionless when at last he spoke.

"Were you planning on travelling somewhere, madam? Without first informing your husband?"

Her wrist was caught in his iron grip. Panic welled in her heart as she sought to free herself. It was at that moment that Jonathan approached them and, speaking softly to his cousin, drew his attention to the watching crowd. Simon smiled frostily down at her. "We seem to have attracted an audience, Katherine." An unwelcome blush crept into her cheeks as she glanced around in surprise at the curious onlookers.

"Why are you here?" She spat the words out contemptuously.

A scornful smile appeared on his handsome face. "Why, I'm here to collect my wife who, through some dreadful misunderstanding, has taken it into her head to fly from my side." He lifted the wrist he was still holding and mockingly kissed her hand, drawing smiles from the crowd, wordlessly assuring them all was well.

They reluctantly turned and once again began boarding the train, eagerly chattering about the events they had just been witness to, especially since it involved Simon Radcliffe and his foreign bride, although most were disappointed that the new mistress of Radcliffe had such a ragamuffin appearance. Many of those watching nodded their heads sagely, agreeing that there was more to this story than met the eye.

Chapter Twelve

The two men flanked Katherine as if she was a criminal intent on escape, and should she be foolish enough to try, they were there to prevent just such an event. They slowly made their way toward the horses tethered at the side of the station. Seething with mounting rage, she stopped suddenly, forcing both men to turn and face her. Jonathan, sensing that his presence was not needed, continued on to the horses, fussing with the reins and saddles in an effort to allow them some degree of privacy.

"Simon, what game are you playing at? Her voice rose in anger as she faced her husband. "I heard you, in fact everyone in the house heard you, declare that your marriage to a penniless Irish nobody was a huge mistake and that you loved someone else." Tears of frustration fell from her green eyes as her voice softened. "Why did you come looking for me? We could have both been free." Her breathing was ragged in helpless, frustrated fury.

His voice was quiet, yet held an undertone of cold contempt. "You're quite right, Katherine, we could have both been free." His voice, becoming loud with exasperation, held a bitter edge of cynicism. "Because that stubborn old man is once again threatening to turn me out without a penny—unless you and I somehow manage to convince him our marriage will survive, despite our stormy beginning!"

"But woman, I will be the one to decide when this union has ended, not you!" He glanced around, noting the inquisitive looks of the station master and others passing near enough to hear his words, not to mention his own cousin hovering within earshot. He seized her roughly by the shoulders, his eyes blazing. "Do you understand me, Katherine? I will be the one to end this marriage!" As he railed at the woman who was his wife, Simon was barely aware that he was striking out at his grandfather, the man who had dominated his mother so completely and, after her death, had tried to dictate how his grandson should live his life.

Biting her lips in dismay, she felt a cold emptiness inside as she listened to the man she was legally bound to. Where would this nightmare end?

Giving her shoulders one last painful squeeze, he led her to where the horses and Jonathan patiently waited. Pulling a flask of whiskey from his pocket, he took a long drink before he grasped her arm brutally, thrusting both her and her bundle at Jonathan. Directing his cousin to take her home, he

96

mounted his horse and galloped furiously away.

They both stared open-mouthed at Simon's abrupt departure until at last Jonathan, after swinging her up onto the saddle, mounted behind her, nudging the horse in the direction of Seven Oaks.

The ride seemed interminable and twice she heard him attempt to speak but shut his voice out until he finally gave up the effort. She felt defeated.

Katherine could feel his sympathy as he held her slender frame against him, but she needed time to digest Simon's words. *What could Simon have meant when he declared he would be the one to end the marriage?*

At last, Seven Oaks came into view and Katherine, having nestled in the security of Jonathan's arms, felt herself stiffen. Everyone would know of her attempted flight, both friends and servants. How could she look anyone in the face?

As they approached the house, she glanced up and there, gathered on the veranda, was everyone she had come to care about. They smiled and waved a warm welcome to her. Astonished, she could only stare at their smiling faces. Jonathan dismounted and suddenly his hands were about her waist, effortlessly lifting her down.

Maggie was the first to reach them. "Oh, Miss Katherine, I'm so thankful that you're safe. I was so frightened for you." She hugged her friend, blinking to hide the sudden rush of tears, her voice becoming chiding. "And just look at you. You are sorely in need of a bath, just as Simon said."

Confusion reigned again. "Simon is here? And he told you…"

Soft laughter rippled prettily from her friend. "Of course, silly. He rode ahead to tell us you had been found and that you and Jonathan were close behind. And he's already got Clover preparing your bath."

Hesitantly Katherine mounted the steps to where Samuel waited, beaming at her in his happiness, grateful that she was back, safe and unharmed. The Featherstone's, standing patiently nearby, were delighted to see her, Mary giving her a squeeze that left her breathless. Freeing herself from her friend's embrace, Katherine turned to Samuel, whose comforting arms soon enfolded her. Teary-eyed, she smiled up at him, noticing that his eyes were damp with emotion also.

"Oh, Samuel. I'm sorry for worrying you but after everything that happened last night…"

"Now, now." He patted her shoulder comfortingly. "Not another word of apology from you. It's that grandson of mine that should be here, on his knees, begging your forgiveness." He dabbed unashamedly at his eyes with his handkerchief. "I've told Clover to have a light lunch sent to your room. I thought you might be hungry." He raised an inquiring brow at her. "And I even have a small surprise for you." Gesturing to someone who had been standing just out of sight, Marie stepped out, a warm smile on her face.

"Hello, cherie. I, too, am glad you're home. I drove out this morning with one gown and some of the undergarments a lady needs." She held up a hand to stop the girl's questions. "I had two of my seamstresses working late into the night to complete as much as they could. I knew Samuel was anxious to see you dressed as befitted the mistress of Seven Oaks."

As Katherine gazed at the small circle gathered about her, she could only bow her head in humble gratitude at their warm reception. It was then that Clover stepped out, beaming at her.

"Miss Katherine, you look a sight. I never, in all my born days seen so much mud on one tiny girl. Now you scoot upstairs. I've already laid out some of your new things on your bed. Oh, and Mr. Simon is waiting for you. He says he needs to straighten some things out with you and doesn't want no audience, so would everyone please give them time alone." Her voice trailed off as she saw the concern on the faces surrounding them.

Samuel's features tightened in worry but he knew he couldn't interfere in matters between a husband and wife. *Besides*, he reasoned to himself, *they do need time to work out their problems, with no audience.*

He smiled reassuringly at Katherine. "Young lady, do you have any idea how fond I've become of you? Hurry upstairs, have a talk with that husband of yours, and then prepare your toilette. Remember, we're having guests tonight."

Samuel's words reminded Katherine that this would be the last day she would enjoy Maggie's company, for she would be leaving with her uncle, to sail to New York to join her husband.

As she looked about her, joy bubbled up inside. She was happy to be back. Turning, she followed Clover up the stairs. As the servant opened the door, Katherine spied Simon, his flask in hand, standing motionless beside her bath. Apprehension coursed through her but she gave herself a shake. *He only wanted to talk, nothing more* she reassured herself.

"You can leave, Clover. I'll call you when you're needed. I believe I'm capable of attending my wife's bath." His words were slightly slurred and Clover, giving Katherine a worried look, nodded. As the servant left the room, he slammed the door, the sound echoing ominously throughout the house. All within hearing distance paused in their conversations, waiting, wondering.

A wave of apprehension swept over Katherine as Simon neared. She could smell liquor on his breath. Wordlessly, he removed her muddy and stained cloak, frowning at the disarray of her auburn locks. His thumb traced a path along her jaw, almost a caress but Katherine shuddered in foreboding at this unaccustomed familiarity and stepped away from him. With no warning, it was as if a dam had broken! All the indignity and humiliation he had been forced to endure under his grandfather's domination suddenly centered on this slight female form, someone his grandfather had come to cherish but only he had complete power over her.

Wordlessly, he spun her around, his strong hands suddenly seizing the back of her mud-spattered gown and tore it open, leaving her shoulders and back bare. Choking back a frightened cry, she recoiled in fear, away from the unfamiliar monster he had suddenly become.

"I promised myself we would resolve our differences, without my grandfather or Jonathan coming to your rescue, and now it's just the two of us."

Shivering as a cool breeze fluttered across her bare shoulders, she turned to the closed door, prepared to flee but he caught her by her hair, twisting it painfully around his hands. He snarled through clenched teeth as he forced her to her knees. "You will beg my forgiveness, for the humiliation you have caused me to suffer today, acting like a petulant child, not just here at Seven Oaks but in Charleston as well. Before I'm finished, you'll crawl to me, apologizing for every humiliation I've suffered since Lord Talbot first proposed I take you as my wife."

Swaying drunkenly, he clumsily seized her wrists and yanked her violently to her feet before flinging her to the foot of the bed. It was then that Katherine saw him retrieve a leather strap from the table. Horror was reflected in her eyes.

"Simon, think of what you're doing. If you want me to beg for mercy…"

A streak of fire raced across the bared skin of her back. Surprise momentarily stopped her from crying out but as he raised his arm to deliver a second blow, she screamed in terror. Voices could be heard, calling both their names as many feet ran up the stairs. Simon, hearing fists beating on the door, quickly sobered. Aware of the strap dangling from limp fingers, he stared in confusion at the angry blood-encrusted welt across his wife's back. His words were muffled as he contemplated his handiwork.

"What have I done?" He flushed, fists clenched angrily, eyes staring skyward. Collapsing on the floor, he hugged his knees, rocking back and forth. "My God, what have I become?"

The door crashed open, revealing an incensed Jonathan, nostrils flaring and grey eyes wild, taking in the scene that chilled him to the core of his being.

He strode forward and seized the leather strap from where his cousin had dropped it. Fists flew but Simon was no match for Jonathan, especially as his reflexes were slowed by the liquor he had consumed since learning of Katherine's flight.

Jonathan grasped the now unconscious Simon by the collar and dragged him through the door connecting the two rooms. Katherine opened her pain-filled eyes to find herself once again the object of pitying and concerned looks as the Featherstone's, Maggie and Marie peered in. Jonathan, returning to her side, draped her nakedness with the nearest cover he could find, her tattered cloak.

"Maggie, send Clover up here, quickly. And try to reassure Samuel that, although Katherine has been sorely abused, she'll be all right."

Maggie rushed to do his bidding, calling for Clover who was already puffing her way up the staircase. Samuel, his face mirroring his concern, stared as his guests made their way silently downward, ashen-faced and numb with shock.

"What's happened now? Is the girl all right?" He waited, strain evident on his wrinkled face.

Maggie took him by the arm and led him into the library, softly explaining what had taken place upstairs. Samuel, white with rage, listened to her account and demanded his grandson face him immediately. It was at that moment that Jonathan appeared, assuring Samuel that Simon was sleeping off the effects of the whiskey and the blow that he had dealt him. Snorting in disgust at this latest indignity that Katherine had suffered, the old man sank into the chair, his hand on his cane, looking up helplessly at Jonathan. Maggie, sensing that her presence was no longer required, withdrew quietly from the room.

"What am I to do? After you leave tomorrow, what will happen to Katherine? You said I had to take care of myself so I could take care of her but I must accept that I'm an old man, no match for Simon anymore. I can't even climb the stairs."

Jonathan, feeling just as helpless, studied the well-loved face and shrugged. "I'm sorry, Sam, but I just don't have an answer. The girl tried to run and he brought her back. I regret helping him, but when he discovered she had flown, I thought he had at last realized what an absolute treasure she was. I never suspected he would flog her like some runaway slave. And Sam, I do have to leave tomorrow. My presence is only aggravating him." At the old man's curious look, he smiled as he explained, "I seem to have witnessed every trial the girl has endured and he resents me for that but I've never had a choice. I was always the one on hand." The old man started to speak but thought better of it and both men sat silently, lost in thought.

Upstairs, after a warm, soothing bath, Clover gently rubbed a salve on the deep red welt, softly proclaiming its healing power to her mistress, assuring her that the cut would probably heal without a mark. Katherine, her mind numb, let the servant talk. Her head was spinning in bewilderment. Why had Simon stopped her from leaving only to deliver a vicious beating? What must everyone be thinking? *Oh, God,* she thought, *if only that train had arrived earlier. She would have been on it and on her way to a new life, a new beginning.* Muffled sounds could be heard from the adjoining room. Sheer fright swept through her but Clover patted her shoulder reassuringly.

"You be fine, Miss Katherine. I just run and let Mr. Sam know that boy be awake now." Moving quickly for one so heavy, she scurried out the door, calling loudly as she made her way down the stairs. Jonathan and Samuel, hearing the urgency in her voice, were already rushing to meet her. Her message delivered, she returned to Katherine. Samuel coldly instructed Jonathan to fetch the miscreant and bring him to the library.

"And Jonathan, let me have my moment with him. He has twice humiliated Katherine publicly and so should make a public apology to her. Should I need assistance, I give you leave to enter but please, not before that."

Bowing his head in silent assent, Jonathan mounted the stairs, anxious to have his own private moment with his cousin. It was some moments later that the two, a scowling but much chastened Simon and a grim-faced Jonathan made their way to the library. As Simon entered, Jonathan pulled the door closed, remaining on the outside as Samuel had requested. He pulled over a chair and sat down, ready to spring to the old man's defense if need be.

* * * *

It was some hours later that Katherine paused at the top of the stairs, nervously smoothing the folds of her new gown. Marie had knocked at her door earlier, offering to assist her in dressing and Clover had gratefully invited her in. The dress, a confection of yellow satin and lace, left her shoulders bare, revealing the tip of the ugly welt. The two women conferred a moment before Clover fetched a piece of soft cotton flannel and together they covered her back, ensuring that none of the salve Clover had applied would leak through and mark the dress while protecting her abused skin from the fabric of the gown. Finally, a delicate woolen shawl was draped around Katherine's tender shoulders, hiding the wound.

She should have been ecstatic with the speed at which Marie had produced such a beautiful garment but her mind fluttered with anxiety, unable to think of anything but the ordeal to come. Clover had convinced her mistress to have a light lunch and a nap before dressing but she had only tossed restlessly, unable to relax.

As she neared the parlor, voices drifted out, giving the evening the appearance of an ordinary affair, but the color drained from her face as Simon stepped into the hallway, having watched as she made her descent. Becoming increasingly uneasy under his scrutiny, she wondered if he had another fiendish plan to torment her but he smiled as if the events of the day had never happened. Warily placing her hand in his outstretched one, he led her into the midst of the small gathering. Entering the sitting room, she read the concern for her well-being on all of their faces. Simon led her to his grandfather, who gallantly bowed over her hand and kissed it lightly. Simon cleared his throat and called for silence, and everyone turned toward him, curiosity written across their faces.

"Friends, before the other guests arrive, I must speak to Katherine, in fact I must address all of you, for I fear I made some very bad decisions today, as you have witnessed. My wife, the beautiful and innocent Katherine, has borne the brunt of these decisions and you have been unwilling observers to our marital differences." He paused and seemed to be assessing the effect of his words on the gathering before he continued. "For that reason, I wish to publicly apologize to her and beg her forgiveness. In my defense, I can only say I was shocked beyond reason when it was discovered that she had fled after hearing the tail-end of an argument between my grandfather and myself, and some rather unfortunate remarks were spoken that should have never been uttered. Later, having arrived at the railroad station just as she was about to board a train, I had what I thought would be one drink but sadly, it was only the first of many, clouding my judgment enormously and turning me into a raging beast. I can only pray that she will forgive me and believe me when I promise it will never happen again."

There was absolute silence in the room as all eyes turned to Katherine, who stared, speechless, at her husband. She stood motionless in the middle of room until he stepped toward her, boldly intimidating.

"Well, Katherine, what is your decision? Can you find it in your heart to forgive me?" Her thick lashes swept downward as she hesitantly nodded her assent. He extended his hand to her. Trembling, she placed her hand in his, looking up into his blue eyes. His smile, which only she could see, held a note of scorn and a warning voice whispered that it had all been an act to mollify his grandfather and cousin. She flinched as he placed a proprietary arm across her shoulders, reminding her of her abused flesh concealed beneath her gown.

It was at that moment that the guests, Captain Hart and Ned, arrived. Greetings and introductions were the order of the day until dinner was announced. After everyone was seated, toasts were proposed, accompanied by much laughter and light-hearted chatter. Ned was saluted by one and all as the hero of the voyage and Samuel, in heartfelt gratitude, rewarded him with a heavy purse for his act of bravery. Ned, eyes shining brightly at the fuss being made over him, glanced across the table at the woman he worshipped but was taken aback by the wistfulness he saw in her eyes. Seeing him studying her, Katherine smiled. As the meal was cleared away, the ladies made their way to the drawing room, leaving the men to their port and cigars. Katherine and Maggie sat together on the sofa, treasuring what could be their last time together for who knew how many years it would be before they met again, if ever.

At last the men rejoined them and, after a pleasurable interval, Captain Hart, checking his timepiece, announced the time of departure had arrived. After the others had said their good-byes, Katherine and Maggie, tears beginning to fall, hugged fiercely, whispering vows of friendship never to be forgotten. As the heavy door closed behind them, Katherine slowly climbed the stairs, calling good night to the others as she made her way to her bedchamber. Melancholy weighed her slender shoulders down, her steps dragging, so different from her usual light movements.

The maid Daisy was waiting as Katherine entered her chamber. Without a murmur, she helped her mistress disrobe and as Katherine crawled between the crisp, cool sheets, she wondered what her life with Simon held but the exhaustion of the day quickly yielded her up to the arms of Morpheus, leaving her no chance to ponder her future.

* * * *

As Katherine entered the dining room the next morning, Simon rose from his chair and bowed to her, his eyes sharp and assessing. "At last, here she is, my wife." His words were cold and impersonal. "I apologize, my dear, but I simply must be off. There is much to do before this day ends. But you will at least have the pleasure of Jonathan's company. Grandfather has requested his breakfast be served in the library and the Featherstone's appear to be sleeping late." Meeting his cousin's aloof gaze, he dipped his head before continuing.

"Jonathan, have a safe trip." Curtly nodding his blond head once more, he walked briskly from the room, calling for his jacket as he strode toward the door.

Jonathan rose and held a chair for her, his handsome face growing reserved as he breathed in the exquisite scent of her, his knuckles tightening on the back of her chair. As she sat down, she grew reflective and, as if sensing her mood, he also became pensive. He resumed his seat across from her, distractedly watching the bustling servants as they went about their duties, quietly withdrawing to the kitchen as their tasks were completed.

He regarded her tenderly, drinking in what could be his last glimpse of her for some time to come. Feeling his eyes on her, she glanced up after daintily sipping her tea. Folding her hands in a pose of tranquility, she let her eyes meet his. A thoughtful smile played about his mouth as he continued to drink in her very essence.

"What will happen to me after you leave?" Her voice was almost a whisper. "Since that first meeting at Marlow Court, you have been my guardian angel. You have always been there to slay my dragons."

Chapter Thirteen

When he spoke, his voice was chuckling and hearty. "Come now, this can't be the same Katherine Maguire Radcliffe who declared to Lady Talbot she would rather jump from a cliff than marry her son, the cowardly Roland." He spoke in an infinitely compassionate tone. "And could this be the same young lady who felt it better to leave all of this," he waved his hand indicating the grandeur of Seven Oaks, "and strike out on her own rather than stay where she mistakenly felt she wasn't wanted?"

Her cheeks heated at his words. Taking her slender fingers in his, Jonathan spoke, his voice a velvet murmur. "I have already promised Sam, and now I'm promising you, Katherine Maguire Radcliffe, that I will return to Seven Oaks as quickly as possible if summoned."

"Thank you, Jonathan. It gives me great comfort to know that you'll still be my knight, even though separated by such a great distance."

He kissed her fingers, his touch sending a thrill through her and then tenderly released her hands. Rising from the table, he smiled at her. "And now, my sweet Katherine, it is time to take my leave of you, for you are too tempting a morsel sitting so innocently across from me. I must speak one last time to Sam before I leave," he paused, "and I believe I hear the Featherstone's coming."

The older couple entered the room just as the words left his mouth. Greeting them warmly as he once again bade them farewell, he excused himself and made his way to the library. Katherine smilingly invited the older couple to join her, ignoring the feeling of emptiness within.

* * * *

The days turned into weeks as Katherine watched the leaves change color before they drifted delicately from the trees to the grounds of the plantation. The Featherstone's, at Samuel's insistence, reluctantly left Seven Oaks to continue their travels up the eastern coast of America. Before setting off, Samuel entrusted his old friend with legal papers to be delivered to an attorney in New York where the elderly couple planned to take ship when they eventually returned to England and their family.

After their departure, Samuel and Katherine grew ever closer. His health failing rapidly, Samuel rarely left his cherished library, a room where Katherine would spend much of each day playing chess or reading to him.

The last of her wardrobe had been completed and delivered by Marie herself, who always joined them in the library for lunch. Katherine would listen as they reminisced about the times they had shared over the years, and again she wondered if she would ever have someone to share her life and make their own memories.

Old friends and neighbors, curious about Simon's new wife and concerned over the rumors of the state of Samuel's health, called often. All who visited Seven Oaks were soon charmed by Katherine's graciousness and her seemingly lack of awareness of her strikingly delicate beauty. It was often remarked on by many of those callers at the devoted care Samuel was receiving from his new granddaughter-in-law, those same visitors wondering at Simon's absence, knowing full well where he spent most of his time. Although Juliana railed at him for the continued good health of his wife, she lacked the audacity to intrude on Samuel's last days and so she and Katherine were destined to never meet again.

Samuel took great joy as Katherine appeared at his bedside each morning, dressed in one of her new frocks. They rarely spoke of Simon who had become almost a ghost, someone who returned most nights after everyone was asleep and left before any other had risen. Samuel formed his plans and then summoned his lawyer from Charleston. The two spent many hours closeted together, as Samuel sought a way to protect his beloved granddaughter-in-law after his death, which he knew was swiftly approaching.

* * * *

Christmas passed almost unnoticed, December giving way to January when Samuel, faced with his own mortality, decided it was time to summon Jonathan to Seven Oaks, sharing his decision with neither Katherine nor Simon. A letter was dispatched and Samuel began to anxiously watch the driveway from his window. His vigilance was at last rewarded late one afternoon when, waking from a nap, he spied a solitary rider approaching the house. Happy that he was alone to receive his guest, he struggled to sit up but the effort proved too much and he fell back on the pillows. Moments later, there was a light tapping at the library door and he bid the caller to enter. The door swung open to reveal the broad-shouldered figure of Jonathan Radcliffe.

He crossed the room, his face a frozen mask as he tried to disguise his dismay at the deterioration of the old man.

"Sam, how are you?" He pulled a chair toward the bed, gently taking the hand being offered to him.

"Jonathan, I'm so very pleased to see you, my boy, and damned grateful that you're here in time." His voice had lost its thunderous quality and he now sounded exactly what he was, a tired, sick old man. "I'm sorry, son, that I had to call on you, what with your wedding only weeks away..." His voice trailed off.

"Nonsense, Sam. I promised that if you called, I would come." He lowered his voice conspiratorially. "Besides, I think Isabella was happy to be rid of me.

105

I believe I was getting in the way of her preparations for the festivities."

Samuel chuckled softly. "You've a kind heart, my boy."

It was at that moment the door opened and Katherine stood, framed in the afternoon sunlight. Jonathan, as the months away from Seven Oaks had passed, had almost convinced himself that she really hadn't been as breathtakingly stunning as he remembered but as he studied her fine-boned features, he felt a familiar inner torment begin to gnaw at him. Quickly crossing the carpeted floor, he took her slender hand in his, drawing her into the room, his eyes glowing with an inner fire.

"Hello, Katherine." There was a faint tremor in his voice as though some undefined emotion had touched him. He heard the gentle softness of her voice as she spoke his name.

"Jonathan, I'm so happy you're here."

He saw a myriad of emotions play across her face until finally she withdrew her hand, as if she was afraid of being thought forward.

"Now I know who Samuel has been watching for so anxiously. And look at him, why, I think that's the first smile I've seen in three days." Suddenly self-conscious in front of them, she quietly fussed with the old man's pillow and blanket.

The three sat and talked over the tea and cakes that the ever-efficient Clover had served but as the last crumbs were brushed away, Katherine glanced at Samuel and saw exhaustion written on his face.

"Oh, Sam, you're tired. Why don't we leave you to have a small nap before dinner and…

He interrupted her with a wave of his hand. "Katherine," Samuel spoke in a gentle manner, "would you mind leaving us for a while? I have some matters to discuss and ultimately to seek Jonathan's advice, and I'm afraid, my dear, you are just too much of a distraction." He looked up at her, his expression pensive.

"Oh course, Samuel, I'll see that Jonathan's room has been readied for him." Smiling at both men, she rose gracefully from her chair, smoothing the folds of her gown as she made her way to the door, closing it softly behind her as she left the room.

"Sam," Jonathan protested when they were alone, "there's nothing that can't wait until after you've rested. I can see how tired you are."

"Jonathan, I must take advantage of every minute I have left." He spoke so quietly the younger man had to lean down to hear him. "That grandson of mine has all but deserted his wife in favor of that hussy, that home wrecker, Juliana Taylor." His complexion reddened with anger as he glanced up at his visitor. "I don't have much time left, boy—days—not even weeks, according to that quack of a doctor, and I can tell by your face that you agree with him." He stopped to regain his breath. "I was worried that I had delayed too long in sending for you or that you might not arrive in time." Beads of perspiration appeared on his brow as he tried to sit up.

"I've reached a decision. I've threatened Simon many times, trying to make him dance to my tune. I was wrong and now, with you standing before me, I freely admit that I want him to have Seven Oaks. He's my only kin, my grandson. But there will be one final condition that he must meet!"

"Sam, lay back and rest. I'm here now and I'll do what I can to put your mind at ease. Now you tell me just what your idea is. Before I left Seven Oaks, you hinted that you were working on a plan of sorts."

The old man glanced up, ignoring the interruption. "Simon has to annul his marriage to Katherine. They don't share a bed, at least not since their arrival from England. And Simon is so besotted by that trollop, I have every reason to believe he'll see the wisdom of setting Katherine aside." He stopped talking for a moment, searching Jonathan's visage for a reaction to his words but the younger man fought to keep all emotion from his face. "I'll make sure he understands that both he and Katherine will be free to each go their own way with no ties, financial or marital."

"You're interfering where you have no right. Perhaps Simon will come around and recognize the absolute treasure he already possesses."

The old man shook his head in vehement denial. "Don't patronize me, son. I'm deeply worried about what will happen to Katherine when I'm no longer here, controlling the purse strings. I shudder at what her fate might be. You're forgetting that I've watched Juliana as she was growing up, and I can only say she is one of, if not the most, vindictive people I've ever had the unfortunate pleasure of meeting. After I'm gone, I'll be beyond her thirst for revenge but I shudder to think of Katherine ever finding herself at the mercy of that one. I've had my lawyer working on the legalities of such a drastic step. And Jonathan, consider this. The gossipmongers will have a heyday with this and no matter how highly they have come to regard her, socially, Katherine will be marked as a pariah should she remain in Charleston, innocent party or not. It would be unfair to expect her to shoulder a burden not of her making." Here he paused, catching his breath and closing his eyes in momentary resignation.

Jonathan, listening intently, knew Samuel wasn't laying all this groundwork without a reason. Curiosity began to eat at him. Did Sam want his help getting the girl back to England? And what would she do once she was back—return to Marlow Court? Impossible!

"I think I know where you're going with this but I have to say I'm against it. What good would it do to send her back? She would be just as unprotected there as she would be if you somehow did convince Simon to divorce her and she was left on her own right here in Charleston."

Samuel, his eyes bright with impatience at the inaccurate conclusion the younger man had arrived at, ordered him to hush a moment and listen.

"Son, I have never considered leaving her on her own, unprotected, fair game for any predator. No, right now my main concern is to get her out of Charleston, away from Simon and his black-hearted tart. I've tried to cover everything but I'll lay my plan out and see if you can find any holes to poke in it."

A gentle tap on the door signaled the arrival of a dinner tray for both of them. Sam merely picked at his food but Jonathan attacked the delectable roast chicken and vegetables, having eaten nothing since breakfast. The fire crackled merrily as Samuel resumed his argument. "Jonathan, I want you to take Katherine with you when you return to Belle Isle." Stunned, Jonathan stopped chewing and stared into the old man's watery eyes. "Yes son, this is the essence of my plan. The rest of it is just detail." He continued, "After my funeral…"

"Sam, I can't listen to this. You might have a lot of time left, more than your doctor or I have given you!" His words trailed off.

"My boy, I'm tired. I'm ready to go." He smiled wanly. "But not before Katherine's future is somewhat assured. As you already know, Marie St. Pierre, the talented seamstress that stitched all of Katherine's wardrobe, is your future father-in-law's cousin twice removed or some such, and therefore has been invited to your wedding. She has already confided that she is travelling to Belle Isle by ship, leaving a week from now. What I propose is you deposit Katherine's trunks with her—she has generously offered to take them to Belle Isle while you and Katherine travel overland by train or, failing that, by horse. Should Simon, for any reason, entertain thoughts of once again preventing her from leaving Seven Oaks, he won't know how she's travelling, nor her destination."

He halted abruptly, fatigue stamped on his face. "Pour me a whiskey, my boy. Both you and my own doctor advised me to curtail my liquor consumption but at this point, what can it matter?" He gave an impatient shrug as Jonathan handed him the crystal glass.

His eyes were sharp and assessing. "Here comes the tricky part. Will your intended and her family welcome Katherine into their home, temporary as that might be?" The challenge hung in the air while Jonathan pondered the question.

"Sam, her welcome is guaranteed. The Beauchamp's are a most generous and caring family, as my own boyhood can attest. Remember, they took my mother and I in after my father died, not only providing a home for us but Phillip Beauchamp also paid for my education. I have no hesitation in offering Belle Isle as a safe haven for Katherine. But Sam, Katherine should be here with us. We have witnessed her streak of independence—do you think she'll take kindly to us planning her future?"

The old man peered up at the younger man. "Leave her to me, my boy. I have all my arguments ready to convince her where her best interests lie. And I have instructed Clover to wake me when Simon returns home, whatever time that might be. I doubt he'll be too upset with any of this."

The two men sat silently for several minutes, contemplating the outcome of Samuel's scheme. At last, Jonathan stood up and stretched his arms. After ensuring the old man wanted for nothing, he quietly left the room.

* * * *

Jonathan could hear voices arguing as he passed the closed library door on his way to the dining room. He hesitated briefly before entering, only to be greeted by Katherine, green eyes flashing with anger as they lit on the intruder, berating him for his part in Samuel's mad scheme. He held up his hand as if calling for a truce just as Samuel, lying back on his pillows, rasped out her name, causing her to cease her tirade immediately.

She crossed the room and began to fuss over the old man, causing him momentary annoyance. In a familiar calming gesture, he took her slender hands and held them between his own.

"I have already spoken to Simon and he has agreed that the two of you should separate—in other words, annul your marriage."

Katherine, although shocked to hear it put into words, felt as if a heavy weight had been lifted from her shoulders but she still bristled at other people making decisions that should have been hers, or at least consulted her.

"Katherine, please, listen to me," he hesitated briefly as if weighing his words. "No, listen to us. We have your best interests at heart." He cast a pleading look at Jonathan. "Help me to convince her, please."

Jonathan, with long purposeful strides, crossed the room. Her enticing scent drifted past his nostrils as he approached her, and he, almost caressingly, pushed stray tendrils of auburn hair from her face.

"Katherine, you must listen. Samuel has convinced me that this is the only way to ensure your safety."

"Am I to once again submit meekly as others decide the course my life is to take?" In as reasonable a voice as she could manage, she spoke with a deceptive calm. "When I was orphaned as a child, the church decided what was to become of me. And I thank my lucky stars that I was sent to my beloved aunt and uncle in England. And then the new owners of Marlow Court arrived in the person of Lord Talbot and his dragon of a wife, Hester. They chose a husband for me, a man I had never met, and a man with whom I immediately set sail across a vast ocean to his homeland! And whilst on this voyage, another man, a sailor, decides that, on his lord's instructions, he is to ravish me before throwing me overboard. And lastly, my husband who is no husband has now chosen to set me aside while he marries the woman he has always loved. Is this my fate, Jonathan?"

Her voice had risen hysterically as she paced the confines of the room. Skirts swirling as she swung around, she glared at the two men who, in unspoken agreement, let her vent her outrage as the course of her life was once again being decided for her. "Samuel, I thought you felt some affection for me. Why are you allowing this to happen?" She continued in a voice shakier than she would have liked. "I don't care a fig about Simon. We don't love each other and, if we lived together the rest of our lives, I doubt that our feelings toward each other would change. But I hate decisions about my life being made for me, even by you."

"My sweet child, you're not listening. It's your safety that we're concerned about." The old man held out his arms and she flew to his side. As she opened her mouth to protest, he held up a hand to quiet her. "My end is near, child. And when I go, who will there be to protect you? Simon, sadly, is in love with another woman. I mistakenly thought to control him by threatening to cut him out of my will if he didn't find a more suitable bride and unbelievably, he found you. But I know now that I should never have interfered with him. It has brought great unhappiness to you and, after I'm gone, I can only foresee disaster. You have never witnessed what a vindictive shrew the woman who Simon wants to spend his life with can be. And I greatly fear that, when I am beyond her reach for revenge, she will turn her attention to you. What will your life be like? That is why I summoned Jonathan. He has agreed to escort you to Belle Isle where, he assures me, you will be warmly received. And after he has returned from his wedding trip, he will help you establish your own home. I promise you will be your own mistress from that time onward. Please, Katherine, you must agree."

She glanced up at him, tears flowing from the depths of her emerald eyes. "Oh, Samuel, please don't talk of your death, I can't bear it. I'll agree to whatever you ask." Both men smiled at her compliance, relieved that she had seen reason.

"You've relieved an old man's mind, child."

Katherine spoke, her voice a question. "But if you are both convinced that Simon, or actually Juliana, might pose a threat to me, and Jonathan is waiting to spirit me off to his Belle Isle in some mysterious manner, what of the wedding?" She could see they weren't following her train of thought and so laid out her concern.

Mentioning the wedding of the man she knew she loved cut through her like a knife but somehow she masked her inner turmoil with a deceptive calmness as she faced them again.

"Jonathan, you are to marry in a few weeks time. Simon is your cousin. Don't you think it possible that he will attend your wedding? What use is all this deception if Simon, Juliana and I are all in the same place at the same time?"

Samuel laughed as the weak spot in their plan was exposed by the very one it was to protect. "She's right, Jonathan."

Chapter Fourteen

Smiling sheepishly at being caught out by this slip of a girl, he nodded his head. "Clever as well as beautiful! You never fail to amaze me, Katherine. I guess we've been so intent on making our plans, we never thought that Simon might have a plan of his own." His grey eyes glowed warmly down on her as she smiled in sheer delight at his unexpected praise.

Samuel, recovering from a fit of coughing, thoughtfully regarded the younger man. "My boy, I have only ever visited Belle Isle once, many years ago when you were but a lad. As I recall, there was a convent some miles away. Doesn't a convent offer safe haven? I'm sure they would if a generous purse was to exchange hands."

Astonished at such a suggestion, Katherine prepared once more to do battle. "A convent! I don't wish to become a nun, Samuel. And there is nothing you can say to convince me this would be the best thing I could do with my life!"

Samuel smiled in amusement. "No one is suggesting that you become a nun. This would be a temporary measure lasting until Simon, if he attends his cousin's wedding, has left Belle Isle. If he doesn't make an appearance, I'm sure Jonathan will send for you immediately."

Jonathan smiled at such a marvelous solution being found. Katherine and Samuel, relieved and excited, were reviewing the plan, examining it for flaws. He heard Samuel speak in a tired, raspy voice.

"Now, child, it's time you and I went over the details of your future." Jonathan, sensing that he was now an intruder, quietly withdrew.

"My dear, there are some papers you must be made aware of. And money, you'll need money. After your experience with Simon, who knows if you'll ever want to marry again and who can blame you. Everything you will need is in the lower desk drawer, buried under some books. Bring it all here, child.'

She retrieved a heavy package and carried it over to Samuel.

"For the time being, we won't even let Jonathan know all the details of your plans. Do you agree?' As she hesitantly nodded, he lowered his voice conspiratorially, causing her to lean closer to hear his words.

"This is a deed to a cottage in the village of Carlyle in New York. Simon, if he ever knew about it, would most likely assume it was sold years ago." He paused, momentarily lost in the past, and then smiled slightly as he studied her face. "When my wife and I first arrived in this country, Somerset Cottage was our home. Later, when we ventured south, we rented it out. I never wanted to sell—there were just too many happy memories within its walls. It's a fair sized house on a small parcel of land and, with a servant or two, you should be able to manage quite well." He pushed the paper aside and drew out a wallet. "There are enough gold coins here to see you on your journey to build your life anew. Your trunk has a false bottom, hide everything in there."

He lay so still Katherine wondered if he had dozed off but as she prepared to leave, he spoke again. "You have probably been wondering why I convinced the Featherstone's to leave Seven Oaks sooner than they had planned. Well, nothing is done without a purpose. Edmond Featherstone is a fine lawyer, and as trustworthy as they come. He carried a letter addressed to a bank up there, ensuring that funds are deposited into an account in your name. He and Mary will also be visiting the cottage, ensuring that it's up to snuff for your imminent arrival. They will also be meeting with an American lawyer who will handle any legal concerns you might have in the future. His name is Harvey Davenport, his address is on this card. Tuck it away safely until you have reached your destination. It is Mr. Davenport who will actually accompany you to the bank with the letter concerning your funds."

A twinkle appeared in his tired eyes as he continued, "Hopefully there is going to be a housekeeper and gardener-handyman awaiting your arrival—one Jamie and Maggie McGregor, I believe their names are."

Her eyes flew open at his last words. "Maggie! Do you mean my friend Maggie, Maggie who was travelling to New York to join her husband, Jamie McGregor?" Tears sparkled once again in her eyes, but they were tears of joy and excitement.

Samuel chuckled at her obvious delight. "Yes, I mean your Maggie. Featherstone has her address and, as long as they haven't moved elsewhere, he will make them a most attractive offer."

Katherine, about to hug him, was struck by his pallor. "Oh, Sam. What has all this scheming cost you? You're exhausted." She rose from her chair and tucked the blankets lovingly about him. Reaching out, he took her hands in his, smiling tenderly at her.

"I'm content with this day's work, sweet child. You run along now and let an old man have a nap." His eyes were already closing as she leaned down and brushed his forehead with her lips. Her slippered feet whispered on the carpet as she made her way to the door. Pausing, she turned and smiled, reflecting on her good fortune in coming to know such a man before she silently made her way up the stairs.

The following day was filled with activity as Samuel and his lawyer shuffled through all sorts of official looking documents, calling her in occasionally to sign her name. Simon was also summoned and given papers to sign. Meeting her as she emerged from the sitting room, he smiled disdainfully at her, his blue eyes resting lightly on her face.

"Well, Katherine, it seems we are now free of the shackles of matrimony that bound us together. My grandfather tells me plans are already afoot regarding your future but declined to share them with me. No matter. I am sure you won't be alone for long but it is a pity that Jonathan is already betrothed to another."

He looked smugly down at her blushing face. Disconcerted, she crossed her arms and pointedly looked away. Simon continued. "As for myself, I am going to marry the woman I should have married." Saying that, he turned and walked toward the door, and, thank heavens, out of her life forever, she prayed.

* * * *

Rain was falling softly as Katherine walked slowly from the small cemetery, the wet grass soaking the hem of her black crepe dress. She was grateful that Sam had insisted that one of her new frocks be a mourning gown. She pulled her cloak closer to ward off the coolness of the day. Jonathan and Simon walked somberly on either side of her, Jonathan's arm lending her support. Samuel had died peacefully in his sleep two days ago, which created a whirl of confusion as preparations were made, friends contacted and consolation calls accepted.

Marie had arrived the night before, quietly making arrangements with Jonathan for the transporting of Katherine's trunks with her to Belle Isle. They had taken Clover into their confidence but the astute servant had displayed no surprise, having observed the lack of marital harmony over the months since Katherine's arrival. "And it sure weren't anything that sweet child could be blamed for, no sir," she had muttered to herself as she packed the gowns carefully away.

In all of the turmoil, Katherine had found little time to mourn the loss of her friend and benefactor. The funeral cortege wound its way toward the house where the mourners could pay their respects to the family. As yet, no one other than those directly involved knew the state of affairs between Katherine and Simon. *Oh, well,* she thought, *soon it will be no concern of mine whatsoever.*

It was later that same evening, as Katherine and Jonathan sat in front of the fire, each lost in their own thoughts, that they became aware Simon had returned home and was standing in the doorway.

"Well, isn't this a charming domestic scene," he sneered upon entering the room. As Jonathan made to protest, he held up his hand. "No, I'm happy you're both here. I have some news to impart and you should hear it from me. I know you leave in the morning and that fits in well with my plans."

Jonathan regarded his cousin warily, wondering what was coming. Katherine sat waiting, trying to anticipate what he intended, worried that their plans would be upended in some way.

"Don't look so suspicious. I am here merely to inform you of my future. Katherine, we are no longer married, and when Charleston society learns that, well, I don't need to tell you about narrow minds and gossip. Juliana and I will be regarded as lepers, in truth we already are. Consequently, I have sold Seven

Oaks."

Jonathan stood up, shock written across his handsome face. "You've done what?"

"I've sold Seven Oaks. Juliana and I are moving to New Orleans, where we can begin life anew." Seeing her incredulous look, his smile grew hard and resentful. "You have no idea, my dear Katherine, of the impact you've had on the folks hereabouts in the short time you've been here. They adore you for your care of my grandfather and, well, Juliana has never been a favorite of Charleston."

He looked somewhat sheepish as he continued. "I am sure Grandfather and Jonathan must have mentioned that Juliana never forgets an insult, and she feels that was what Grandfather did to her when he bullied me into travelling across the ocean in search of what he considered a suitable bride." He turned the hat he was holding through his fingers before he resumed. "Also, servants, whether slave or free, talk to their own kind, and our sham of a marriage, my dear, has become quite a hot topic of conversation. And, since I was approached months ago by a neighboring planter about selling after I inherited the property, the decision to leave was an easy one. I've just signed all the legal documents and then we'll travel down to New Orleans to find a house, after your wedding of course, Jonathan, then back to Seven Oaks to pack whatever furniture we'll be taking with us." Nodding his head curtly, he turned on his heel and left the room, his footsteps the only sound to be heard as he mounted the stairs.

Katherine and Jonathan faced each other, both stunned by his announcement. "Well, that settles it. They will attend the wedding and so it's off to the convent for you. And somewhere between Charleston and Belle Isle, you'll have to come to a decision as to whether you would prefer to wait at the convent until Isabella and I have returned from our wedding trip or travel to Belle Isle once Simon has departed the place. I know Isabella's father, Phillip Beauchamp, will be captivated by you and will have no hesitation in offering you a safe refuge." Seeing her troubled face, he tried to comfort her as she gazed absently into the fire.

"I have time to make that decision, don't I, Jonathan?"

"Of course you do. But for now, I think we should get some sleep. God knows what tomorrow will bring." Katherine, brow furrowed in thought, silently climbed the stairs, leaving a deeply contemplative Jonathan staring into the fire.

* * * *

Katherine and Jonathan, both outfitted in riding clothes, ate breakfast just as the sun appeared on the horizon. The slaves, although no announcement had been made, somehow knew their young mistress was leaving for good, stood on the front steps as she and Jonathan stood, ready to mount their horses. A tearful Clover hugged the slender girl one last time.

"You takes good care of yourself now, Miss Katherine. And don't let anyone push you into something you knows is wrong. And you, Mr. Jonathan, you make sure this precious child is protected from anyone wants to do her harm."

Both nodded solemnly at her admonitions as they mounted their horses. They waved a final farewell as their mounts turned down the lane. Katherine, looking back one last time at the house that hadn't had time to become her home, spied Simon at the window, watching her departure. She gave him the slightest nod before facing forward, not waiting to see if her gesture was acknowledged.

As the horses turned down the dusty road, Jonathan faced her, a look of concern on his face. "I spoke to Simon this morning, Katherine, and learned that they will be travelling by train, leaving this afternoon, the same train we would have taken. And the ship Marie boarded yesterday has already sailed and, again according to Simon, there will be no other ships sailing for at least three days. All avenues seem to be closed to us except for our mounts and long days in the saddle. It's going to take at least two extra days travelling by horse before we reach Belle Isle." He studied her closely, waiting for her reaction.

"I've never ridden more than a few hours in one go but I'll try not to be a hindrance and keep up." She sniffed in indignation at what she perceived as an implied criticism. "And if I can't keep up, please feel free to ride on and I'll make my own way." She continued irritably, "I certainly don't wish to be the cause of the groom arriving late for his wedding."

Jonathan, choosing to ignore the last comment, chuckled at the thought of Katherine somehow riding all those miles without becoming lost. "No need to worry, Katherine, I won't abandon you."

Skirting much of Charleston by keeping to the outlying roads and passing few others along the way, they rode on. Katherine, determined not to admit defeat, climbed stiffly down when they stopped to eat the lunch Clover had packed but it seemed only minutes before Jonathan was urging her to remount. Long hours passed with few words exchanged. She studied the countryside they were passing through, charmed by the flowers growing wild by the side of the road. As evening closed in on them, Jonathan at last found a spot not too far off the road where he thought they might safely spend the night. As he helped her dismount, Katherine looked around in tired confusion.

"Where are we? Is this where we're to spend the night? I see no inn."

He laughed softly as he walked to the centre of the clearing. "I apologize, madam, but the closest inn is at least a day's ride from here. And looking at you, I think your derriere might have reached its limit today."

Katherine blushed at the reference to her much abused bottom and as she turned away spied a pretty little brook sparkling in the setting sun.

"Oh, Jonathan, I admit to feeling the effects of that horse in every bone of my body. But where will we sleep?"

She wandered about the glade, walking off some of her stiffness before kneeling beside the stream, cupping her hands to sip the clear water.

"You fetch the bread and cheese left from lunch while I get a fire going," he said. They worked companionably together, preparing a light supper. After they had finished eating, Jonathan spread their blankets chastely on either side of the fire. Katherine, returning from the stream where she had washed as well as she could, studied the sleeping arrangements and the gathering darkness.

"Ah, Jonathan..." She licked her lips nervously. "Don't you think we're rather far apart? What if some wild animal should wander over to see exactly who dares to invade his kingdom?"

His mouth twitched in amusement. "Why, Katherine Maguire Radcliffe, this is a side of you I never thought to see. You, who have fought so many adversaries, now fret over the possibility, small as it is, of an animal coming to investigate intruders in his hunting ground. If such a beast does appear, let us hope he doesn't realize what a delectable morsel you are. Now be a good girl and go to sleep, and I promise tomorrow night will be spent at an inn."

Somewhat mollified, Katherine lay down and wrapped her blanket around her, turning over his remarks in her head. She listened to the fire crackling, glad of its comforting warmth before sitting up once more and peering into the darkness, making out the outline of Jonathan as he eased under his blanket.

She heard her voice, stifled and unnatural. "Jonathan, tell me of your Isabella. Other than casually mentioning that you were to be married, I have never heard you speak of her." Her voice faded to a hushed stillness.

Chapter Fifteen

The rich timbre of his voice carried over the crackling of the flames. "You already know most of my history. My mother and I were taken in by Phillip Beauchamp as soon as he learned how poverty-stricken we were following my father's untimely death. He explained to me years later that he had always felt a debt of gratitude he could never repay when my father, a lawyer fresh out of law school, won him an inheritance, allowing him to live in the style which he felt he merited."

He continued speaking, a certain huskiness lingering in his tone. "His wife had died in childbirth, leaving him with a son, Edmond, and an infant daughter, Isabella. Sending for my mother and me helped him almost as much as it helped us."

"Edmond was some years older than me but he tolerated me trailing after him just as I, in turn, tolerated Isabella following me about as she grew older. And then, last year in pure exasperation, she made her feelings for me very obvious." He faltered in the silence that engulfed them. "You see, I had always thought she regarded me as an older brother. And Phillip, very subtly, let it be known that a match between us would have his blessing. It's not that I don't love Isabella, she's a beautiful woman. But I feel," he said, his voice unsteady, "I feel as if all my decisions had been made for me, much like what you were arguing about with Sam. Anyway, my mother had died the previous year and I felt an enormous debt to Phillip for all he had done for us. And Isabella has always been my greatest admirer, and I know it will be a good marriage."

Katherine sat quietly, surprised that someone as strong as Jonathan would feel indebted enough to marry a woman who he probably loved more as a sister than one he wanted to spend his life with.

She glanced across the fire at him and saw that he was wrapping himself up in his blanket. "I've spoken too freely, Katherine, please forget what I said. Sitting around a fire always makes one reach out and share more than was intended. Go to sleep now." And with those words, he turned his back to her, successfully cutting off any reply she might have made. Feeling somewhat rebuffed, she curled up in her blanket, watching the flames as she drifted into a deep sleep.

* * * *

In spite of sleeping on the hard ground, Katherine awoke feeling refreshed, her youthful resilience ready to face another day on her horse. Few words were spoken as they rode along, for the road had narrowed to a path, a thick growth of underbrush on either side. Again, they met few travelers as they wended their way ever southward. It was toward evening that they approached a small town, a place Jonathan was obviously familiar with as he led the way toward a well-lit structure. Snatches of song and raucous laughter drifted out into the crisp night air. He gave the waiting stable boy the care of their mounts after lifting their saddlebags from the tired horses.

Jonathan leaned forward and lowered his voice after she dismounted. "Katherine, stay close to me and keep the hood of your cloak covering your face. There are some rough characters in here and I would prefer not to have to defend your honor again. I'll arrange rooms and have supper sent up to you." He glanced down at her to be sure his words had been heard. Stung by his remark about not wanting to defend her again, she gave an almost imperceptible nod, following as he led the way towards the inn.

Reaching them before they crossed the threshold, a woman's screeching voice was proclaiming some unseen villain to be a thief, expressing her great displeasure with someone she called Wolf. As they entered, a woman brandishing a broom chased a lanky figure in their direction. Jonathan found himself pushed into a wall but the fleeing figure, realizing she was a woman, caught hold of Katherine's slender form before she fell. As the flickering light from a lantern fell on her, her hood slid from her head, revealing startled green eyes, an auburn cloud of hair framing beauty exquisite and fragile. Jonathan, recovering quickly, forced the man's hold on her to loosen and, as the miscreant cast a look at Jonathan's enraged countenance, was convinced a threat deadlier than Molly faced him now and he fled into the night. Assuring himself that Katherine wasn't hurt, they walked toward the woman who stood watching from a doorway.

"Well, well," a mocking voice greeted them, "Jonathan Radcliffe, I didn't expect to see you again so soon. Sorry about that little fracas but that Wolf—I give him odd jobs to do now and then but he's taken advantage of my good nature once too often!"

"Molly, how are you?" Jonathan's smile was reserved as he ushered Katherine into the brighter light of the inn. Neither the innkeeper nor Jonathan noticed the rogue creeping back toward the door, hoping for another glimpse of the vision he had held so fleetingly.

Katherine, glancing curiously toward the husky voice, saw a woman, faded red hair tucked into a frayed hairnet, her blotchy complexion bearing silent witness to a fondness for liquor. Dark inquisitive eyes examined her in return, causing Katherine to feel uncomfortable as the woman thoroughly scrutinized her from head to foot. She concluded that the rotund figure was almost as wide as she was tall. A dingy, stained orange shawl hugged rounded shoulders, covering a massive though sagging bosom. A black nondescript dress, shiny with wear, completed her skirmish with fashion.

"Is this a prospective employee you've brought me, Jonathan?" She stepped from behind the counter and circled Katherine slowly, causing the younger woman to draw closer to her escort, feeling much like a cow at market.

"Now Molly, stop right there." His mouth twitched with humor. "This young lady is my cousin-in-law, Katherine Radcliffe. She is travelling with me to attend my wedding. Her husband, Simon, who you've met in the past, was unavoidably detained and will follow as quickly as possible but until then Katherine is my responsibility. We left Seven Oaks Plantation too late for either the train or ship. What I need from you, Mistress Molly, are two rooms, just for the night."

The innkeeper threw back her head and let out a great shriek of laughter. "Well, Jonathan, if you don't beat all. You expect me to believe your cousin is allowing you to travel across the country, unchaperoned mind you, with this stunning creature. And when did Simon get married?" Tears of mirth rolled down her plump cheeks. The din from the other room had quieted at the unaccustomed sound of Molly's laughter and Jonathan glanced uneasily at the doorway, hoping none of the patrons felt curious enough to investigate the cause of such a rare sound.

He ground out the words between clenched teeth. "Molly, all I'm looking for are two rooms for the night, supper and a bath for the lady, in her room. Can you accommodate us or not?"

"All right," she spat out, suddenly concerned over the possible loss of coin, "I can take care of you. You can have room six and the chit can take room three, the room I reserve for new girls to..." she paused before continued bawdily, "to conduct "interviews" in." Pleased with her drollness, another burst of laughter rang out, revealing blackened teeth and gaps where teeth had once rested. The unseen listener felt his heart beat a little faster at her words as he crept silently away, satisfied with what he had garnered, for he knew that Molly always put the new girls in room three.

She lifted a small lantern from a hook on the wall and gestured for them to follow as she led the way up a narrow flight of stairs. As they gained the second floor, Jonathan saw that they would pass an open gallery where Molly's 'girls' could parade their wares to those drinking and gambling below. Jonathan moved to Katherine's side, attempting to shield her from the unwelcome notice of any who might glance upward before they reached the narrow hallway.

Pausing outside a door with the number six painted on it, Molly wordlessly indicated to Jonathan that they had arrived at his room. Stepping inside, their eyes surveyed the stark furnishings within the narrow confines of the dingy room. A double bed, as well as a tiny chest of drawers on which a wash basin and jug rested, occupied most of the floor space. Below a threadbare curtain covering a dingy window was a chair. Despite the shabbiness of its furnishings, Katherine was happily relieved as she spied the freshly laundered bedding, silently praying that her own room had been as well tended. Jonathan carelessly threw his saddlebag on the bed and the three withdrew from the room. He claimed the key from the landlady's clutching fingers and locked the door against any chance intruders.

Once again, they followed Molly as she waddled down the short corridor, stopping before a door that was within plain view of the saloon and its patrons below, a fact that left Jonathan feeling uneasy. The door was wordlessly pushed open, and they stepped inside.

Both of them could only gawk speechlessly at the tawdry interior of the room that Molly claimed was kept for 'new girls'. Countless years before, two of the walls had been painted a garish purple while the other walls had been wallpapered in a flamboyant purple pattern, both now peeling with age. A chintzy purple curtain hung over a tiny window, completing the tasteless decor of the room. Katherine's eyes fell quickly on the double bed, thankful that the linen appeared to be freshly laundered. A chair and small dresser completed the furnishings with a jug and cracked basin resting on it. Cocking a questioning eyebrow at Katherine, he received an almost imperceptible nod of acceptance. Jonathan turned to Molly and coins changed hands, Katherine watching wearily as he dropped her saddlebag onto the bed.

"And I believe I mentioned earlier that supper was to be brought up to the lady, as well as a hot bath, Molly. Will you see to it?

Another coin was quickly snatched up by pudgy, grasping fingers. The rotund innkeeper, with a curt nod, crossed to the stairway and began her descent down the protesting stairway. Observing her departure, Jonathan ushered Katherine into her room, casually checking the sturdiness of the door and its lock before turning his attention to the window, which he judged too small to admit anyone but a child.

A timid knock at the door signaled the arrival of a dented bathtub, delivered by two panting and flushed young maids. On spying the handsome man standing in the doorway, both shyly ducked their heads, giggling as they pushed their burden into the room. Seeing Katherine sitting on the bed, they set the tub down, promising to return presently with supper and hot water.

Jonathan took both of Katherine's hands and pulled her to her feet. She gazed at him apprehensively, sensing he was about to leave her. A burst of male shouting followed by a roar of laughter floated up the stairs into the room, and she looked questioningly at the door. Lifting her chin, Jonathan gazed into her green eyes.

"You're safe here, Katherine. Keep the door locked unless it's the maids returning with your supper or bath water, although I expect it will take them several trips to fill that old tub. I'm going to eat downstairs and perhaps try my luck at poker. You get some sleep because I can't promise you anything but the hard ground tomorrow night." Smiling at her, he closed the door waiting on the other side of it until he heard her slide the bolt across before he made his way down to the main floor.

* * * *

The two giggling maids made the first of many trips as they tipped bucket after bucket of hot water into the waiting tub. Finding a sliver of soap in the wash basin, Katherine quickly claimed it as her own and, after eating as much of the hearty stew as she could manage, she began to undress. Sighing as she examined her soiled shirt and wishing she had another to change into, she thought longingly of the gowns and delicate undergarments that Marie St. Pierre was transporting to Belle Isle for her. Quickly, before the maids returned with more water, she rinsed out the shirt and undergarments, laying them over the back of the chair, hoping they would dry by morning. And then, knowing there were still some buckets of water to come, she could no longer resist and slowly sank into the tantalizingly steaming water, luxuriating in the wet warmth of it.

* * * *

As Jonathan joined the poker game, he failed to notice the man Molly had been soundly berating when he and Katherine had arrived. Wolf, standing unobtrusively outside the inn, studied the comings and goings from Katherine's room through the large window.

Scratching his be-whiskered chin, he reflected on all of the wrongs done to him that he could lay at Molly's door. True, she had occasionally hired him to sweep the tavern and perform odd jobs in order to earn a few coins but she had banned him from using any of her girls after they had complained of his brutality. In fact, they had all agreed he was nothing but a barbaric savage. Grinning wickedly he continued watching, thinking this new one must be very special indeed if Molly was letting her have a bath in her room instead of going down to the kitchen like the others occasionally did. And that story from the tall bloke about escorting her to a wedding because her husband was busy—he knew that even Molly didn't believed him.

Wanting nothing more than to avenge himself on Molly, a plan began to form in his mind, a way to gain so much more than a night of pleasure with that tempting piece he had almost knocked over. He took a last pull on the bottle he had liberated – the very reason Molly had expelled him from her establishment.

He would snatch her right from under the nose of the snooty fellow who brought her here and use her until they reached a brothel he knew of in Savannah, where he was certain he could sell her. Something as tasty as that one should fetch him more than the few coins Molly doled out.

His scalp, pink and shiny, was devoid of hair, his brows and lashes so fair he appeared to be completely hairless. His build was lean and sinewy although his arms and legs were thickly muscled, warning the fainthearted not to challenge him thoughtlessly. Glancing once more at Jonathan, Wolf reassured himself that the stranger was involved in playing cards, even ignoring the fawning attentions of the women who hoped to entice him upstairs.

The bald man watched as more buckets of water were carried up the stairs. With sly animal cunning, he crept round to the seldom used backstairs, thus avoiding drawing unwelcome attention to himself. The unlit stairwell creaked slightly as he slowly crept upward, swaying drunkenly from the hours he had spent consuming his ill-gotten gains. Peering blearily down the hallway, he spied the maid as she once more left the room he was seeking, carrying an empty bucket. She spoke softly to the occupant but her words were lost to him.

He skulked warily down the corridor, only vaguely aware of the clamorous din from the tavern, reaching his destination undetected. Stubby fingers grasping the doorknob and, heart hammering excitedly, he licked his lips in anticipation of what he was going to do to the hapless trollop who waited behind the door for him. He paused, wondering if he would have time to have his first taste of her in her bed. Cautiously he turned the handle, the unlocked door opening noiselessly as he stepped inside.

* * * *

Wet hair covering her breasts, Katherine felt the breeze from the open door, and she laughed softly.

"Goodness, is that you Jenny, back again. I really don't think I need more water." Receiving no response, she pushed her hair back and twisted around, her smile turning to a look of puzzlement as she saw a strange man leering down at her. She heard his quick intake of breath as he studied her.

He giggled evilly and Katherine crossed her breasts with one arm in an attempt to shield herself from his leering eyes as her other hand groped frantically for the bath sheet that she had dropped when she'd first stepped into the tub. Seizing a corner of it, her shaking fingers covered herself as well as she could, clasping the ends together as she rose, dripping, from her bath.

The trespasser continued to stand, mute and motionless, seemingly bewitched by his prey.

"You're the one who bumped into me downstairs. What do you want here? You're in the wrong room." Her voice rose an octave as she slowly edged away from the intimidating intruder, trying to put some sort of distance between them. But for every step she retreated, he advanced the same, slowly, menacingly. In desperation, she spoke in what she prayed was a voice of authority. "Leave this room—immediately!"

"And, my beauty, what if I don't?" He persisted in his advance, forcing her to continue her retreat deeper into the room.

As Katherine felt the back of her legs touch the bed, she knew she could withdraw no further. Desperation goaded her to attempt to flee past him but his muscled arms caught her as she neared him, enfolding her in what seemed an unbreakable iron grip. Opening her mouth to scream, he clamped a hot, sweaty hand over it.

"Scream, my lovely, and it's the last sound you'll ever make. I'll snap your scrawny neck like a twig. Do you understand me?" Tears of fear and frustration filled her eyes as she nodded her understanding, terrified at the ominous sound of his voice. Gratefully she felt his hand leave her face.

Still struggling madly, she could feel his arms tighten around her. The sheet, which had been all that protected her modesty slipped, unnoticed, to the floor.

He stood back, taking in the fairness of the prize he had captured, his face sweating profusely in excitement, his breathing uneven and ragged

Katherine could smell the liquor on his foul breath, causing her to wretch in revulsion as she realized he was going to kiss her. As he momentarily loosened his hold on her arms, her hand shot out, frantically pummeling him, fingernails raking his face.

Incensed, he slapped her with such force that she felt her neck snap back. She shrieked in agony as his yellowing teeth bit into the tender flesh of her shoulder. Tears of pain filled her eyes, her struggles growing desperately wilder as she fought to escape his clutches but his one arm continued to hold her own in a vice-like grip as his other hand roamed freely over her body, brutally kneading her soft flesh. Screeching in indignation as his fingers violently pinched her, her cries seemed only to inflame him further. Holding her thrashing body, he glanced at the inviting bed and picked her up, his intention clear as he threw her on it, trapping her flailing legs to prevent her escape as he began tugging at his shirt. In absolute disgust, Katherine watched as he yanked it off, baring his chest and arms. She shuddered again in revulsion.

He scowled at her as he began to undo his trousers. Katherine, horror-struck, felt her legs, which had been trapped between his own, momentarily freed as he lowered his pants, revealing his engorged manhood.

With little thought, Katherine lifted her legs rapidly and kicked toward the solid flesh of her attacker. A look of surprise crossed his face, which contorted into angry disbelief as the sensation of overwhelming agony rushed to his brain. He bellowed in rage and excruciating torment, sinking slowly, helplessly, to the floor.

It was at that moment that the maid, returning to see if anything else was needed, opened the door which Wolf, in his lust and excitement, had so carelessly forgotten to bolt. Her mouth formed a startled O as she took in the scene before her. Katherine, seeing the door opening, seized the moment and screamed, the sound floating eerily down the stairs where groups of talking, laughing men and women paused, wondering at such a cry of distress.

Chapter Sixteen

Jonathan, recognizing the origin of the scream, was already running toward the stairs, catching the maid as she stumbled down, seeking help.

Jenny clutched at his arm and breathlessly pointed upward toward Katherine's door. "Wolf is up there with that poor lady, and I know he means to harm her. Oh, please sir," she begged, tears coursing down her pale, pock-marked cheeks as her fingers clutched at his shirt, "help her."

Jonathan felt his blood run cold at the thought of the peril Katherine was facing alone. He shoved the slight girl aside and almost flew up the stairs. The door stood open, just as the maid had left it. He drew a small revolver that had been hidden within his jacket and cautiously entered the room where a moaning Wolf lay on the floor, writhing in pain.

Jonathan, tucking the gun away, turned to where she stood, pale and shaking. "Cover yourself, Katherine, quickly. I hear footsteps approaching and I can't fight them all if they see you looking like that."

He stepped in front of her, shielding her as she hastily pulled the coverlet from the bed and wound it around her bruised and battered body.

Incredibly, Molly was the first to appear, with the maid Jenny close behind. Swiftly assessing the scene, the tavern keeper turned to the curious crowd who were peering over her shoulder, trying to see the cause of the furor. "Nothing much happening here, boys. You might as well go back down and continue whatever it was you were doing."

Much mumbling and muttering could be heard as the crowd made their way downstairs, certain they were missing out on something exciting.

After whispering orders to her, Molly dismissed the maid who, with one final inquisitive glance, hurried off to do her mistress's bidding. Molly shut the door against any chance passer-by and studied the man who, as the pain in his groin began to subside, stared shamefaced at the floor.

"Wolf, you great oaf, what were you thinking?" she exploded. Attempting to utter a reply, she held up a hand, implying that she wasn't really interested in his excuses.

"Well, sir, what do you want done with this brute?'

"I really don't care what you do with him, Molly, as long as I don't see him again before we leave in the morning. And if I do spy him anywhere, for any reason, I won't hesitate to put a bullet between his eyes."

Jonathan was satisfied to see Wolf, listening closely, shiver in apprehension at his words.

She nodded thoughtfully. "All right, I can mix a little something that will send him off to sleep until you're well on your way. But it means he would have to spend the night in this room where I can hire someone to watch him. I'll get the sheriff to fetch him in the morning. What do you propose to do with her? She obviously can't stay the night in here, and the rest of my rooms are taken." She lifted an inquiring eyebrow.

Jonathan, glancing at the hulk that lay on the floor quietly listening, saw no way out of the dilemma she presented.

"Well, it's too late for us to head out now, and I'm too tired. I'll take her into my room and we'll work out something." He frowned darkly at the knowing smirk that fleetingly crossed Molly's face. Turning to where Katherine still huddled in the blanket, he smiled at her.

"Once again you're in the middle of an uproar not of your making. I'm aware this would be frowned on in polite society but I can think of no other solution so gather your things and we'll move you to my room."

Wolf looked up, leering hungrily at the girl as she moved about the room. Watching him, Jonathan gestured at Molly who had also seen Wolf's eyes following the girl's movements as she collected her things.

A knock at the door announced the return of the maid, bearing a tray of bottles and glasses. Molly mixed a strong sleeping potion, standing over Wolf until he finished it, thereby assuring everyone a restful night. Jonathan patiently waited for the concoction to take effect, wanting to be sure it had the desired result.

Waiting, he gathered Katherine to him, seeking to reassure her that she was safe from harm. She flinched at his touch, light though it was, causing him to see the wound Wolf had inflicted in the throes of his passion. Molly, glancing at the torn flesh, took a bottle of whiskey from the tray and, as Wolf began to snore unconcernedly on the floor, Jonathan gently cleaned her wound.

Assured that her attacker was no longer a threat, Jonathan gathered up Katherine's belongings and, nodding his thanks to Molly, poked his head out the door to see if anyone had been foolish enough to loiter outside the room. Seizing a bottle of wine and two glasses from the tray, he put his arm lightly around Katherine's slender waist, and guided her blanketed figure down the deserted hallway to his room.

Unlocking the door, he ushered her inside, putting the bottle and glasses on the table and tossing her things beside his onto the bed before sliding the bolt on the door. Crossing the room in easy strides, he carried the one chair to the door, propping it against the door to prevent any chance intrusion. Katherine, suddenly aware that beneath the blanket she wore nothing, moved toward the bed and her small bundle. Picking up her shirt and undergarments, still damp from her laundering, brought a sudden rush of tears coursing down her pale face.

Jonathan, glancing at her, took the clothes and felt their dampness. Helplessly, he searched the depths of her green eyes, sparkling with tears. His tone was gentle when he spoke. "What happened to your clothes? I thought that animal surprised you in your bath."

Glancing up at him, she sobbed even harder as he continued to hold the damp clothes. Haltingly, she explained, "I'd rinsed them out before taking my bath."

Understanding dawned quickly and he smiled as he took the garments, shaking them before laying them out, just as she had done earlier. Smiling through her tears, she gazed in what appeared to be adoration at him. Obviously, she was grateful he'd rescued her from yet another perilous situation he thought, as he continued to prowl the room.

Apart from the bed, drawers and the chair propped against the door, there was no other furniture in the room. His thoughts raced as he weighed all the possibilities, knowing that they both needed a place to sleep. He, as a gentleman, would take a cushioned chair, if such a thing existed in this confined space. Certain that he could find such an item downstairs, he was reluctant to make his request to Molly and face her smirking, knowing expression again. There was no help for it, he thought, they would have to share a bed. All he had to do was convince Katherine that it was a necessity and not a ploy to finish what Wolf had started.

He cleared his throat, suddenly as nervous as a schoolboy. The girl, lost in her own misery, started at the sound. At the sight of tears still falling, he sat beside her, taking her hands in his. "What are the tears for, Katherine? You're safe now and I promise not to leave your side again."

Her sobs continuing, she murmured, "I'm sorry, Jonathan. I know you said you didn't want to defend me or my honor but…" Her words were lost in a torrent of tears. Helpless in the face of such misery, he held her tenderly, his arms aching to crush her to him.

"Katherine, my sweet Katherine, I will always be ready to defend you, be it from a dragon or any other monster that threatens you. Ignore my words, I was tired and out of sorts when I spoke earlier." He kissed her chastely on her brow before releasing her and standing up, all too aware of her lack of clothing and their seclusion.

He cleared his throat again, uncertain how to proceed. Her eyes, still bright from tears shed, looked up, trusting, adoringly, once more.

He gulped as he considered the state of her undress. How was he supposed to sleep, lying next to this goddess who was totally dependent on him?

"Katherine, I, uh, I…" He trailed off.

Smiling at him, she waited patiently for him to speak.

"Katherine, the truth of the matter is that we'll have to share this bed," he blurted, "just for tonight, you understand. If there was another solution, I would take it but unfortunately, there is none." His tone had become brusque.

Katherine, puzzled at the curtness in his tone, shrugged her shoulders and smiled her acceptance. Standing, she turned the covers down, still hugging her own covering to her, before climbing into bed.

"Jonathan, there is no one in the world I would trust more than you. Of course, we can share a bed. We are friends, even if we can be nothing more, ever."

Jonathan groaned inwardly. Did she have no idea of the imaginings and passions that coursed through a man's mind just from looking at a woman such as her? She played the innocent so convincingly but she had been married for some months, and though at Seven Oaks, it had been whispered that they never slept together, he knew Simon had shared her bed on at least one occasion before they had left England. Did she think him so insensitive and unfeeling that a woman would be safe with him, no matter how he might be provoked?

Seeking to send her off to sleep before he dare lie beside her, he remembered the wine he had taken from Molly. Opening the bottle, he raised an inquiring eyebrow and, with her approving nod, filled two glasses.

A shapely arm reached for the glass he offered. Taking a sip, she wrinkled her nose before she laughingly spoke.

"This reminds me of the wine Simon and I shared on that first night of our marriage, except it's not as bitter." The mention of Simon's name reminded him that he also had someone else in his life but he quickly squashed all thought of Isabella, focusing only on Katherine.

She hugged her protective cover tightly, unaware of the picture she presented. Her thick auburn hair, tousled from the events of the evening, hung in glorious disarray, the flame of the candle highlighting the creaminess of her face and shoulders. Cheeks faintly flushed from the wine, she smiled up at him. Swallowing the liquid in one gulp, he poured himself another while Katherine continued to sip daintily at hers. She placed her near empty glass into his outstretched hand, watching as he placed both goblets on the tiny table before turning to her.

"Katherine," he began hesitantly, suddenly tongue-tied as she smiled once more. As their eyes met, her heart began to dance with excitement. Her hold on the blanket that protected her modesty lessened, slipping midway down her breasts as slowly and seductively, his gaze slid downward. She found his nearness overwhelming, swallowing tightly as he dropped down next to her. A delightful shiver of desire raced through her. His arms encircled her, one hand in the small of her back as he drew her to him. Hesitantly, she wound her arms around his neck, just as his mouth hungrily found hers. Raising his lips from hers, he stared into her eyes, seeking to reassure himself that he wasn't frightening her before losing himself in their emerald depths. His lips seared a path down her neck and shoulders, stopping at her breasts as he planted tender kisses on the pink tips.

She was shocked at her own eager response to his touch. He broke away as he tore at his own clothing, eager to feel the satiny touch of her skin against his. His body imprisoned hers in a web of growing arousal. She gasped as he lowered his body over hers, feeling his hardness searching, probing, as she instinctively spread her legs, welcomingly. As he entered her, a shriek tore from her lips at the burning pain. Astonished, he stopped, amazement written across his face but his passion could not be contained and he resumed his thrusting movements.

Katherine, after the first shock, let his ardor carry her along with him, and together they found the tempo that bound their bodies together. The turbulence of his passion swirled around her until at last they soared to a shuddering ecstasy. As they lay together, his arms drew her near, her soft curves molding to the contours of his lean body. Nestling into each other, they fell asleep, wordlessly and deeply.

It was still dark outside when Katherine felt herself being shaken awake. She lay there, subdued, until Jonathan sat on the bed, softly caressing her, his touch causing her skin to tingle. The sheets beneath her were twisted and, as she threw them off, a bloodstain became visible. She looked at him in confusion.

"Well, my love, this is undoubtedly the most perplexing thing I have ever heard of, something never mentioned in my medical studies." There was a trace of laughter in his voice. "I certainly never expected to bed a virgin last night, a woman who has not only been married these many months past but a woman who I personally rescued from rape not once but on three separate occasions." There was a slight tinge of wonder in his voice. "Now I know the assaults weren't successful but the marriage bed? What happened, or should I perhaps be asking, what didn't happen?" His grey eyes gazed questioningly at her but Katherine, shaking her head in confusion, looked about her, seeking an answer she didn't have.

"Katherine, think! Simon, on the morning after your marriage, told me that Edmond Featherstone had apparently barged into your chamber and saw both of you in a state of undress, sharing a bed. Something must have happened!"

Her pink tongue nervously licked her dry lips, desperately trying to recall those events, which seemed to have happened in another life. "We went upstairs after dinner. While I was changing into my nightgown, Simon went downstairs to fetch a bottle of wine. It wasn't very good wine, it tasted very bitter."

Jonathan nodded as he recalled her words from the previous evening. "I really didn't want any but he was insistent, watching me as I drank it down. And then I must have fallen asleep." She rubbed her forehead as if trying to draw more memories forth but failed. "I awoke when Edmond Featherstone knocked at the door and Simon bade him to come in. Poor Edmond! I don't know which of us was more embarrassed, him or me." She blushed slightly, while laughing softly at the memory.

"But what happened during the night, when you were alone with him. Did Simon exert his husbandly rights?"

"I don't remember, Jonathan. When I awoke that first morning, I was naked and so was he. I tried for days to remember that night but couldn't. We shared a bed until we boarded the ship but I awoke as I went to sleep, fully clothed, and he came in after I was sleeping." She spoke in a weak and tremulous whisper. "You know the sleeping arrangements on the ship and, once we reached Seven Oaks, he maintained his own bedroom, never seeking my bed, much to Samuel's chagrin."

"But what of those afternoons, few though they were, that you spent alone with him while we crossed the ocean?"

"I read to him, nothing more. We didn't have a proper conversation, ever. He always dismissed me late in the afternoon and we would meet again at dinner."

There was a slight tinge of wonder in his voice when next he spoke. "That's it, of course." Excitedly he grabbed her shoulders, a hint of laughter in his voice. "Don't you understand, Katherine? He drugged your wine that first night, undressed you and set the stage for Featherstone to walk in on you in the morning. For some reason, he needed a witness to your bedding and I wouldn't do."

In his excitement, he paced the narrow confines of the room, talking more to himself than her. "But why? Why would he go to such lengths?" The answer hit him suddenly. "Of course—Juliana! Samuel was totally against their marriage—some sort of feud between the two families. Simon told me he would be cut off without a penny if he married her. And having no other prospects, he had to fall into line and do as Samuel wanted. He did confide that if he entered into a second marriage, Samuel had agreed the choice of bride would be his. But how could he resist playing the husband to you? He must have had ice water in his veins." Shrugging, he tossed her now dry clothes to her.

"Get dressed, my sweet, or I'm afraid our departure will be delayed even longer. I'm worried that Wolf might stir before we've put enough distance between him and us. We can talk more as we ride." He bent and kissed her, his hungry lips caressing hers. He broke away, leaving her feeling achingly empty. He smiled warmly but determinedly moved about the room, gathering their belongings, his last act to take the stained sheet, folding and packing it into his bag, ignoring her questioning look.

"Why give Molly something to dwell on?" Sensing his urgency, she dressed quickly, brushing her hair and pinning it up as best she could. Noiselessly, he opened their door, motioning for her to follow. Creeping down the stairs, they were met by Molly.

"I thought you would probably leave by first light, so I had the cook prepare a few things for your journey. And your horses are saddled and ready to go.

Jonathan, taken aback by this display of generosity, kissed her lightly on her forehead. Relieving her of the bundle, he nodded his thanks and, holding Katherine's hand tightly, led her to their rested horses and, without a backward glance, they rode off.

Chapter Seventeen

Again Jonathan chose roads that were less travelled although, he admitted to himself, his motives were no longer cautionary but with a keen desire for privacy. While aware of Katherine riding at his side, he continued to turn over the puzzle of his cousin in his mind, examining it from all angles. At last he stopped his horse and dismounted. Grasping her about her waist, he deposited her on the grass beside him. She smiled in delight as she viewed the secluded glade.

Tilting her head at him, he nodded. "Yes, my love, this is where we'll have breakfast."

He tied the horses and took the parcel Molly had given him. As he glanced about, he saw Katherine standing, her eyes admiring the countryside. He felt a surge of emotion as he studied her, realizing she was his with no one to say nay, especially her. All those months, when he had not dared dream of such a possibility, the unimaginable had happened.

His long legs covered the distance separating them and he took her in his arms, moving his mouth over hers, devouring its eager softness. Spreading his cloak on the rough ground, they sank down as slowly, worshipfully, he undressed her, his lips teasing each pink-tipped nipple in turn. Instinctively her body arched toward him and soon they were lost to anyone but themselves, their bodies once more moving together in perfect harmony.

It was much later, as they talked and ate, that Jonathan suddenly straightened, his handsome face alight with excitement. "I have it! I have fitted the pieces of the puzzle together, my love. Featherstone was not only a lawyer but Samuel's trusted friend. Simon said something aboard the ship about the futility of having a marriage witnessed if that witness was travelling with you to the same destination." He glanced at her, wondering if she followed his reasoning and, satisfied, he continued.

"His plan already foiled, he had to come up with something new—hence Spanish Jack." Katherine shivered as she recalled that evil, odious creature. "My darling, do you recall that, after having his plans thwarted, he started to say something about 'the Lord' just before Simon shot him? We all thought, since he was of a religious bent, that he was referring to God or at least his twisted version of God but I've just now recalled coming upon Simon and Spanish Jack one evening, deep in conversation. They broke off as I approached but the sailor, as he was leaving us, said, "Good evening, lord" to Simon. I even teased him about his rise to the nobility." In his excitement, he seized her shoulders and kissed her, once again setting off a golden wave of passion and love flowing between them and, when at last they were satisfied, they succumbed to the numbed sleep of contented lovers.

* * * *

Mounting their horses some time later, she turned an inquiring eye on her beloved. "I'm still unsure of your meaning about Simon and Spanish Jack."

Smiling, he said, "Simon hired Spanish Jack to murder you."

Katherine gasped, unable to digest what he was stating as fact. Sadly, he nodded his head. "My theory is simple. Samuel refused to allow Juliana to become a member of his family and so forces Simon to seek a bride elsewhere. He travels to England, meets and marries you, an orphan who, should you disappear, no one will ever come looking for. His plan to have Featherstone attest to the happy couple occupying the marriage bed is foiled when Edmond announces he and his wife will be sailing with us to America, to visit his old friend and to see something of the world before he's called to meet his maker. So Simon moves on to Plan B. He befriends and bribes Spanish Jack who agrees that, after tasting the delights of your body, will throw you overboard, leaving poor Simon a heartbroken widower returning home, his bride lost at sea. He had to shoot the sailor to protect himself."

"But he never succeeded, thanks to you and the cabin boy, Ned. But I still stood in his way. What changed?"

"Once we reached home, I think he realized Samuel was dying. All he had to do was convince Juliana to be patient a while longer. What he didn't count on was Samuel at last understanding the wrong he had done by forcing his grandson to marry where he didn't love. He was agreeable to your marriage being dissolved so that you would no longer be in danger. If that hadn't happened, I think you would have quickly followed Samuel to your grave. In spite of the annulment, I don't believe Samuel entirely trusted Simon, or more likely Juliana, to leave you alone."

Katherine shuddered at the thought but her face quickly brightened. "All that is in the past, my darling Jonathan. And now we have our whole lives ahead of us." Turning away, she didn't see the shadow that passed over his handsome features.

They rode on in silence, anxious now to put more miles behind them. Each time she looked at him, her eyes were sparkling with happiness, a radiance seeming to encompass her entire being, for he was her future. And so they rode on, stopping often as lovers are wont to do, before moving ever southward, toward Belle Isle.

It was to be their last night on the road and Katherine began to gather wood for their fire. Jonathan seemed lost in thought as they ate and Katherine strolled over to the brook to wash what few dishes there were. After completing this wifely task, she decided to wash herself and so, confident of their solitude,

132

stripped off her clothes and waded in, splashing, laughingly calling to Jonathan to join her. He strode over to the brook, looking at her with fierce longing but turned away.

Stepping out of the water, she dried and wrapped her blanket around her, sitting before the fire, knowing that soon she would be in his arms, safe and loved. He sat on the opposite side of the fire, his face solemn and unsmiling. Unsure of the cause, she smiled lovingly at him, and thinking to cheer him, began talking about the future, their future, but stopped as she saw him moving about restlessly.

With a faint tremor in her voice, she spoke. "What is it, Jonathan? You've been melancholy most of the day. Is it the thought of hurting your betrothed that worries you?" Katherine decided that must be what worried him; breaking off his engagement to his betrothed.

He gazed across the fire at her, his eyes brimming with tenderness and love. "It isn't the thought of Isabella that is causing this pain in my heart, my darling." He stopped, suddenly lost for words. "Katherine, you know I love you, more than life itself!" Her green eyes shone brightly in the pale light of the moon as she studied his face, uncertainty filling her heart. He moved to her side, sitting but making no move to take her in his arms.

"I love you, my sweet, but there is no future for us."

She gasped, aware of a deep, icy coldness wrapping itself around her heart. She heard his voice, as if at a great distance, as he continued, sighing heavily, his voice filled with anguish. "I have thought of nothing else since our first night together. In spite of my overwhelming love for you, I still intend to marry Isabella in a few days. I can do nothing else. The debt I owe Phillip Beauchamp for rescuing my mother from a life of poverty and hardship when I was but a boy is too great and, remembering his joy when Isabella told him we were to be wed, it's too much. Please my darling, forgive me."

Katherine, her mind in turmoil, rose wordlessly and stumbling, made her way back to the brook, breathing raggedly. What was he saying? He loved her but was still planning to marry another? She heard his footsteps approaching. His arms reached for her but she angrily shook him off.

"Get away from me," she hissed, "and never, ever touch me again."

Throwing off the blanket, she quickly donned her clothes. Her thoughts flew in all directions until at last, unsure of what she should do, she sat once more beside the fire. Tears stung her eyes and she angrily brushed them away. Looking into Jonathan's tortured face, she knew he was suffering as deeply as she was, but that thought held no comfort for her.

"Katherine, please, listen to me. We don't have to part." His voice held a note of desperation. "Belle Isle isn't far from Savannah. I'll buy a house for you and visit as often as possible." His words held a note of excitement and hope.

Jumping up, she looked at him. "And what then, Jonathan? You expect me to become your mistress? What of children? Have you given any children we might have a thought, how society would call them bastard? And what would society have to say about me, a kept woman?"

Her voice was shrill as she tried to wound him as deeply as he had her. Grabbing her blanket, she moved as far away from him as she could and, turning her back to him, wrapped herself in her blanket, trembling with anger and unshed tears. Eventually she heard him sigh as he lay down, far from her. It was only then that she allowed her tears to fall, unheeded, as she contemplated how bleak her life would be without him by her side.

They slept little that night, both tossing in total and wretched anguish, until finally the black night faded into a sullen grey dawn. Silently they mounted their horses, riding toward their destination, each adrift in their own private sea of misery.

Where once they would have stopped and reveled in their love, they now plodded on, wordlessly, until at last Katherine called out, her tone as cool and clear as ice water.

"I have decided to stay at the convent, for the time being." Her words, crisp and clipped, asked for neither approval nor argument from him, so he merely nodded.

Long hours passed before he slowed his horse and walked beside her.

"I've done nothing but think of your decision to stay, temporarily at least, at the convent and I can't help but agree that perhaps it would be best." With each word he uttered, she felt a knife twisting in her heart. "But, my love, we must have a care for you so I am asking you to let me do the talking. If they knew or even suspected your marriage had been dissolved, no matter the reason, your welcome might be less than cordial, if you were allowed to stay at all. I think it best if we let them assume you a widow."

In spite of her anger, Katherine could only agree with his wisdom. Not trusting herself to speak, she merely nodded her agreement and fell back, forcing him once more into leading their small party of two, the pastoral beauty of the countryside unnoticed by either as they rode on.

* * * *

It was early afternoon before they turned from the main road and followed a narrow path bordered by towering pines. A stone wall loomed up before them as their tired horses trudged wearily on and Katherine guessed that they must be nearing their destination. Halting before a pair of heavy wooden gates, his face rigid and solemn, Jonathan dismounted and then turned to help her down. She felt her heart skip a beat as his hands grasped her about the waist but she gave no sign of her inner turmoil as she stood back, waiting for him to once more lead the way.

Taking the reins of both horses in one hand, he banged at the gate until finally a tiny window slid open, brown eyes peering curiously out at them. Sensing no threat, the unseen gatekeeper unlocked the portal and allowed it to swing open very slowly. Two women, one tall and bony, the other plump and matronly, both wearing nun's habits, stood before them, barring their entry.

The taller of the two looked Jonathan in the eye, almost challengingly. She held her ground, speaking in a voice of authority. "No men allowed inside, sorry."

Removing his hat, he courteously requested a meeting with the head of the convent, promising that his stay would be a very short one. Studying both arrivals with sharply appraising eyes, Sister Ursula turned in the direction of the buildings enclosed within the stone walls and beckoned them forward. Jonathan tied the horses to a small tree before following her, Katherine distancing herself as far from him as possible, the shorter nun bringing up the rear.

As they walked down the stony path leading to the small cluster of buildings, Katherine surveyed the grounds. A few nuns labored in a large, well-tended vegetable garden whilst three others hung laundry out to dry in the hot sun, everyone seeming to be engaged in one task or another. The enticing aroma of bread baking carried on the breeze to them, a reminder of the meals they had missed this day. Reaching the entrance of the smallest of the buildings, they followed their guide through the open doorway into a cool stone structure, bringing welcome relief to the weary travelers. The nun stopped in front of a dark wooden door and knocked, fidgeting with a cross that hung from her neck, until she was at last bid to enter, leaving the visitors outside. The other nun smiled warmly at them, gesturing toward two chairs where they could take their ease while they waited.

Short minutes later, the door was opened and they were summoned inside. A large silver crucifix hung on a whitewashed wall, the only ornamentation in the starkly furnished room. Under it sat a tiny woman with bright curious eyes, also garbed in the habit of a nun, ledgers spread before her. Silvery-grey eyebrows were raised questioningly at the unexpected intrusion of two strangers, and one of those a man. She rose from her chair, a diminutive figure but one that wore the mantle of authority well. Looking up at Jonathan, she spoke in a voice that was neither welcoming nor warm.

"Somehow, sir, you have convinced Sister Ursula to allow you to gain access into a community of women, although she claims it was the sadness in the face of the young woman who accompanies you that she was concerned with. And I can see what my nun meant, now that she stands before me."

Jonathan, hat in hand, advanced further into the room, his hand on Katherine's elbow, silently urging her into the chamber. "Mother Superior." His voice was calm and steady. "My name is Jonathan Radcliffe and this is," he paused, his hand drawing a reluctant Katherine forward until she stood beside him, "is my cousin-in-law, Katherine Radcliffe. We are seeking a safe haven for her, perhaps for one week or several, I can't really say how long." Sensing the need for complete privacy, the Abbess of the convent dismissed Sister Ursula and Sister Claire, instructing them to wait outside. Nodding obediently, they closed the door softly as they stepped from the room.

Intelligent eyes glanced from one visitor to the other, attempting to gauge their characters. She turned to Katherine and looked deeply into her eyes. *What could be troubling this child, this beautiful child, that she has such a look of desolation and anguish?* Turning back to Jonathan, she asked him some very pointed questions, studying him for any sign of deceit, but as wily as she was, she had met her match in Jonathan Radcliffe.

"Why do you seek refuge here? And from what, or should I be saying from who? Why would you turn to a convent rather than an inn?"

Jonathan smiled, astonished at the astuteness of her questions, and so chose his words carefully. "We seek a sanctuary that will be safe and what place on earth could be safer than a convent? I am to be married in a few days and will no longer be free to protect the young lady. And she does need protection, madam. Since her husband is no longer able to stand by her side, the task has fallen to me." As the nun's eyebrows shot up in surprise, Jonathan held his hands up beseechingly.

He paused, allowing her to digest the information. "As to why here, well, I admit it's still only a suspicion, but I feel the one who might seek to do her harm will possibly attend my wedding, hoping to find Katherine and finish what was started some months earlier. Before he died, her husband's grandfather, Samuel Langtree, thought that this, *The Convent of Saint Mary Magdalena*, might be the safest place for her and I couldn't agree more."

At her startled look, he rushed to reassure her. "Not that we know for certain that there is someone who seeks to harm her, Reverend Mother, but do you not agree it is better to err on the side of caution?"

Once again the nun looked at Katherine, who smiled tremulously back at the wrinkled face. Reaching a decision, she took Katherine's hands in hers. "All right, perhaps against my better judgment, she can stay."

Jonathan smiled in relief. Unthinking, he tried to hug Katherine but she recoiled at his touch, a movement not lost on the nun. Resuming his business-like demeanor, Jonathan moved stiffly away from the girl and faced the nun.

"It is not expected that you perform such an act of kindness for nothing." Saying this, he laid a bag of coins on the table. The nun, always vigilant in her search for money to support the convent and the nuns living within its walls, seized the purse and peered inside. Satisfied, she nodded at him as she dropped it into a pocket hidden deep within the folds of her robes.

"Thank you for your generosity, Mr. Radcliffe. But now, I'm afraid I must ask you to leave. My nuns will be all-a-twitter at the thought of a man within our walls but you may rest assured that your little cousin will indeed find a safe haven for as long as she resides with us." She rang a small bell and Sister Ursula appeared in the now open doorway. "Mr. Radcliffe is leaving now, Sister. Please escort him to the gate and ask Sister Claire to take our guest to the guest room upstairs."

Jonathan turned to Katherine, covering her unwilling hands with his. "This is not good bye, Katherine. As soon as I return to Belle Isle, I will send for you. I know you will be welcome to stay at Belle Isle for as long as you wish."

She reclaimed her hands and, determined to show him how unconcerned she was with his departure, spoke in her wonderful low voice, her words soft and clear. "Will you please have my trunks sent over here, Jonathan?" She paused, aware that the three nuns stood listening to them. She continued. "My best wishes for your future happiness and please convey my thanks to your bride for allowing you to escort me on this journey." With that, she turned her back, hoping she wouldn't break down in front of everyone.

Jonathan blanched at the coldness of her words, sensing their finality and knowing he had lost her, perhaps forever. Bowing stiffly to the women, he turned and with long strides that Sister Ursula couldn't hope to match, marched from the room, his footsteps echoing thunderously down the hallway.

Katherine, at a signal from Mother Superior, turned and followed Sister Claire down a cool, dimly lit hallway and up a set of narrow stone steps. Pushing open a door, the nun ushered Katherine into an austere chamber containing a single bed and a tiny wooden table. Sunlight streamed through a tiny casement window, which Sister Claire eased open in the hope of catching a stray breeze.

Glancing beyond the stone wall that surrounded the convent, she saw the distinctive figure of Jonathan as he rode away, out of her life forever. His whole being appeared unyielding as he disappeared down the trail. Sister Claire murmured that she would return for her when it was time for the evening meal.

Katherine, alone at last, sank down on the thin mattress, gulping hard as scalding tears rolled down her cheeks. She sat in lonely silence, listening to the unfamiliar sounds of convent life as its inhabitants chatted, prayed and toiled their way through the day. Angrily she wiped the tears away, vowing not to cry, for she felt that, once started, she might never stop.

* * * *

Sitting alone in the tiny herb and flower garden, Katherine was soothed by the comforting splash of the fountain in the centre of the courtyard. The flower garden, with no one seeming to take an interest in it, was slowly being overtaken by weeds when Katherine first discovered it. She toiled away that first day, unaware of time passing and, when the Abbess observed Katherine from her window, instructed Sister Claire to offer her the use of a spare habit, at least until the girl's baggage arrived from Belle Isle.

At her first evening meal Katherine learned the garden had once been tended by Sister Agnes who had died some months previous and, as yet, no one had been assigned to it so it had become sadly neglected.

Within a week of her arrival, her two trunks had been delivered but she had been in the kitchen when they arrived and so had missed the opportunity to ask if there was any message for her. *It's just as well* she had thought later that night as she lay in her narrow bed. *He's a married man by now, and I am long forgotten as he lies in the arms of his beloved Isabella.* Tears had again flowed until at last exhaustion delivered her into the arms of Morpheus.

* * * *

Wearing the robe of a nun made her feel more accepted by the others, and all welcomed her wherever she might wander, happy to break the routine of convent life. Most were curious about her as the convent rarely allowed an outsider to stay more than a night or two.

They had been told she was a widow, seeking sanctuary for an unspecified amount of time but Katherine could not bring herself to reveal anything about her past, knowing that her experiences since meeting Simon and Jonathan Radcliffe would shock these cloistered, unworldly souls. She had learned that most of the nuns would likely spend their lives in this particular convent but some, like Sister Ursula and Sister Claire, were teachers and were destined to work in orphanages or schools, wherever the Church felt they were needed.

Putting the book of poems she was reading aside, she watched bees buzzing lazily from flower to flower. Ten weeks had passed since her arrival and she indeed found the convent a haven, although she knew the time was approaching when she would have to return to the world that bustled unseen around them. She had labored long hours in an effort to drive Jonathan from her mind and often felt she had succeeded, at least to some degree. Eventually, she thought, *I won't even remember what he looks like and perhaps then my heart will stop aching so.* If any of the convent residents noticed her tears, they assumed she was mourning her lost husband, and left her to grieve.

The sound of hurrying footsteps approaching broke into her reverie and turning, she spied Sister Claire hastening toward her, her plain face wreathed in smiles.

"Oh, Katherine, it's so exciting", she bubbled, "Mother Superior has just received word that Sister Ursula and myself are to leave shortly for *St. Bernadette's Orphanage* in New York." She paused to catch her breath before continuing on, her words tripping over each other. "We'll travel by ship. I've never been on a ship but Mother Superior says the journey will take only a few days." She hugged Katherine in her exuberance.

"Sister Claire, I'm happy for both of you but I know everyone here will miss you dreadfully.'

The nun, blushing at the kind words of the young woman, hurried off with a promise to speak to her later. Katherine, watching her new friend bustle away to spread her news, wandered restlessly about among the flowers, the question of her own future once more looming before her. She chopped away at the weeds with renewed vigor but dropped her hoe suddenly as she recalled Samuel's words so long ago. *Here is a deed, Katherine, to a cottage up north in New York.*

Katherine, in a swirl of black skirts, hastily made her way up to her tiny room, closing the door behind her. Excitedly she pulled the larger trunk into the centre of the room, lifting out the carefully packed gowns until at last it stood empty. Running slim fingers over the smooth wood, she released a concealed catch and lifted out the false bottom, revealing a leather pouch which contained several documents. Quickly sorting through them, she at last found the one she was seeking. Unfolding it carefully, her eyes flew over the pages. Her cottage was indeed in New York, in the village of Carlyle. And there was the name of the lawyer who would help her, Mr. Harvey Davenport, and his address in New York City. Excitedly, Katherine repacked her papers into the false bottom and laid her gowns neatly on top. Returning the trunk to where it had been sitting, she left the room, her feet swiftly carrying her downstairs.

Chapter Eighteen

A voice rang out, neither welcoming nor unfriendly, bidding the visitor to enter. Katherine pushed the door open hesitantly, suddenly wary. What if her plan was not acceptable to this most esteemed of nuns?

Seeing who her caller was, the nun beckoned her into her private sanctuary, away from the burdens of running such an establishment. The old woman studied her visitor and intuitively knew that this was not an ordinary visit.

"What may I do for you, my child?" Indicating a tea service resting on a corner of her table, she asked Katherine if she would care to join her. Nodding her acceptance, Katherine sat down on the chair indicated. Barely able to suppress her excitement, Katherine, like a young child, wriggled on the hard wooden chair.

"Oh, Reverend Mother, Sister Claire has just told me that she and Sister Ursula will be leaving soon for an orphanage in New York." Pausing, she saw the gentle nodding of the nun's veiled head.

"I have never spoken of this to anyone before but I own a cottage in New York, in the village of Carlyle. My husband's grandfather, sensing things were going wrong for me, transferred over the deed but cautioned me to say nothing about it to anyone."

She stopped speaking, uncertain the Abbess was even listening as she sat with her eyes closed, her lined face turned toward the sun streaming through her window. Her eyes fluttered opened, wondering why Katherine had stopped speaking. Raising a thin grey eyebrow at the girl, Katherine continued.

"I have enjoyed your hospitality, Reverend Mother, but it is time I took charge of my own life. Samuel knew I would need somewhere to live after leaving your convent and so I thought, with Sisters Claire and Ursula travelling there, I would have someone to accompany me on my journey." Stern blue eyes looked across the table at her and Katherine's words of hope faded away.

The nun spoke in a calm soothing voice. "Child, there is no need for you to hurry away from here, at least not yet. Your benefactors were most generous in their gift to the convent and, should you so desire, you could stay a year. And if I'm to be entirely truthful, I have been entertaining the hope that you might become a novitiate. It is not uncommon for a widow to choose to join a convent."

"I thank you for all your kindnesses and I do admit that, for a short time, I did think seriously of taking vows, but as the weeks passed, I realized becoming a nun was not what I was meant to do with my life."

The nun's voice rose slightly, quivering testily with age as she faced the younger woman. "What could possibly have happened in this quiet backwater that would convince you to look elsewhere for something to give your life meaning?" Her voice took on an incredulous tone. "Have you had a vision, Katherine?"

"No, Reverend Mother, I've not had a vision." Katherine sat straighter in her chair, her slender fingers twisting uneasily in her lap. When she tried to speak, her voice faltered. "The simple truth is that I am going to have a baby." As the words left her mouth, she heard a startled gasp of surprise from the other woman.

"A baby!" She sank back in her chair. It was not by accident she had been made the overseer of the convent, and she quickly recovered from the shock and began planning. "Hmm, yes, I can see that you must leave the convent. But child, to go so far away, where you know no one. And how do you propose to travel, unmolested." She paused, thoughtful, before continuing. "You are a comely young woman, Katherine, and even though you would be accompanied by two nuns, it might not be enough to fend off a determined admirer. And as cynical as this might sound, there are men out there just waiting for an innocent such as you to fall into their clutches."

Katherine smiled, surprised at this woman of the Church having such a worldly grasp of the evil man visited upon man, or in her case, woman. "Firstly, Reverend Mother, you're wrong to think that I'll be alone. Samuel was arranging for a dear friend, Maggie and her husband Jamie McGregor, to be housekeeper and handyman, doing whatever might be necessary to upkeep the cottage and the land. I left Seven Oaks before hearing that they had been found and had accepted his offer, but I'm full of hope. Samuel also arranged for a lawyer in New York, a Mr. Harvey Davenport, to handle my affairs."

"And, Reverend Mother, I have formed a plan of sorts." Her hands again moved restlessly in her lap. "You have generously allowed me to wear the robe of a nun. What if I were to complete the outfit with a nun's veil? Who would bother, or for that matter even look, at three nuns travelling to an orphanage?"

The old nun, at first stunned by Katherine's words, laughed and clapped her hands at the audacity of the plan. "All right, child. You seem to have thought this through, from the dilemma of travel to the solving of the problem of living alone. I will arrange to purchase your passage on *The Flying Eagle*, departing shortly for New York." She stood and began pacing slowly about the room.

"I've just had a thought, my dear. Nuns are noted for the parsimony of their wardrobes and thus it would be most unusual to find such a one travelling with two trunks of her possessions. In case they have to be opened for some unforeseen reason, we'll pack a few of the books and children's clothes on top of your own belongings. And, oh yes, a letter must be sent off posthaste to this lawyer, Mr. Davenport, acquainting him with the probable date of your arrival. I'll also ask him to contact your Maggie and Jamie McGregor, advising them that you will soon be taking up your duties as mistress of your cottage in Carlyle." She stopped, snapping her fingers as she suddenly remembered one last point. "And Katherine, I will need Mr. Davenport's address if this letter is to reach him before you do."

Nodding her head happily, Katherine rose from her chair, intent on fetching the address in question. As she closed the door, she heard the old nun call her name. Poking her head inside, she saw the nun's fingers beckoning her back inside. "And what of Jonathan Radcliffe, Katherine?"

She stood frozen in the doorway, suddenly unsure of herself. Meeting the speculative gaze of the older woman, she shrugged dismissively. "Jonathan is a married man now. His responsibility is to his wife and his medical practice. He can't be escorting me about the country any longer." Bowing her head to indicate the matter closed, she quickly spun around and left the room, the tapping of her heels against the cold stone floor attesting to her hasty retreat up the stairs.

It was late the following morning that Katherine received word her passage was indeed booked and a letter had been dispatched to Mr. Davenport.

The convent became a hive of activity as everyone threw themselves into the task of seeing two of their number begin what was, for them, a journey into the unknown. After dispersing a few articles of clothing and books into Katherine's trunks, boxes containing clothing and school supplies were bundled and bound together, as well as the meager possessions of the departing nuns. Katherine's own trunks were added unobtrusively to the pile. And finally, one bright morning, a hired wagon appeared at the gate, signaling that the day of departure had finally arrived.

Everyone gathered for a final farewell as their driver, a wizened leprechaun of a man, whistled cheerfully as he loaded the baggage before helping the three women clamber up.

Katherine, clutching at the unfamiliar headdress as a breeze fluttered softly about her face, gave one final wave to the inhabitants as they slowly disappeared from sight, feeling as if another chapter of her life had ended with as much finality as the gates of the convent closing behind them.

The wagon, after a dusty, bumpy ride, at last reached the harbor which, to the three women accustomed to the quiet serenity of the convent, seemed chaotic with sailors moving to and fro, lugging crates and bales onto waiting ships, calling out to each other, their words lost in the crash of the waves against *The Flying Eagle*, the vessel which would carry them to New York.

Their cheerful driver who, along the road, had instructed them to call him Alf, helped them alight, bidding them to stay by the wagon and their goods while he boarded the ship to enlist help with the trunks and boxes. Just as Katherine began to think he had fallen into the sea he reappeared, followed by four burly sailors. Tipping their hats respectfully to the three nuns, they mumbled to each other as they effortlessly heaved everything onto their shoulders, indicating that the women should follow them.

With a quick wave to Alf, the two nuns excitedly crossed the gangplank as Katherine, recalling a previous voyage, followed slowly behind. Impatiently she submerged her thoughts, not wanting any reminder of the past to haunt her as she began her new life. The small party crossed the deck quickly, trailing behind their guides as they were led to a tiny cabin.

They had barely settled into their temporary quarters when there was a thunderous knock, one that threatened to separate the door from its hinges. Opening it, Sister Ursula found herself looking into the steely eyes of a man who unceremoniously introduced himself as Caleb Greenaway, Captain of *The Flying Eagle*. He stood just outside the door, as if unwilling to strain the walls of the crowded cabin further, explaining to the women that they would be sailing with the tide and, with any luck, the voyage to New York would be a short one, probably just days since they would be hugging the coastline as much as possible as they sailed northward, hopefully missing any chance squalls or storms.

His resonant voice went on to say they were his only passengers, directing them to remain in their quarters, where all meals would be brought to them, including this evening's meal. As the crew would be too busy to have them on the main deck, it was strongly recommended that they remain in the tiny cabin until someone came for them in the morning. Nodding their veiled heads in understanding, they watched as he closed the door firmly behind him.

Unwilling to let such a gruff character dampen their enthusiasm, the two nuns tried to draw their companion into what they saw as a great adventure but Katherine, feeling the strain of the past week, quietly lay down and was soon fast asleep.

* * * *

The docking of the ship in New York went smoothly, due in large part to Captain Greenaway's years of sailing experience. The voyage had been what he had promised, uneventful. Neither Katherine nor the two nuns were molested in any way. In fact the crew had behaved most respectfully toward them. Katherine's shrewd assessment that men, be they sailors or any other, would pay little attention to women who were already married to the church had been proven correct.

As they stood on the deck, a sailor delivered a message from the captain, directing the ladies to remain on board until he was able to secure transportation for them. In any of their brief conversations with the captain, they had confided that they were travelling to *St. Bernadette's Orphanage*, the captain assuming all three passengers were seeking the same destination.

Standing at the railing of the ship, the three women watched the hustle and bustle of the docks. As crates and boxes were unloaded, Sister Ursula spied a handsomely appointed carriage heading toward *The Flying Eagle*. Nudging the others, they watched as it slowly approached, until at last it drew opposite the ship. A balding man, hat in hand, seemed as interested in them as they were in him when the carriage came to a stop. The lone passenger climbed down, placing the hat he had been holding firmly on to his head.

Captain Greenaway, having observed the stranger as he approached the gangplank, obviously planning to board the ship, met him as he set his feet on the deck. The nuns, willingly or not, could overhear the exchange between the two men.

"Good day to you, sir. Would you by chance be Captain Caleb Greenaway?' At the other's nod of agreement, he continued. 'My name is Harvey Davenport, a lawyer by profession. I received word some days ago that a Mrs. Radcliffe would be arriving in New York on board *The Flying Eagle*. I prudently hired a boy to keep watch and, upon spying your vessel, he hightailed it to my office to say you had indeed reached port."

"Well, Mr. Davenport sir, most of your facts are correct as indeed you can see *The Flying Eagle* has docked but unfortunately there is no passenger by the name of Mrs. Radcliffe on board my ship."

It was at that moment a feminine voice called out. "Mr. Davenport, I am the one you seek." Katherine stepped forward, quietly amused at the shocked expressions of both men as they confronted a nun. The lawyer was the first to recover his wits.

"You must excuse my surprise, Sister, but I wasn't expecting a member of a religious order." His unspoken questions hung in the air but Katherine merely smiled before turning to the other man.

"Please forgive me for my lack of honesty, Captain Greenaway, but it was felt the safest way for a single woman to travel unmolested was in the company of nuns, and the easiest way to blend in was to become a nun myself. Do forgive me for my charade, but…" her voice trailed off, uncertain of his reaction to her little deception.

There was a perceptive sparkle in his eye as he looked closely at the youngest of the nuns for the first time. Laughing, he lifted her fingers to his lips and kissed them.

"Well, madam, I confess that, though hurt by your lack of confidence in myself, I salute the author of such a ruse, and having now observed the loveliness beneath that veil, I don't wonder at the necessity of it all." Bowing to the others, he instructed some passing sailors to carry the ladies' belongings ashore to the gentleman's carriage. He bowed once more to the small party before he moved off to oversee the unloading of the remainder of his cargo.

With some judicious juggling, the carriage soon held all the baggage and the two extra passengers. As they drove away from the hubbub of the harbor, the three women gazed out at the passing scenery, the lawyer waiting patiently for their curiosity and exclamations about the countryside, so different from their own, to subside somewhat.

It was Katherine who spoke first. "I feel I owe you an explanation, Mr.

Davenport. For many weeks, I have been residing at a convent. It was felt there were forces who might wish me ill, and Samuel Langtree, my husband's grandfather, arranged for my stay there. When I heard that two of the nuns, Sister Ursula and Sister Claire, were travelling to New York, I knew that opportunity was knocking. I prevailed upon the Abbess of the convent to allow me to journey with them, garbed as a nun myself, thus avoiding any unwelcome advances or threat of personal danger. It is amazing, don't you agree, Mr. Davenport, that, as a presumed member of a religious order, in men's eyes I ceased being a woman as such and became someone who you paid respect to but never anything more, for which I will always be most grateful."

The lawyer nodded, surprised at her perceptive assessment, spoke with quiet conviction. "Obviously a very wise plan, young lady." He glanced at the two nuns who, having heard these scanty details of Katherine's life from the Reverend Mother, were now nodding off. "Mrs. Radcliffe, I wonder if we might speak freely now or would you prefer to stop at an inn where we might have some degree of privacy." His voice trailed off in awkwardness as three pairs of eyes met his.

Her pretty laugh rang out as she assured the lawyer that Sisters Ursula and Claire were no threat to her need for secrecy as their journey would continue upstate where they were to take up residence at *St. Bernadette's Orphanage*. Both nuns, who were also her friends, understood the danger she might face if they let any chance traveler know her whereabouts.

Nodding his head uncertainly, he opened the leather satchel that had been resting beside him, clearing his throat importantly before he began. "Some months ago, as I am sure you are already aware, dear lady, I received a visitor by the name of Edmund Featherstone. He presented impeccable credentials attesting to the fact that he represented your grandfather-in-law, Samuel Langtree." He paused momentarily. "I surmise that he has since passed on, since Mr. Featherstone was adamant that you would not leave Mr. Langtree's side while he lived." At her tearful nod, he patted her hand awkwardly. "You have my deepest sympathy, dear lady."

"That being said, on to the business at hand. I was instructed to ensure that Somerset Cottage be prepared for your arrival. For the last few years, it has been rented by a Mrs. Spooner, who, most conveniently, died some months ago and the cottage has been sitting vacant ever since."

The lawyer heard a collective gasp at his tactless remark and glancing across saw the nuns cross themselves, whispering a small prayer for the repose of this recently departed soul.

Fussing uncomfortably with the cuff of his jacket, he met the sparkling eyes of the youngest of his three passengers, and was somewhat relieved to see he at least hadn't offended her. She nodded encouragingly for him to proceed.

"Well, the upshot is that your Mr. Featherstone was searching for a housekeeper for you, preferably one who was married and whose husband could act as a sort of groundskeeper for you. The last I heard, he had located such a couple and was arranging for them to be waiting on your arrival at your new home. Unfortunately, the Featherstone's couldn't wait any longer for you since they had booked passage on a ship that sailed back to England less than a week ago."

Disappointed as she was at not seeing Edmond and Mary Featherstone one last time, Katherine excitedly broke into his rambling discourse. "Did you learn their names?" At his blank expression, she stopped. "Oh, please do remember, Mr. Davenport, the couple that Edmond Featherstone hired. Was it Maggie and Jamie McGregor?"

Pausing at this unexpected interruption, Mr. Davenport peered at her over his spectacles. "Why, I really had no idea the names of potential servants would mean so much to you but if you just give me a moment, I must have it in my papers somewhere." He began shuffling through his satchel until at last, in exasperation, he stopped. "I do apologize, Mrs. Radcliffe, but it appears that is the one piece of paper I don't have."

Somewhat disappointed, Katherine gazed out of the window, recalling her arrival in this vast country and driving by carriage to Seven Oaks, full of hope. *Oh, please let it be Maggie and her Jamie awaiting my arrival. I know I can manage everything if I just have a friend beside me.*

"I have also taken the liberty of arranging to spend the night at the only inn the village has to offer, Mrs. Radcliffe. I thought it best, unaware that you would be providing such irreproachable chaperones." He nodded at the softly snoring nuns. "It is my understanding that there are at least two bedrooms so the good Sisters will be able to help you settle in before continuing on their own journey. I will collect you in the morning, madam, and will escort you to the bank, ensuring that your interests will best be served there."

"How far is it to Somerset Cottage, Mr. Davenport? I confess I weary of this constant bouncing." The two nuns nodded in agreement, sleepily revealing their interest in the conversation but the lawyer merely consulted his timepiece before returning it to his pocket.

"By my reckoning, we are drawing near. It is about two hours from the city so I doubt you will travel there too often but you are just outside Carlyle, a pleasant little village, or so I've been told. I imagine you will be able to make any necessary purchases there. And who knows, a pretty little thing like you, perhaps it is there you will meet your next husband." He smiled, genuinely unaware of the indelicacy of his remark. He settled back in his seat, pleased that his commission was nearing its end, at least for today.

Looking out the window to avoid commenting on his boorish remarks, Katherine saw they were now on the outskirts of a village. "This must be Carlyle", she said to her fellow travelers.

The nuns glanced out the window, delighted at the thought of leaving the bouncing carriage and dusty roads behind them. Katherine spied all manner of shops lining the dusty road, with men and women strolling about, all intent on some manner of business or another. She wondered if this village would prove to be as friendly as Charleston. Time will tell, she thought, gathering her belongings together.

* * * *

As the carriage rattled to a stop, Mr. Davenport alit, assisting each of the three women down. Katherine stood there, gazing in awe at the cottage, which now belonged to her.

Smoke curled lazily from the chimney, filling the air with the welcoming smell of burning wood. Vines had begun their annual climb up the walls of the cottage and smaller shrubs and budding flowers filled the ground all around the neatly kept house. The door stood slightly invitingly ajar, the open windows carrying the scent of the spring flowers indoors. After a gloomy, mist-filled morning, the sun chose that moment to poke out from behind the clouds, shining brightly down on her as she slowly walked up the flagstone path, the others falling in behind.

An unseen hand pushed the door open fully and a young woman, alerted by the sound of a carriage stopping, stepped out. Spying three nuns standing there, she hesitated, peering inquisitively into each face.

"Miss Katherine, is that you?" Uncertainly, she looked into familiar green eyes. Puzzled she asked, "Have you taken the veil, Miss Katherine?"

Smiling, Katherine shook her head in denial as Maggie stepped quickly down the two stone steps, holding her arms open as the younger woman ran to her.

"Maggie, Edmond did find you. Oh, I'm so happy. But what is all this 'Miss Katherine' about? Blushing, Maggie quickly explained that their friendship was somewhat altered now that she was her hired servant. Katherine nodded uncertainly, the joy of seeing her friend once again overwhelming her. The two women hugged warmly, babbling on to each other of their joy in being reunited. Seeing her friend eyeing her black robe, she explained the need to assume some sort of disguise whilst travelling to avoid any unwelcome attention and Maggie, recalling Spanish Jack and his plans for Katherine as they crossed the Atlantic, nodded in agreement.

The brim of a jaunty cap peeked around the corner, followed by a smiling, curious face. A tall man, lean and clean-shaven, stepped out, puzzlement written across his face as he gazed at the three nuns. Maggie laughed and took Katherine's hand, beckoning her husband over. Somewhat reassured by his wife's smiling face, he joined the small party.

"Jamie, my love, this is Mrs. Katherine Radcliffe. And no, she hasn't taken the veil. She wore it to discourage any unwelcome advances from amorous travelers."

Jamie and Katherine took an instant liking to each other, their affection for the happily grinning Maggie their common bond. Katherine turned to the three who stood watching, introducing Sister Ursula and Sister Claire and finally the somewhat stiff and austere person of Mr. Davenport. It was quickly established that there was indeed room for the two nuns, as Maggie explained that she and

Jamie lived in the small cottage behind the main house, leaving the three bedrooms of Somerset Cottage for the owner.

Linking arms, the two friends chatted happily, as they entered the house, the nuns following quietly behind with Mr. Davenport bringing up the rear.

Katherine felt she had indeed come home as she followed Maggie across the gleaming wooden floor of the parlor and tiny dining room. She merely glanced into the kitchen as Maggie claimed it as her domain and, as Mr. Featherstone had explained, she was there to cook and to oversee the housework done by village women hired for that purpose and Jamie, unless the work was too heavy, could tend the garden and livestock. Jamie, with the reluctant assistance of the driver, had unloaded all of the trunks and boxes, carrying them upstairs under the watchful eyes of the nuns. He deposited Katherine's trunks in the largest of the bedrooms as she and Maggie stood admiring the handsome furnishings and linen. The rest of the baggage was carried into the second bedroom, where both nuns now waited.

It was a short time later that Mr. Davenport took his leave, again promising to fetch Katherine in the morning for the much anticipated meeting at the bank.

Thanks to Mr. Davenport's foresight in sending word to Maggie of Katherine's probable date of arrival, she had prepared a mouth watering meal, confirming that she indeed ruled the kitchen.

There was much laughter and chatter around the dining room table until at last the nuns, looking exhausted, begged leave to seek their beds. Jamie, recognizing that his Maggie and the new mistress of the house had much to talk about, quietly left to tend the livestock. At Katherine's questioning look, Jamie laughingly informed her that she was the proud owner of a horse, a cow, three piglets and several chickens, all capable of contributing to the well being of Somerset Cottage and its larder. Chuckling at the amazement on her face as she contemplated the extent of her great good fortune, Jamie left as Maggie called out to him that she would return to their cottage before it grew dark.

The two women, friends rather than servant and mistress, washed and dried the dishes until the last plate was tucked away and they sat in front of the small fire in the tiny sitting room, drinking tea and renewing the bonds of their friendship. Katherine told Maggie of Samuel's death, tears flowing freely from their eyes as they recalled the fondness they had both felt for the old man, Katherine feeling she was at last mourning him as he deserved.

Katherine, unsure of Maggie's reaction to the fact that she was now a single woman, studied her friend's face in the firelight. Sensing a certain reluctance, Maggie, wisely and patiently, let her lead the conversation.

Straightening her spine in a way Maggie had come to recognize as a sign that her friend had reached a decision, pressed her hands warmly, reassuringly. Katherine sighed and at last confided to her friend what Samuel had proposed, a legal parting of the ways for Simon and herself, leaving Simon free to marry his love, Miss Juliana Taylor, the woman he should have married in the first place.

Katherine, giving only the barest of details, told of Samuel's plan for her to accompany Jonathan when he returned to Belle Isle and his bride-to-be and their reasoning for depositing her at a nearby convent. They hoped to escape Simon, or more correctly Juliana's wrath, should there be second thoughts on the dissolving of their marriage. She spoke softly as she recounted only that part of the journey where he left her at the convent. She couldn't share, even with Maggie, the realization that she had fallen deeply in love with him, and to speak his name, even after these many weeks, still felt like a knife twisting in her heart.

"Now, Maggie, before you seek Jamie's bed, there is one more thing. I'm going to have a baby."

Chapter Nineteen

Shocked, Maggie met the now defiant eyes of her friend. "Does Simon know?" she whispered.

Tearfully Katherine locked eyes with her friend, aware she was twisting the truth but feeling nothing would be gained by publicly acknowledging that Jonathan, not Simon, was the father. "No, Maggie, he doesn't know. And the possibility that he will ever learn of it is too unlikely. The nuns at the convent, including Sisters Ursula and Claire, and even Mr. Davenport, all believe I am a recent widow. Will this bit of deception be a problem for you and your Jamie, Maggie?" She held her breath as she waited for an answer.

"I know Jamie will agree with me that you are more in need of loyal friends than ever before. Of course we'll stand by you." Maggie, suspecting there was something she wasn't being told, buried her suspicions and smiled at her friend.

Katherine, unaware she had been holding her breath against Maggie's answer, began to breathe again. After hugging each other, laughing and crying together, both women felt the bonds of friendship had been cemented together forever.

An excited Maggie eagerly began to ply her with questions about the imminent arrival and the state of her health, which Katherine willingly answered, laughing in delight at having someone to share and rejoice in her news. As a clock chimed, the two realized the hour was indeed late and hugging affectionately, Katherine watched as Maggie made her way to her own home.

* * * *

Bright sunlight streamed through the window when Katherine opened her eyes. Glancing about, she snuggled deeper into her bed, happier than she had been in what felt like forever. She was home. Nobody could take this from her. Delicious aromas assailed her as she reluctantly arose and began searching through her trunks for a frock that would serve as a declaration of her 'widowhood' to the village where, hopefully, she could raise her child in peace and safety.

Settling on the black dress she had worn for Samuel's funeral, she silently thanked Marie for designing a gown in the French fashion, gathered just below her breasts, leaving the rest of the gown to flow loosely to the floor. After donning the garment, she studied her reflection in the looking glass, satisfied that anyone observing her would surely respect her 'widow's weeds' and leave her to mourn in solitude. A pang of conscience stabbed at her as she thought of the friends she was deceiving but this was the path she had chosen, and she felt confident that it was the safest way for all concerned.

At Maggie's knock, she brushed at the gown and opened the door to her, smiling. "Oh, Maggie, dear, I had such a delicious sleep but I must admit I am famished." Laughing, Maggie helped her arrange her hair in a simple knot, tied with a black ribbon. The two were still chattering as they made their way downstairs.

The two nuns smiled as their former travelling companion entered the dining room, happy to see their young friend so cheerful. In a burst of exuberance, Katherine kissed each of them on their lined cheeks.

Flustered at this unaccustomed display of affection, they regarded each other across the table, delighted at her happiness. Katherine took her place at the table and began to study her surroundings. Small though the room might be, the tasteful furnishings did not overpower it. On one wall stood a matching sideboard, its shelves laden with elegant dinnerware. A bouquet of fresh flowers graced the table as the three women chatted over their breakfast until they heard the wheels of a carriage drawing up and Katherine knew Mr. Davenport had arrived.

Maggie wrapped Katherine's cloak about her shoulders as the lawyer stood watching, impatient to be on his way, for once finished with this business, he doubted he would ever have occasion to grace the environs of Carlyle again.

Signaling his driver after assisting Katherine into the carriage, they were soon travelling the same dusty road they had taken the day before. After a few polite exchanges concerning the weather and such, both lapsed into silence, Katherine again surveying the countryside they were passing through.

Earlier she had toyed with the idea of transferring the gold coins from within the hidden recess of her trunk into the bank's keeping but had then argued with herself that it had been a lack of coin that had kept her at Marlow Court, making it possible for Simon to claim her as his bride. No, she decided, it would be better to have money near to hand.

Sinking back into the cushioned seat, it seemed no time at all before they were stopping before an imposing brick building, the sign above the door proclaiming it to be the Bank of Carlyle.

Again, Mr. Davenport was there to assist Katherine as she alit from the carriage and, offering her his arm, the two entered through the sturdy wooden door. The usually hushed atmosphere of the bank became alive with whispers as the two tellers and the men they were serving stared inquisitively at them, all four gazing appreciatively at the breathtaking loveliness of this new arrival. Both tellers recognized Mr. Davenport as the gentleman who had called in the day before to ensure that Mr. Henry Percival, the owner of the bank, would lend his full attention to Mrs. Radcliffe and the arranging of her financial affairs, under the lawyer's supervision, of course.

The younger of the tellers, a thin, serious looking chap with a pockmarked complexion, was instantly smitten by the face that peered out from beneath the hood of her cloak. Excusing himself from the customer he was serving, he knocked quietly at his employer's door to announce their arrival. His pale blue eyes followed the vision as she and her escort crossed to where Mr. Percival now stood waiting, greeting them effusively as the love-struck youth made his way back to his patiently waiting customer.

Inside the over-furnished office, the banker seized Katherine's hand and brushed his lips across her slender fingers in what he thought was a cosmopolitan gesture, almost falling over himself in his haste to be the one to offer her a chair. He indicated with a careless nod of his head, the chair Mr. Davenport should occupy before returning to his own place behind a handsome oak desk.

Katherine, studying him, saw a man who she guessed to be about thirty-five years, hair already thinning and which, in a futile effort to conceal that fact, had combed what strands remained across a pale pink scalp. A moustache, pencil thin and black, perched below a slightly hooked nose. His lips were thin but when he smiled, his teeth appeared sound. His chin had a strong and determined look. He fussed with the papers strewn about his desk, at last locating the ones he sought before he met the eyes of the two who sat patiently waiting.

Mr. Davenport made the introductions, feeling the formalities must be followed, even in this backwater. Reminding the banker that the purpose of their being here was to open an account for Mrs. Radcliffe, just as her grandfather-in-law, the late Mr. Samuel Langtree, had instructed, he added that he himself would expect a yearly accounting from the banker. He handed over a Letter Of Credit, which the banker barely glanced at, unable to take his eyes from the divine creature sitting opposite him, nodding his head in agreement to everything the lawyer said.

"Well, I can't see anything amiss, Mrs. Radcliffe. This note authorizes my bank to deposit this rather large sum into your personal account. Yes, quite a large sum indeed. You are to have full access to this money, a fact I find a trifle disturbing." He paused, smiling condescendingly at his captive audience. "Ladies, even widows, are not usually capable of administering such large amounts of money but Mr. Langtree obviously had full confidence in your abilities and so I shall abide by his instructions. But if ever, dear lady, you find yourself in need of male guidance, please do not hesitate to call on me. Now, if you will just sign these papers, our business for today is concluded."

As she signed the documents put in front of her, Katherine struggled to maintain her composure as she listened to his pompous words. The gall of the man! Assuming because she was a woman, she was incapable of managing her affairs. If only there was another bank in this sleepy little hamlet, she would take her trade there but, according to Mr. Davenport, this was the only one. *So smile,* she chided herself, *and allow this mincing fop to imagine that one day I might actually seek his guidance.*

Rising in one fluid motion from her chair, she turned to leave but again the banker caught her hand and lifted it to his lips. She stepped back, suddenly aware of the sourness of his breath. Hastily, she snatched back her hand, and glided silently from the bank, oblivious of the eyes that followed her.

The village, already aware that a young widow had settled in Somerset Cottage, and in spite of her widow's weeds, those who first saw her that day could attest to their fellow villagers of her uncommon beauty and grace as they watched as she was once again handed into Mr. Davenport's carriage.

Instructing his driver to give Mrs. Radcliffe and himself a tour of the village so she might become familiar with the shops and what they had to offer, they slowed before the various storefronts, affording the curious a chance to peer into the carriage, to be met by Katherine's shy but warm smile. Some stared back impassively, reserving judgment of Carlyle's newest resident but others waved and returned her smile.

It was late afternoon before they returned to her cottage and she felt obliged, after all his kindnesses, to invite the lawyer to stay for dinner. Seeing the lateness of the hour, he decided to spend another night in the village, declaring his intention of leaving at first light.

As they sat at the table that night, Sister Ursula spoke. "Katherine dear, I'm afraid Sister Claire and I must also be on our way. After all, our mission is the orphanage where we are sorely needed. We promised Mother Superior that we would see you safely settled and I feel we have accomplished that."

"Mr. Davenport, could I impose on you one final time?" Katherine, disappointed they were leaving so soon, smiled beguilingly at the prim gentleman before she made her request. "Could you see your way to accompany my friends back to New York and see them safely on to the next leg of their journey?" Feeling maneuvered into agreement, he grudgingly nodded his head and the two nuns murmured their gratitude, promising to pray for his soul as soon as they were settled into their new post, while Harvey Davenport frowned balefully at the ceiling.

* * * *

As the leaves began to display the riotous colors of fall, Katherine watched with fascination as her body changed progressively with each passing month. She and Maggie, conferring, judged the baby would be born sometime in late November.

The three occupants of Somerset Cottage began to attend the village church on Sundays, meeting the townspeople and forming friendships. The men respected Katherine's fecundity and her widowhood whilst the women sensed no threat from the newcomer as she faithfully continued to drape herself in her widow's weeds.

She had had Jamie take her into town soon after her arrival to search out a seamstress and, although Belinda Ross wasn't as clever with a needle as Marie St. Pierre had been, the simple black frocks she stitched were more than satisfactory for Katherine's purposes.

While chatting with some of the women of the village, Maggie had discovered there were two midwives, sisters in fact, who had delivered most of the children in the area and had secured promises that one or both of them would attend Katherine when her time came. The more curious of the village were the first to ride out to the cottage, followed shortly by the rest of the village, most bearing welcoming gifts of pies and breads, all accepting tea and cakes in Katherine's cozy parlor. And so the weeks passed.

In her waking hours, Katherine was able to keep herself busy, pushing all thoughts of Belle Isle and its inhabitants away but she spent the nights tossing and turning, helpless against the grief and despair that tore at her heart. After such nights, she would descend the stairs, pale and downcast, unable to throw off the cloak of despondency until Maggie, her heart aching to see such misery, would surprise her with a tiny garment she had sewn or a toy that Jamie had carved, reminding her of the coming child and the bright future ahead.

But Maggie was also angry, angry at the man who had deserted her friend. She recalled Katherine's words that first night at Somerset Cottage and knew that Katherine, for some unknown reason, wanted Maggie to believe Simon to be the father. But she had seen the way Jonathan and Katherine had looked at each other when they thought no one was watching, yet she voiced her suspicions to no one, not even to her beloved Jamie.

The falling leaves chased each other in colorful swirls of reckless abandon down the road as Katherine watched the season change from the warmth of her window. She sewed tiny garments, thankful for her aunt's exacting lessons in needlecraft and Mary Featherstone's knitting classes as they crossed the Atlantic. With each passing day, her shape became rounder, her steps slower.

* * * *

Maggie, the eldest of a large brood of children, had helped her own mother prepare for her lying in, and so she watched over Katherine carefully. Although they were so far childless, she and Jamie had great hopes for a large family, and so Jamie also watched her with interest as Katherine maneuvered her increasing bulk around obstacles of furniture and narrow doorways, ready to fly for help should Maggie give him the nod.

It was early morning when an ashen-faced Katherine appeared in the kitchen doorway. Maggie had noticed some days ago that her burden had dropped and so had told her the time was near. Maggie was busily cooking breakfast when she spied Katherine, still in her nightgown, standing in the doorway, nervously twisting her hands. No words were needed as Maggie efficiently returned her to her bed, and after a few questions, admonished her not to move from there until she returned.

The girl ran swiftly from the house, calling frantically for Jamie. Startled chickens flew clumsily about the yard, squawking furiously at this inexcusable interruption to their breakfast. Jamie, hearing her calling, poked his head from the barn where he had just finished milking the cow. One look at his wife's face told him all he needed to know.

"How far along is she, Maggie? Should I be leaving for one of the sisters now or should I bide a wee while?"

"Oh, Jamie, I don't know. Whenever I helped my mother, she had the answers to my questions before I knew what to ask. But none of us have gone through this. Perhaps one of the sisters will know. Ride now, Jamie, and bring back at least one of them."

Instructions given, she whirled around and rushed back to the house. It was short minutes later that she heard the wheels of the carriage turning as her husband sped from the tiny courtyard.

Rushing up the stairs, Maggie breathlessly entered Katherine's bedchamber, where she found her friend pacing the floor, frightened at the ordeal she was about to endure alone. *The father of this babe should be here with her* the faithful Maggie thought, as she tried unsuccessfully to coax her back to her bed.

Maggie, sitting with Katherine, saw that her pains were still far apart. *I don't care if I have acted hastily. I'll feel much better when one of the midwives arrives.* She finally convinced Katherine to lie down and rest if she could, knowing she would need all her strength in the hours that loomed ahead. After tucking her in, Maggie stirred the fire, laying another log on before retreating to the kitchen to fetch everything that would be needed. Just as she was gathering the last of it, she heard the carriage pull into the yard. Rushing out, she saw both sisters had arrived with Jamie. He assisted them down and, after being assured that Katherine was doing well, led the horse to the stable.

Both sisters, Mrs. Simpkin and Mrs. Granger, turned to Maggie as she held the door open in welcome relief. Mrs. Granger, with a soft Scottish burr, questioned Maggie about the progress the expectant mother had made thus far.

Smiling, Maggie ushered them into the kitchen and, after relieving them of their wraps, offered them tea, which they politely refused 'for the now'.

They appeared to be middle aged and of a plump build, their brown hair pulled back neatly into identical tight buns, wearing starched white aprons over blue gingham dresses.

Bustling about the neat kitchen, they checked what Maggie had already gathered, smiling and nodding their approval at her foresight. Spying a washbasin, the sisters filled it with hot water from the kettle and began washing their hands, right up to their dimpled elbows. Satisfied at last and smiling kindly at Maggie, they asked to see the patient.

Following in her wake, they climbed the stairs, pausing as they heard a small moan from within the chamber. Rushing in, Maggie found her friend drenched in sweat, lying helplessly on the bed. The sisters, accustomed to each other's ways, shooed Maggie out despite her protests, suggesting that she make that lovely husband of hers a cup of tea.

Jamie was just coming through the kitchen doorway when her feet touched the last step. Hurrying to him, they quietly held each other, concern for their friend written across both their faces. As they sat sipping tea, they could hear an occasional moan and footsteps overhead as the midwives tended their patient.

The clock in the parlor ticked on, chiming each passing hour. Jamie, unable to bear sitting by helplessly, had gone out to the barn to tend the animals and Maggie, unused to being idle, soon had soup simmering on the hob, her hands covered in flour as she mixed up a batch of scones.

Throughout the day, the sisters took it in turn to come down for tea or a bowl of soup, both looking more disheartened as the day wore on. Her heart beating faster at the sound of footsteps once again descending the staircase, Maggie smiled hopefully at Mrs. Granger as she peeked into the kitchen.

"My dear, we're at our wit's end. It's been too many hours since her labor began with little progress being made. She calls constantly for her husband. In desperation, we have come up with a very outlandish idea but for it to be successful, we first need your blessing and then your husband's help." She paused, giving Maggie time to digest what she had said before continuing. 'We thought that, since she calls for her husband, perhaps your Jamie could answer for him. We know Mrs. Radcliffe is a widow but we both feel she's close to giving up, and my dear, she's so very weak, I doubt she would see through this wee deception. Do you think your husband would be willing to play the part?"

Maggie, without pause, whirled out the door, calling Jamie as she ran. It took only a minute to explain what was needed before both were racing back to the kitchen where Mrs. Granger patiently waited. One look at their faces gave her the answer she had hoped for. As they both turned to the stairs, a daunting voice stopped them in their tracks.

"And where, might I ask, would you two be going?"

Startled, they both turned and stared at Mrs. Granger, unable to fathom what game she was playing at. Eyes twinkling but arms crossed, she pointed to the washbasin, which she had just filled with warm, soapy water. She admonished them that, unwashed, they would not be allowed across the threshold of the lying-in chamber. Impatiently they both plunged their hands into the water and it wasn't until Mrs. Granger was completely satisfied that they were allowed to proceed up the stairs.

Hesitantly, they entered the bedroom where a very pale and exhausted Katherine lay, fitfully moaning and mumbling. Mrs. Simpkin, spying Jamie, smiled brightly and beckoned him to the corner of the room furthest from the bed. She whispered her instructions and he nodded, understanding the need for haste. With a hurried glance at Maggie, knowing this charade had her blessing, he moved toward Katherine's bed, sitting on a wooden stool that had been moved there for him.

Taking Katherine's limp hand and rubbing it softly, he murmured into her ear, something he had watched his father do as his mother lay giving birth and no midwife had been available. As Maggie watched, tears streaming down her face, she recognized her helplessness and bowed her head in silent prayer.

Katherine's head twisted in denial at something Jamie said but he kept talking softly, and gradually she calmed. Leaning forward, he kissed her cheek and then her slender hands, lacing his own fingers through hers, urging her to help the midwives deliver her baby. She nodded imperceptibly and, grasping Jamie's hands, gathered the strength needed to bring this new life into the world.

The women worked together, encouraging her to push when needed, telling Jamie when to comfort her, and thus it was much later when Katherine gasped, "Jonathan" as a tiny head emerged. As Mrs. Simpkin gathered the squirming body into a warm cover, Mrs. Granger stepped back in surprise.

"Sister", she exclaimed, "there's another one coming. Keep talking to her, Jamie, for this little lady is about to become the mother of twins."

Chapter Twenty

Many hours later, as the four of them sat around the table eating more of Maggie's delicious soup, the two sisters confessed how close their patient had been to giving up, and without Jamie acting the role of her dead husband, there might now be two orphans upstairs instead of two babes sleeping peacefully beside their mother.

It was at this point that Maggie realized that when Katherine had cried out, it hadn't been for Simon, who was neither dead nor her husband any longer, but Jonathan Radcliffe. Recalling Katherine's words when she had confided to Maggie that she was pregnant, she had said only that Simon didn't know and was unlikely to ever find out. Maggie had assumed it was bitterness that made her speak in such a manner, but now her suspicions had been confirmed. She tucked this bit of information away and listened to the sisters as they continued their assessment of Katherine.

Mrs. Granger, in her no-nonsense voice, was speaking. "There was some damage done delivering those two babies and I doubt that Mrs. Radcliffe will ever conceive another child but fortunately for her, she has two already and will not likely feel too deprived," she looked uncertainly up the stairs before murmuring, "at least I hope she doesn't."

Early the next morning, Jamie waited patiently by the carriage for the two sisters, who had stopped to give Maggie more instructions for the well-being of their patient. They thought, in Katherine's weakened state, a wet nurse would be needed and fortunately, they knew of just such a person, a Mrs. Bridgette Murphy. Mrs. Granger again took charge of the conversation. "Mrs. Murphy has fallen on hard times, her husband just up and running off and her with a wee son, ready to be weaned, mind you. We could stop and have a word, and she could return with your Jamie." Without hesitation Maggie agreed, hoping Katherine would be of the same mind.

Somerset Cottage did not lack visitors in spite of the inclement weather. The ladies of the village ventured out to view the babies, which Katherine had named Declan and Christine, after her parents. Bridgette Murphy, a morose being, plain of face and stick thin, had jumped at the chance to begin life anew and, with her young son, had been installed in the third bedroom of the cottage.

Katherine's strength returned gradually, due in no small part to the tender nursing she received and, while understanding the need for a wet nurse, it was with reluctance that the babies were turned over to Bridgette when they needed feeding but otherwise she had complete care of them. While the babies slept, and after all chores and cooking were finished, the three women would gather over a steaming cup of tea, waiting for Jamie to finish his chores before sitting down to their evening meal.

Bridgette, loudly and often, lamented the loss of her husband, vowing dolefully that if he ever came back to Carlyle, she would welcome him with open arms. Katherine and Maggie, trying to reason with her, pointed out that if he had left her once without a backward glance, he would likely do so again, should he be bold enough to ever return. She would listen politely as they tried to sway her with their arguments, stubbornly certain that one day he would return, seeking her and their son.

Green shoots began to cautiously poke through the cold ground, harbingers of spring. Windows were thrown open, welcoming the warm breezes. The babies grew apace, happy and content. When Katherine found something was needed, she would have Jamie drive her to the village, visiting the various shops and making whatever purchases were necessary for the running of her small holding.

Her black dress proclaimed she was still in mourning but with each visit to the village, as she leisurely strolled along the main street, Henry Percival seemed to emerge through the doors of his bank and walk along beside her, seeming intent on impressing her with his position in the village and even finding occasion to mention the advances socially that he seemed to be making in the city. He often lamented the lonely life of a bachelor, subtly hinting that a meal at the home of his favorite depositor would not go amiss but Katherine managed to avoid issuing such a coveted invitation.

As the months passed, Katherine delighted in watching Declan and Christine develop from babes in arms to infants who in turn became toddlers, following her footsteps as she busied herself about the cottage. Both twins had the grey eyes and black hair of their sire, although Christine seemed to have the delicate slenderness of her mother while Declan promised to grow tall and broad shouldered. And if a memory stirred, she pushed it away and slowly her nights became peaceful as the past became a faded, tarnished dream.

* * * *

Christmas passed as quietly as it could with two toddlers and a small child taking up everyone's attention. Brigitte, hired as a wet nurse, had become Maggie's helper, as the twins grew and needed her less and less.

Invitations for afternoon tea were accepted and other than attending church on Sundays, that was as far as Katherine was prepared to go toward establishing a social life for herself, thus becoming something of an enigma to the villagers.

The women at first had been prepared to rebuff this striking newcomer but as time passed and no flirtations or dalliances with husbands or beaus occurred, they relaxed and slowly welcomed her into their lives. The few unattached men, other than Henry Percival, were intimidated by the widow's weeds that

Katherine wore like a shield to discourage unwanted attention.

Bridgette, true to her word, accepted her errant husband back into her forgiving arms when he reappeared, hat in hand. Katherine knew her small holding had no need for a second man and, since the twins were now weaned, she reluctantly released Bridgette from her service when the reunited family announced they were heading west.

* * * *

Two more years passed, time Katherine spent watching and delighting in the growth of the twins, seeing them turn from chubby toddlers to self-assured individuals, curious about everything that touched their world.

It was on the morning of her twenty-second birthday that Katherine decided she had played the part of grieving widow long enough and threw off the black dress she had just donned, selecting in its stead a cream colored gown trimmed with moss green ribbons and buttons. As she entered the kitchen, both Maggie and Jamie paused in their tasks, slowly surveying their mistress and friend. Maggie rushed over and gave her a warm hug while Jamie looked on, smiling his delight. The twins, eating their porridge, paused and appraised this unfamiliar figure and, as they confirmed in their own minds it was indeed their mother, crowed their delight, sharing in the laughter of the adults around them.

"Where might Madam be going, dressed in such finery?"

Katherine blushingly stirred uneasily in her chair. "Maggie, hush now. I have merely decided to wear some of my other gowns for I am indeed done with black." She turned to Jamie. "Do you have time to take me into the village, Jamie?" At his nod, she smiled. "Maggie, would you care to come with us? We could do whatever shopping is needed and perhaps all of us could have lunch at the hotel." Looking at their smiling faces and listening to the squeals of the excited children, she had the answer. "Well, it's settled. Come Maggie, help me get the twins ready."

Those villagers who were already going about their business recognized the carriage, nodding as the small party drove by. As Jamie handed his passengers onto the wooden walkway, he smiled. Katherine saw how those who were passing by sent her welcoming smiles and she relaxed at her first social jaunt into the village. Looking about, she was surprised at the attention they were garnering. Smiling uncertainly, she and Maggie led the children to the entrance of the bank. Directing Maggie to sit with the children on a wooden bench outside the bank, she stepped through the doorway. The bank was bereft of customers when she entered and the same young teller who had been so smitten with her when she had first arrived and on each subsequent visit, looked up and smiled his delight at seeing her.

"Mrs. Radcliffe," he stammered. "How very breathtaking you are." He gasped and Katherine grinned. The poor boy was surprised by his words and blushed to the roots of his blond hair. "I...I mean, are you here to see Mr. Percival?"

Laughing, Katherine shook her head. "No, Mr. Marshall, I'm just making a small withdrawal from my account."

The teller, recovering his composure, nodded and stepped back behind his counter. After they had finished conducting her business and he had handed her the money, he stepped out from his post once more. Licking his dry lips nervously, he took her fingers lightly in his own, escorting her to the door. Just as he opened his mouth to speak, Mr. Percival's door opened and the owner of the bank stepped out, spying Katherine immediately.

Crossing the room, he hissed through clenched teeth, "Marshall, why wasn't I informed that Mrs. Radcliffe was here?"

The slightly built young man blanched at the rancor in the bank owner's words. Turning his back on the embarrassed teller, the banker bowed over Katherine's hand before raising it to his lips. "Mrs. Radcliffe, what a very pleasant surprise. And don't you look fetching." He glared at his employee before snapping angrily, "Return to your post at once."

Head down, the younger man slunk behind his counter, watching helplessly as his employer and Mrs. Radcliffe stepped outside. When Katherine emerged, Maggie and the twins rose to greet her.

"Ah, Mrs. Radcliffe, I wonder if you have heard there is to be a picnic after church next Sunday. I believe most of the town will attend and I would be most pleased to act as your escort, for I see you have laid aside your mourning. Why, when word gets out, all manner of suitors will be knocking at your door."

Katherine, surprised at the bluntness of his words, opened her mouth to decline but looking at Maggie and the twins, she realized if she chose not to attend, neither would they and after the long winter, an outing would be good for them.

"Why, thank you Mr. Percival. I know the children will be happy to meet others their own age. I have allowed us to become far too isolated but this will all change now."

Katherine hid her grin, seeing how Henry Percival appeared taken aback at her response to his invitation. She saw him glance disdainfully down at her children and her back stiffened, realizing the invitation was not meant for all of them.

"By all means," he agreed weakly, "picnics are made for the young. And Mrs. McGregor, you and your good husband must also be my guests." His smile was magnanimous, yet Katherine doubted his sincerity. "There, that's settled. We'll meet up after church." Once again he bowed over Katherine's hand before returning to his bank.

The two women, each grasping a toddler's hand, stopped at various shops along the way where they were greeted warmly and the children were fussed over. It seemed everyone was eager to confirm that the widow of Somerset Cottage was no longer in mourning. Soon they reached the hotel where Jamie and lunch awaited.

* * * *

Some days later, with the sun shining brightly the twins, eager for any new adventure, hopped about in a state of unbridled excitement, impatiently awaiting the eagerly anticipated picnic. Only the dire warnings from their mother kept them sitting still through the sermon until the minister, taking pity on all the squirming youngsters of the congregation, gave the final benediction before throwing open the doors of his church.

Greetings were extended as the villagers milled about in the churchyard, all calling out plans for meeting each other at the site chosen for the picnic and soon wagons were rumbling by, the smiling children contained within excitedly shouting to their friends.

Mr. Percival, having joined Katherine and her party in their pew, effusively complimenting her on her plum colored gown and matching bonnet, led the way out of the churchyard. His carriage, liveried driver standing smartly by the open door, waited.

Katherine, perceiving a problem, turned an inquiring eye on Jamie and Maggie but Jamie, having already spied the banker's conveyance, knew they would have to take two carriages, for their own could not accommodate another and the banker's carriage was meant for two. Unseen by the others, a surreptitious grin played about the banker's face as he led a mildly protesting Katherine away from her family and into his carriage.

The day passed quickly as all the children of Carlyle, free of parental restraints, ran wildly about, squealing their happiness in unrestricted delight. The town folk wandered about, chatting and laughing to each other, all the while keeping a watchful eye on their offspring.

Katherine, finding the banker's attentions wearisome, was grateful that her own children took up much of her attention, for she had insisted that Maggie and Jamie have time to stroll about without the added burden of Christine and Declan.

Henry Percival was beginning to feel thwarted in his goal to have her to himself until at last the twins were led off to play a game with the other youngsters of the village. Seizing the opportunity and ignoring her protests, he led Katherine into the woods toward a secluded glade. When at last his steps halted, he turned to her, his eyes boldly raking over her before his hungry gaze fell on the creamy expanse of her breasts.

Katherine, her mind distracted by the children's absence, suddenly found herself crushed in his arms, his mouth hard and searching as they found her lips. Shocked at his boldness, she struggled to free herself.

"Mr. Percival!" She ground out his name through clenched teeth, her green eyes flashing angrily. "Release me this instant!" The sound of her hand striking his face echoed in the surrounding trees.

Realizing he had just possibly ruined any chance to claim her as his own, he stuttered out an apology, professing to have been overcome by her winsome beauty. A shadow of annoyance crossed his face as she, retracing her steps back to the safety of the others, ignored him as he continued to stammer out his regret.

"Please, dear lady," he begged, "I'm a helpless victim of your charms. Oh, please, please, let me prove to you that my intentions are honorable."

At last, reaching the other picnickers, he seized her hand. She hid her annoyance in front of any chance onlookers and, encouraged by her silence, the banker continued to plead his case so earnestly, she felt herself almost relenting. Now, wanting only to be rid of the man, Katherine nodded distractedly as she searched for her children, finding them just as they were being lifted into the carriage by Jamie.

Nodding a cool dismissal, she made her way to her little household and safety, barely hearing his voice as he shouted his intention to call on her soon. Aware that some of the townspeople might have noticed her abrupt departure, he brushed at his tailored jacket self-consciously, waving one last time at the departing carriage before returning to his own transport, brusquely ordering his driver to get him home with all speed and leave these picnicking revelers to enjoy their amusements without him.

* * * *

Slowly the passing of summer and autumn once more proclaimed the coming of winter.

Henry Percival did indeed receive his heart's desire as Katherine reluctantly issued the invitation that he seemed so desirous of receiving. He gradually became a constant visitor to Somerset Cottage, although she was wary of being alone with him and so always had Maggie bustling about the kitchen, the clatter of pots and pans a reminder of her presence. If any others were interested in the comely widow, they soon fell by the wayside, intimidated by the banker's formidable financial prowess, certain that someone as fair as The Widow Radcliffe was beyond their reach.

And the married ladies of the village, matchmakers one and all, smiled at what they saw as a budding romance. The single women bewailed the unfairness of it all, moaning that the widow had already had her chance and was leaving them with no hope of catching the eye of the prosperous banker, the most eligible bachelor in town. None of them would have guessed that, much to the banker's chagrin, he was forced to share Katherine's attention with her twins or the constant interruption of Maggie or her meddlesome husband.

It was on a frosty afternoon early in December that the banker braved the brisk weather and rode out to Somerset Cottage. He had been courting the widow these many months, he thought, and the time to propose marriage was at hand. As the carriage made its way along the bumpy road, he wondered if an attractive woman such as she ever pondered the lack of other suitors, other than himself. Arrogantly, he doubted that she was aware of the influence he exerted over the town, his interest in her enough to ward off any potential rivals.

He had plotted his course very carefully after bungling so badly at that blasted picnic, almost ruining his chances completely. But he was certain that, with such a coveted invitation tucked safely away in his pocket—that should overwhelm her when she was reminded once again of his distinguished social connections. After all, an invitation to the Christmas Ball at the home of John and Sarah Stevens!

And Mrs. Stevens' brother and sister-in-law, Lord and Lady Deniset of England were visiting! Only the cream of New York society would be there, their manor situated closer to Carlyle than the city. What a feather in his cap to have received such an accolade after being overlooked for so many years. He patted his pocket smugly, certain the fetching prize he lusted after, in the person of Katherine Radcliffe, was finally within his grasp. *I'll propose to her on the way home, and perhaps, in sheer happiness, she'll fall into my arms.* He twisted the thin ends of his moustache, lost in thought. *But I'll insist we wait for the nuptials to be performed. That should convince her she's made the right decision.* He rode on, mulling over his plan, examining it for any flaw. *And her attention-stealing brats—well—they'll soon be of an age to be sent off to distant boarding schools. By then, she'll have a new babe or two at her breast and won't even notice them gone.* He chuckled to himself, pompously pleased with the rosy picture he was painting in his mind.

Arriving at the cottage, he was ushered inside and, once tea had been served, Maggie disappeared with Christine and Declan in tow, their childish voices protesting their banishment to the kitchen. The banker, unable to contain his excitement any longer, reached into his pocket and drew out the white card, handing it to Katherine to read.

"Why Henry, aren't you the fortunate one to receive such an invitation."

Surprised at her lack of enthusiasm, he wondered if she was being deliberately obtuse as he lightly patted her hand. "You've misunderstood, my dear. If you but take a closer look, you will see it is addressed to Mr. Henry Percival and Guest. I am requesting your sweet self to be my guest."

Not entirely surprised at his including her on such a grand occasion, she withdrew her hand and picked up her teacup. Although he had been a model of decorum since that debacle in the summer, she had been careful to keep him at arm's length. She fretted that attending this ball might serve to place her in an awkward situation but the thought of an evening of dancing and gaiety weakened her resolve. Unexpectedly, Jonathan's face flashed before her, and she was momentarily lost in the past. *No! He no longer existed, at least not for her!* Her decision made, she lifted her chin, smiling at Henry's hopeful expression. *Here, in this room, was a man who seemed to care for her but,* the thought nagged at her, *could she could learn to love him or any other man?*

Her thoughts flew to her wardrobe. She had the perfect gown, one that Samuel insisted on buying for her first Christmas in Charleston—deep green velvet, with the skirt slashed to reveal a white satin underskirt, and the sleeves, also slashed with white satin, displayed tiny seed pearls and green satin rosettes elegantly accenting the neckline and sleeves. It had looked wonderful on her, she thought but sadly, with Samuel so ill, Christmas had never been celebrated at Seven Oaks while she lived there.

Smothering her misgivings, she voiced her acceptance. *I just want to be young, to laugh and dance the night away. I've been alone and lonely for too long.* Henry, in a burst of passionate exuberance, shattered her calm with the hunger of his kiss, devouring the lush softness of her mouth.

Lost in her nearness, he felt her stiffen before she pushed him away. Apologizing for forgetting himself so completely, he brushed a gentle kiss across her forehead as he took his leave into the cold night air, afraid that if he stayed another minute, she would decline his invitation. As she watched his carriage disappear down the road, she struggled to suppress the misgivings she felt.

* * * *

The carriage ride was overlong, Katherine thought, as Henry droned on about the importance of his social connections and his prosperity. She burrowed deeper into her fur-lined cloak, trying to ward off the cold, wiggling her toes on the hot brick the driver had placed beneath her slippered feet.

Maggie had spent the day with her, overseeing her bath and dressing her hair, twining a string of pearls through the abundant auburn tresses and finally, slipping the gown over her head. Together they chose a pair of emerald earrings and matching necklace, another gift from the generous Samuel. A finely knit wrap, to ward off any chills while at the ball, was settled on her shoulders before they made their way down the stairs and into the kitchen.

The twins had clapped their hands with excitement, exclaiming she looked just like a fairy princess. Since Katherine would most likely arrive home late, Maggie was taking them to her cottage to spend the night.

At last they pulled up before the manor house where footmen were assisting new arrivals from their conveyances, and maids stood inside taking cloaks from the guests. Henry held Katherine's arm possessively, tightening his grip when she attempted to withdraw. They, along with many others, were directed toward the grand salon, the strains of a waltz drifting out to greet them.

On entering the tastefully decorated ballroom, Katherine was delighted to see such elegantly dressed women being whirled about the dance floor in the arms of their handsomely turned-out partners.

Henry drew Katherine into the receiving line where they were presented to Mr. and Mrs. Stevens and their aristocratic visitors from England. Both Mr. Stevens and Lord Deniset spied her as she approached, and both men, although long past middle age, portly and standing next to their wives, preened themselves hoping to impress the stunning creature that stood before them, murmuring a polite greeting first to their wives and then turning to them. Backs stiffened and stomachs pulled in, both men attempted to present as favorable a picture as they could as each in turn bent over her extended hand, lightly kissing her slender fingers in a courtly gesture. Their wives, seeing their would-be Lotharios trying to impress the young beauty, snickered behind their fans, knowing that one so fair would not deign to look at their two old fools.

As Katherine at last reached the end of the receiving line, she was met by a gathering of unattached swains who stood waiting, all vying to claim a dance with the most beautiful woman any of them had ever seen.

Another waltz was just beginning when the boldest amongst them stepped forward and, seizing her hand, introduced himself as Maxwell Henderson, Esquire. As the young man requested the pleasure of this dance, Henry, feeling honor-bound to make similar introductions, introduced her as the Widow Radcliffe and himself as Henry Percival, Banker. The two men bowed to each other before Katherine, turning to Mr. Henderson, Esquire with a tiny smile, allowed herself to be whirled onto the dance floor, a diamond among swirling, colorful precious gems.

The music had ended when a reluctant Maxwell Henderson returned her to the side of a sour-faced Henry Percival. Spying another eager young man approaching, the banker spun her out onto the floor before that hopeful gentleman could reach them. Agitated, he held her too closely and as she tried free herself, he ignored her and the bounds of good taste, pulling her even closer. Dourly, he whirled her about the room, glaring at any male who looked like he was even considering approaching them. The music ended at last, much to Katherine's relief.

Glancing at her escort's sullen features, a flicker of apprehension coursed through her. A passing servant offered them wine and Henry, knowing he was behaving churlishly, took two of the crystal goblets and presented her with one, almost as a peace offering

Wordlessly, they stood back and watched the flowing gowns as the dancers floated past them. Katherine heard his sharp intake of breath as what he perceived as another potential rival's approach, bowing to Henry as he requested the pleasure of the next dance with Katherine.

It was painfully obvious to him that word had spread that the striking lady in green was presently unattached, a widow in fact. This time, without a word or glance, she handed her wine to the banker before she moved onto the dance floor, smiling warmly up at her partner.

And so the evening passed, with Henry becoming more petulant as the minutes ticked by. It was a relief to be away from him, she decided. As she danced, she could feel eyes following her, and she caught herself glancing uneasily over her shoulder. As her eyes nervously swept the room, she finally glimpsed him deep in conversation with their host and his brother-in-law. Relieved, she hoped that being singled out by the men he held in such esteem would put Henry in a more pleasant frame of mind. At last, the music ended but as her partner started to return her to the banker's side, she spied a familiar face.

"Mr. Davenport!"

The lawyer, somewhat astonished at hearing his name, turned and recognized her. Bowing his head in greeting, he admired the picture she presented as she sent her dance partner on his way. Smiling, he led her toward a small knot of people who watched them approach.

"My dear Mrs. Radcliffe, may I present my wife, Lorna and her sister, Larissa." The three women exchanged polite smiles. "Is that the banker, Henry

Percival, across the room? He seems most interested in one of us. By any chance, would he be your escort this evening, my dear?" Seeing her reluctantly nod, the lawyer, thoughtful for a second, continued with the introductions. "And this is my son, Herbert, and his wife, Selma. And for an extraordinary bit of coincidence, I believe you already know this rogue who, I believe is champing at the bit to claim you for the next waltz." A tall figure stepped forward.

Chapter Twenty-One

"Jonathan!"

She stared at him in utter astonishment, confused thoughts and feelings tumbling about her, as he gathered her in his arms, whirling her back into the sea of dancers.

When at last he spoke, his voice was tender, almost a murmur. "Katherine, my sweet, lost love."

With those words in her ears, she tried to pull away but his grip was like steel and, unless she wanted to create a scene, she realized she would have to finish the dance. There was a slight tinge of wonder in his voice as he continued to whisper in her ear. "I've been searching for you for so long, my darling." Again, she tried to extract her hand but he wouldn't release her.

"How did you find me? And why were you even looking? Doesn't marriage agree with you any longer?" The tremor in her voice betrayed the depth of her emotions. A tiny, nagging voice in the back of her mind questioned the wisdom of Samuel imploring her to keep Somerset Cottage and the village of Carlyle a secret, even from Jonathan 'for the time being'. *Good advice*, she silently argued, *his future was with Isabella, her own life no concern of his!*

"Don't speak, my love. Just let me hold you." His voice was low and purposefully seductive. As he whirled her about the room, the two of them were unaware of the many eyes following them as they moved in perfect harmony across the floor.

The music had ended but he continued to hold onto her until a hand clamped on his shoulder. He turned and met the scowling face of Henry Percival. Smiling disarmingly, he bowed to the enraged man. "And you, I take it, are Katherine's escort?"

"Jonathan, may I introduce Henry Percival, owner of the bank in Carlyle." She spoke quickly over her choking, beating heart, becoming aware that they were still on the dance floor, the object of much curious scrutiny. "Please, let us move away from here," she entreated both men. "People are beginning to stare."

Henry, lips compressed tightly together, barely glanced at her. "You have given my name to this intruder, madam, but I have yet to hear his, and also an explanation as to why he feels he has the right to continue to fondle you."

Katherine, fearing an explosion, faced him, hesitantly explaining that he was her husband's cousin, deftly assuring him they hadn't seen each other since shortly before she had donned widow's weeds. As soon as the words were out, she caught Jonathan's startled look. Dropping her eyes before his questioning gaze, she missed the wry but indulgent glint that appeared in his steel grey eyes. Henry gave a snort of derision, sensing he wasn't being told the whole story.

Jonathan nodded his head in the direction of the banker. "Mr. Percival, a pleasure to make your acquaintance, sir." His grey eyes flashed mischievously as he handed Katherine over to her escort. "Katherine, it's been wonderful seeing you once more. Perhaps we'll have a chance to reminisce before the evening ends?" Taking her hand, his lips brushed her fingers.

Henry curtly nodded his dismissal of the man he was swiftly coming to regard as an interloper. Whistling a cheery tune, Jonathan turned and walked away, Katherine's eyes following him until he was swallowed up in the crowd.

It was only a short time later that dinner was announced. Henry, grasping Katherine's elbow, steered her toward the dining room. There, the usual long tables, where one's conversation was restricted to the person on either side, had been replaced by more intimate round tables seating eight people. Individual name cards were at each place setting, causing Henry to guide her about the room searching for their names. Finally, with a grunt of satisfaction, he held out a cushioned chair, which she sank gracefully into. Taking no notice of the other names, he smugly assured himself that she would be his alone for the duration of the dinner at least. His pompous, self-satisfied air soon disappeared as Harvey Davenport and his party approached their table. Glancing up, the banker could only groan inwardly as they smilingly seated themselves, leaving an empty chair directly opposite Katherine, which was soon occupied by a broadly grinning Jonathan Radcliffe.

"What are the odds of something like this happening?" Mr. Davenport chuckled in amusement.

"Yes, what are the odds?" No one but Jonathan heard Henry Percival mutter these words, offering the banker a cheeky grin. Looking at the smug expression on Jonathan's face, the banker speculated whether this impudent fellow had had the impertinence to switch the place cards around to suit himself.

As course after course was served, Katherine barely touched the delicacies placed in front of her. The Davenports, sensing undercurrents between their dining companions, tried to distract the others with light, witty conversation.

Harvey, the senior Davenport, hoping to dispel the somber mood, thought to regale the company with his first meeting of Katherine. As he recounted the spectacle of three nuns making their way down the gangplank, and one of the three answering to the name of 'Mrs. Radcliffe', he wondered at the wisdom of telling the tale as he saw the sudden pallor of Katherine and the shocked countenance of Jonathan.

The banker leered speculatively at the downcast expression of the young woman but the others, taking in her angelic visage, could only sit back in amazement at such daring.

Katherine blushed as she saw their admiring looks and, smiling shyly, she accepted their words of praise, all the while avoiding Jonathan's questioning eyes.

It was Lorna Davenport, her eyes twinkling, who asked the obvious question. "But why, my dear girl, did you find it necessary to disguise yourself as a nun?"

Laughing softly, she met the older woman's warm gaze. "It was self-preservation, madam. A woman travelling alone would be considered fair game but three women belonging to a religious order, why, they cease being women and become black robed and untouchable." Once again, laughter rang out, all but one of the party admiring her ingenuity.

Her bewilderment at the reappearance of Jonathan in her life was something of which Henry was very keenly aware. His suspicions aroused, he held his questions. Time enough on the ride home. At last, the meal ended and, as the throng began to leave the dining room in small chattering groups, Katherine knew she could not endure another moment, her much anticipated evening now lay in shambles.

Excusing herself from the others, she mounted the grand staircase and withdrew to a small room where several of the ladies were resting or having their stays loosened by maids hovering nearby. Sinking into the deep red cushion of a chair, she examined her options. She couldn't stay here, not with Jonathan haunting her steps. Pausing, she recalled their very limited conversation. He hadn't actually said he was here because of her, he had just cleverly whispered those empty words of love he so excelled at. She brightened. Of course, that was it. It was happenstance. He obviously knew nothing of the life she had made for herself. She deliberated further. Henry was becoming a very serious problem also. The easiest course would be to claim sickness and use his carriage to make her way home. Would he agree? He must!

Rising purposefully from the deep cushion of the chair, she straightened her shoulders, prepared to do battle. Descending the stairs, she found Henry loitering in the main hallway, unsure of where she had disappeared. Unveiling her plan she felt her heart sink as he vigorously declared that travelling home alone was the last thing he would allow her to do.

As he arrogantly instructed a servant to have his carriage brought round, he spied an inconspicuous alcove, which he insisted she secrete herself in until his return. At her weary nod, he left to make his excuses to their hosts and collect their cloaks. Unhappy that he was so adamant about accompanying her, she was at least grateful that, should Jonathan be casting an eye about for her, he would never find her, tucked away as she was.

At last the banker returned and, as he helped her don her cloak she felt a trickle of apprehension as his lips brushed her bare shoulders. Making their way toward the door, Katherine held her breath, expecting Jonathan to magically appear as he had done so often in the past. Unchallenged by anyone, they were soon safely ensconced in the carriage, with Henry solicitously tucking a travel rug about her and fussing with a small lamp until the interior of the carriage glowed dimly as it turned onto the road to Carlyle.

They had been travelling only a few moments when Henry took her slender hand in his. "My dear Katherine, I have been waiting the whole night for this moment." He paused, his words stumbling and clumsy, before heedlessly continuing his suit. "Katherine, will you do me the very great honor of becoming Mrs. Henry Percival?" Uncharacteristically nervous, he stroked his thin moustache, suddenly apprehensive at the empty silence.

Stunned, Katherine could only stare at the man, shocked, not just with his proposal but also because of his appalling behavior all evening. "Henry, this is so unexpected. I, well, I simply never expected such a declaration from you." She stumbled over her words, uncertain of his reaction if she refused him outright. After all, they were miles from anywhere and he had already demonstrated a quick temper when crossed.

Holding on to her hand, he ignored her words, which he thought were not quite a refusal and continued, almost feverishly. "I would make you happy, my beloved. And you'll never want for anything. I'm quite a rich man, you know. I can well afford to send your children to the best boarding schools. And before you know it, there will be the pitter-patter of little feet when you bring Henry Percival the Second into the world, and any other babies that come along will also be welcome."

"Henry, stop!" She held up her hand, refusing to let him take it again, her tone coolly disapproving. "Heed me well, Henry. Never would I consider sending my babies away, to boarding school or any other place you might have in mind." Staring uneasily down at her lap, her fingers fidgeted as she selected her next words carefully. "Henry, I must tell you something. Perhaps I should have told you earlier but I never guessed the depth of your feelings." She gazed into his dark eyes as he waited impatiently for her words. "Henry, I cannot have another baby. When the twins were born, something went wrong and there will be no other children, ever." With a shattered look, he withdrew from her, digesting this devastating revelation.

As the carriage sped along, he seemed to reach a decision. Wordlessly, his arm stole around Katherine's shoulders, pulling her close. Annoyed at being mauled, she stiffened and moved away. Not discouraged in the least, he kept his arm about her shoulder while his other hand crept inside her cloak until his grasping fingers brutally squeezed her breast. With a cry of outrage, Katherine pushed him away. "Henry, behave yourself."

Incensed at the rejection to his advances, he seized her slender shoulders and, leaning his face close to hers, he snarled, "Why, you brazen harlot!" His words spilled from his mouth, filled with such venom that Katherine recoiled in fear. "You think you can dance the night away with anything wearing trousers and then act the innocent when I draw near?"

He lifted her face upwards as he crushed her to him, smothering her cries with angry, punishing kisses. Struggling to free herself, she could feel him once more groping for her breasts. Beating helplessly at his chest, she screamed for the driver to stop the carriage but the poor man had earlier been instructed to stop only if he, his employer, should personally bid him to do so. She felt the frosty air caress her bare skin as her attacker succeeded in freeing her breasts from the confines of her gown.

Frantically she screamed again, helplessly, hopelessly, and as tears of frustration coursed down her cheeks she felt her strength ebbing until unexpectedly, her small fist connected painfully with his eye, and his face contorted with rage.

Mercilessly he pinched her breasts, his smile grim as her shrill scream carried across the crisp, cold air. Raking his face with her fingernails brought forth another string of curses from his tightly clenched mouth. He was now beyond caring how badly he hurt her, his hand drawing back to deliver what he hoped would be a mind-numbing blow, but he had time only to bellow in surprise as the door of the carriage flew open. Katherine, surprised and very grateful, breathed a sigh of relief as Jonathan daringly leapt from his galloping horse through the narrow doorway.

"Good evening once again, sir. Please forgive me for dropping in so unexpectedly."

The banker, snarling his contempt of the man, let his hand drop casually to a concealed panel below the seat.

"I wouldn't try anything so foolish, Mr. Percival", he chided mockingly. Glancing down, the banker saw that Jonathan was holding a gun and so returned his searching hand to his lap. Jonathan eyed the disheveled Katherine. "Is all well with you, my sweet?" His voice was calm, his gaze steady. At her nod, his eyes swung back to the banker. "Mr. Percival, I believe Mrs. Radcliffe is ready to part company with you. Would you be so kind as to have your driver stop the carriage and we'll be on our way."

Glowering his displeasure, the banker signaled his driver to stop. Following Jonathan's lead, Katherine moved cautiously to the carriage door. Whistling sharply, his horse galloped up to him. Cheekily saluting his adversary, Jonathan mounted his restive horse and, reaching across, lifted Katherine onto his steed. They both heard a bellowed command for the driver to proceed and, without a word, the carriage trundled on.

Katherine, hugging her cloak tightly about her, shivered in the wintry night air as snowflakes whirled about them. Jonathan pulled his cloak around her, his arms enfolding her. She leaned back, soaking in his warmth and strength as he urged his horse onward, following the trail of the carriage, which was quickly disappearing from sight. There was a gentle softness in his voice when next he spoke. "You will have to direct me, my love, for I have no idea where we are or where we are heading."

Katherine assured him that they were indeed on the road to Carlyle and she lived but a short distance beyond. A sharp blast of icy air hastened them on until at last Somerset Cottage came into view.

Jonathan lowered her to the snow covered ground before dismounting himself. Holding her arm as her slippered feet cautiously followed the icy path to the cottage, he released her at the door before turning his horse toward the barn.

Katherine stepped into the welcoming warmth of her snug home and, as she added wood to the fire Jamie had left burning, her cloak fell open, revealing another gown ruined by a man's lust. Anger coursed through her at the memory of the disastrous evening. A gentle tap on the door signaled Jonathan's arrival. *Well,* she thought, *at last I will get some answers,* as she called for him to come in.

Hugging her cloak tightly about her, she welcomed him into her home, this man who had haunted her dreams for so long. She watched as he glanced about, a spark of some indefinable emotion in his eyes. Seeming satisfied with what he saw, he smiled, warm grey eyes gazing into the icy emerald depths of her eyes. Finding his nearness disconcerting, she moved back to the fireplace to stir the embers. Again her cloak fell open and, cheeks flushing with embarrassment as his gaze fell on her bare skin, she hastily pulled it closed. He swore softly as he proclaimed his intention of seeking out the banker on the morrow.

Katherine's head snapped up at his words. "Please, no great harm was done but if you were to seek revenge, that would start tongues wagging." Smiling ruefully, she tugged the cloak tighter. "You really must excuse me so I might change my gown before someone spies me like this and attributes its cause to you."

Saying that, she turned on her heels and fled up the stairs as if a demon was chasing her, into her bedchamber where she swiftly changed her torn gown for a warm frock, one that would preserve her modesty with the visitor downstairs. As she noiselessly descended the stairs, she was able to observe her unexpected guest as he stared thoughtfully into the leaping flames in the fireplace. He turned at her approach, smiling as he followed her into the kitchen where, wordlessly, she moved about, putting the kettle on the fire as she prepared tea. At last, they faced each other across the wooden table.

"Well Jonathan," she spoke at last, hoping he couldn't hear the wild beating of her heart, "you owe me some sort of an explanation. You said you had been searching for me and yet, purely by chance, we both attend a Christmas ball, a ball to which neither of us had been personally invited. I was Henry Percival's guest and you were with the Davenports. How did such a coincidence come about?"

"It's no great mystery. I have been searching for you these many months past but the nuns, including the Abbess, refused to admit to any knowledge of your whereabouts." Pausing to clear his throat, he continued with his tale. "I returned there one last time to plead my case and was again refused. But this time there was a difference. An old nun with a romantic soul escorted me to the gate. She told me you had left the convent with Sister Claire and Sister Ursula, who had been sent to an orphanage somewhere in New York. And so I closed my practice, left Georgia and travelled north." He paused, sipping the hot tea she had poured, gazing adoringly and openly at her, as if she were the woman he loved above everything else in this world.

"As to how I came to attend the ball, that's really not a mystery either. I travelled to New York City to begin my search there. After all, how many orphanages could there be? By chance, I met an old school chum, Herbert Davenport. We studied medicine together. He kindly invited me to dinner where I met his wife, Selma." He smiled at a distant memory. "Selma saw me as an eligible bachelor and for weeks paraded one unmarried friend after another before me. I challenged and frustrated her matchmaking abilities to no end."

Sitting opposite each other, he tried to take her hand but she pulled it back. Shrugging, he continued his tale. "As the weeks wore on, I eventually met Herbert's parents, Harvey and Lorna. Harvey commented on the name Radcliffe, finding it an amazing coincidence that he should know three people bearing it. When questioned, he admitted to knowing Samuel and having business dealings with him. For some reason, he was hesitant about the second person bearing that name but I continued to badger him until he admitted knowing you, but declared it was only in a legal capacity. I told him that I had been searching for you for many, many months, and begged him for news of your whereabouts. The only information I could wring from him was that you were in the state of New York but he refused to divulge exactly where, promising that he would write and ask your permission before doing so. The letter was only just dispatched so you won't have received it yet."

He changed the course of the conversation abruptly, taking her hand and holding it, despite her effort to free herself. "Herbert, upon learning I had left my practice in Georgia, invited me to join his surgery in New York." When he spoke again, his voice was tender, almost a murmur. "Would you consider moving to the city, Katherine?"

Impatiently, she ignored the question. "What of your wife, Jonathan, your precious Isabella?" Her eyes were sharp and assessing as she awaited his answer.

Unspoken pain was alive and glowing in his eyes as he answered her. "Isabella is dead." His voice became crisp and clear. Her eyes widened in surprise as she waited for him to continue. "She died in childbirth."

Chapter Twenty-Two

Contrite, she murmured, "I'm sorry, Jonathan, truly I am."

He smiled at her. "We didn't have a happy marriage, Katherine. After leaving you at the convent, I found it impossible to pretend any depth of feeling for her and she sensed it. Often she would ask me who I was thinking of whenever she caught me daydreaming, which was far too often for her liking. One day she asked if it was you I couldn't forget." He paused, his eyes downcast as he recalled the accusations and arguments. "If you remember, I always returned to Belle Isle after meeting you. In the beginning, I told her only about Simon and his treatment of you. Perhaps it was the way I looked when I mentioned your name, or perchance I talked in my sleep," he chuckled softly, "but she began to accuse me of having more than cousinly feelings for you. I denied it at first but..." He shrugged his broad shoulders. "Your name became a thorn in her side."

"She was forever accusing me of being in love with you, no matter how many times I denied it—to her as well as myself. I tried to be a husband to her but her incessant jealousy wore me down. Her father and brother knew things weren't right between us but thankfully they left us alone, hoping we would sort it out." He paused. "And when she fell pregnant..." He ran his fingers through his hair. "It was a difficult pregnancy and by the time she went into labor, well, I think she just lost heart and both she and the babe died." He sat for several moments, lost in the past.

Reluctant to intrude into his thoughts again, Katherine poured a second cup of tea for each of them. Glancing out of the window, she saw the snow still swirling about, covering the ground completely. Yawning delicately behind her hand, she cleared her throat as she rose from the chair.

"The snow hasn't stopped, Jonathan, and since you don't know the area, you'll have to spend the night here." Seeing his expression change from astonishment to a speculating smile, she stiffened. "You can sleep down here on the sofa or, if you don't behave, out in the barn with your horse." Hurrying up the stairs, she quickly returned carrying a blanket and pillow. As she lay the bedding on the sofa, he seized her hand.

"And what of you, my sweet Katherine? After vanishing in the guise of a nun, how did you come to live here, in this tiny village of Carlyle?"

The heavy lashes that shadowed her cheeks flew up. She stared wordlessly

175

up at him, her heart pounding. Finding his nearness disturbing, she moved away from him. "Samuel transferred ownership of this cottage to me just before he died. Even Simon didn't know of its existence or, if he did, Samuel thought he would most likely assume it had been sold years before. He cautioned me to say nothing of it to anyone, including you. He arranged for the Featherstone's to locate Maggie and her husband in New York and offer them the post of housekeeper and groundskeeper which, to my great good fortune, they accepted. After leaving the convent, I travelled north and found them waiting for me. I have lived here quietly ever since, or at least I did until this evening. It strikes me as strange, Jonathan, that I could live unmolested in this hamlet until the day you chose to enter my life again." Turning from him, she walked gracefully to the staircase.

His voice rang out in frustration as she slowly mounted the stairs to her bedroom. "Then, madam, the men of this village must be blind and near dead to have been able to ignore your presence so completely. How did you accomplish such a feat, Katherine?" His voice, at first mocking, become harsh and demanding as he moved toward her.

Irritated by his scornful tone, she spun around, giving him a hostile glare. "I resorted to a harmless deception, Jonathan. I became "The Widow Radcliffe" and wore mourning until a few months ago." There was a bitter edge of cynicism in her voice. "And do you know something, Jonathan Radcliffe? The men of Carlyle respected my so-called grief and left me alone." She tossed the words out contemptuously before fleeing up the remainder of the stairs, the slamming of her bedroom door echoing through the cottage while he, astounded once again at her ingenuity, could only stare bemusedly after her.

* * * *

A great clatter of pots and pans woke Katherine the following morning and, as she stretched languidly, the sound of an unfamiliar masculine voice drifted up the stairs. Sitting up, memories of the entire disastrous evening flooded back.

A string of profanity reached her ears along with the sound of breaking china. Hurriedly she scrambled out of bed and, after performing the briefest of ablutions, she slipped into her dress and hastily made her way downstairs. Entering the kitchen, she had to stifle the urge to giggle for there was Jonathan, obviously unfamiliar with the workings of a kitchen, surrounded by broken china, a boiling kettle and a look of complete bewilderment on his handsome face. Pushing him gently toward a waiting chair, she became a picture of efficiency as she poured water into the waiting teapot and then turned to the task of sweeping the remains of the shattered cup from the floor. She could feel his eyes following her every move. Glancing out the window toward Maggie and Jamie's homey abode across the way, she knew Maggie, spying the lights on, would soon be over.

"I can only offer you tea, Jonathan. I know you prefer coffee but I could never acquire a taste for it and, having no one to please but myself, I never buy it. Luckily, both Maggie and Jamie also prefer it, and when any of the ladies of Carlyle come calling, they seem content." She babbled mindlessly on while flitting about the kitchen, clearly on edge about something. Jonathan finally stood before her, intimidating and bold.

"You're as nervous as a cat." He grinned wickedly. "Does my being here upset you so?" His voice was low and purposefully seductive. "Or are you perhaps worried about Maggie and her good opinion of you?"

Taking a deep, unsteady breath, she stepped back. "You flatter yourself, Jonathan. You rescued me from an awkward situation last night, and for that, you have my gratitude. But please, don't think for one moment that I want to pick up where we left off so long ago." Her voice trailed off. "It's getting light now and I think you should leave."

As the words left her mouth, the door opened, a familiar face peeking into the room, uncertainty written across her face. "Maggie!" Jonathan called out, delighted at seeing her again and relieved at the interruption.

"Why, Mr. Radcliffe." she sputtered, confusion written across her face.

Sensing an undercurrent of tension in the mistress of the cottage, Maggie hesitated. "I merely thought to get breakfast started, Miss Katherine. The children are hungry but are helping Jamie clear a path to your cottage and the barn." As her words faded away, excited voices could be heard as the door opened once more. The new arrivals smiled at the two women but stopped abruptly as their eyes spied the unfamiliar figure standing in the tiny kitchen.

The little boy, always the leader in their childish games, looked Jonathan up and down, his young mind trying to understand why a visitor would come calling so early in the morning. "Mama" he began, watching the stranger warily, "who is this man?"

Maggie gently squeezed his shoulder, admonishing him about his manners and Jonathan, expecting her to make the introductions to her brood, smiled at both the children and the lanky man who now stood in the doorway. The little girl, shyly hiding behind Maggie's skirt, squinted upward at him and smiled. Suddenly both children left the safe haven of Maggie and darted across the room into the welcoming arms of their mother.

Jonathan, speechless for an instant, realized his mistake and turned to her, shock written across his face as he surveyed the exchange of hugs and kisses. "Katherine," he stammered, "are these children…?"

Disdainfully she raised herself to her full height as she faced him, lifting her chin and meeting his questioning gaze straight on. "Yes, Jonathan," her voice clipped and cold, "these are my children, Declan and Christine Radcliffe. Say hello to the gentleman, children." There was defiance in her tone as well as a subtle challenge.

Declan stepped forward. "Good morning, sir." But Christine, shyly hiding her face in her mother's skirt, would only peek out and whisper a greeting. Dazed, he looked about him, realizing he was under intense scrutiny by the three adults. He bent down and faced the boy, taking his small hand and shaking it solemnly. "Good day, Declan, I'm very pleased to make your acquaintance." The small boy beamed at Jonathan. He leaned over and quietly informed Jonathan that his sister was very shy, not like him at all.

"Well, Declan, that is sometimes the way of little girls. I hope she will talk to me before I have to leave."

Katherine, confused at the exchange between the two, turned back to the doorway and the one who lingered there. "And this is Jamie McGregor, Maggie's husband." The two men eyed each other suspiciously before giving the slightest of nods, Jamie recognizing the name of the man Katherine had called out in her labor.

Katherine herded the children into the parlor, listening to their exciting tales of sleeping away from home, leaving the kitchen to Maggie to cook breakfast for them all. Aware that Jonathan had followed them, she watched as he wandered restlessly about the room. The children withdrew to a corner of the room to play, near enough that Declan felt he could keep a watchful eye on this unexpected visitor.

Jonathan dropped down on the seat opposite Katherine. She imparted an air of calm and self-confidence as she waited for him to speak. Hesitant at first, he was unsure how he should broach the subject.

"Katherine, why didn't you tell me..." his voice, thick and unsteady, trailed off.

Her voice was heavy with sarcasm as she faced him, eyes blazing, shaking her head in dismay. "Tell you!" she exploded. Realizing how loudly she had spoken, she lowered her voice, smiling reassuringly at both children as they watched the scene unfolding before them. She continued, speaking softly. "You were a married man, Jonathan. What would you have had me do, invite you and your wife to the christening?"

Both children, alert to the sharp edge of her voice, moved protectively to their mother's side, ready to do battle with this tall stranger if need be. Katherine, aware that they were apprehensive, strove to lower her voice, smiling at them as she assured them that all was well. Aware of Jonathan, hands locked together behind his back as he glared impatiently out the window, she hugged both offspring just as Maggie called that breakfast was on the table. Young appetites hooted in glee as they quickly headed off toward the dining room, leaving Jonathan and Katherine alone.

She shifted uncomfortably under his dark and unfathomable gaze. His hand, suddenly tender, pushed stray tendrils of hair from her cheek. "Madam, I believe we've been summoned to the breakfast table." There was a trace of laughter in his voice. "And I confess I am most eager to become better acquainted with young Master Declan and Mistress Christine Radcliffe." He tucked her arm into his as he escorted her into the dining room where the others awaited.

Jonathan was captivated by the twins, seeing both Katherine and himself in each of them. After they had eaten breakfast, he sat on the floor, talking and playing, whilst Katherine watched, almost unnoticed, as she plied her needle to a basket of mending. Maggie and Jamie had discretely left the cottage after breakfast, returning only to set out lunch before they disappeared once more. After lunch was eaten, Katherine insisted, despite the protests of all three, that naptime had indeed arrived. Tugging at Jonathan's hands, both begged him to read them a story as they were led by a smiling Katherine to their room. As the adults later made their way down the stairs, they shared a companionable silence.

Reaching the bottom of the stairs, Katherine found herself being spun around, Jonathan's nearness making her senses reel. She quickly moved into the parlor, sinking gracefully into an overstuffed chair. He stood before her, a dark figure of a man, big and powerful. Glancing up, green eyes meeting grey, she felt his strong hands pulling her to her feet. His eyes travelled over her face, searching the depths of her eyes. His arms encircled her, her soft curves molding to the contours of his lean body. His mouth covered hers hungrily, devouring the softness of her lips and she returned his kisses with reckless abandon, savoring the moment. A light tapping at the window broke them apart and Katherine, breathing shakily, laughed softly as she spied a small branch from a nearby tree tap once more. As he moved to take her in his arms again, she stepped back, holding up her arms in a forbidding gesture.

"Jonathan, stop!" She quickly withdrew a few paces as he moved toward her, his eyes glowing with a savage inner fire.

"Damn it, Katherine. I've been dreaming of this moment for so many long, lonely months. Let me hold you at least, nothing more." His voice, deep and sensual, sent a ripple of awareness through her. Unyielding, she shook her head and retreated to the chair she had been sitting in short moments before.

"Jonathan, we have to talk. You're going too fast for me." Her green eyes bored into his, daring him to cross the barrier she was trying to erect. Frustrated, he made an elaborate bow and sank down into the chair opposite her.

"Why have you been searching for me, Jonathan?"

Not entirely surprised at her question, he again studied her beloved face. "Do you really have to ask?"

"Jonathan, the last words you spoke to me before abandoning me at the convent were that you loved me more than life itself and, oh yes, you offered to buy a house to keep me and any bastards I might have in." Tears stung her eyes as she again felt the pain he had dealt her on that most horrible of days.

"I tried to explain to you, Katherine—it was a debt I owed to Philip Beauchamp. He rescued my mother from a life of penury and financed my education, believing that he was assuring his daughter a life of ease, married to a doctor." His voice was thick and unsteady. She glanced at him, uncertainty making her hesitant.

"And now, Jonathan? I no longer need you to buy me a house to keep your bastards in. And if I'm careful, I have enough money to live on for some years.

Samuel was determined to take care of me, even from the grave." Her voice was mocking, as if hoping to make him feel some of the pain she had endured a lifetime ago.

His tone was contemptuous when next he spoke. "Is that what you think, madam? That I want you as my mistress!" He spoke the words with the certainty of a man who could never be satisfied with only a dream, his voice low and smooth. "I told you that day that I loved you more than life itself and that hasn't changed. The only difference today is that I am released from a burden I neither contracted nor wanted. I can freely and most lovingly ask you to be my wife, to share my life and let me take care of you and those two imps sleeping so innocently upstairs. Don't they deserve to know their father?" There was a faint glint of humor in his eyes when he spoke again. "And it's the only way I can think of to always be on hand to protect you from the Spanish Jacks and Henry Percivals of this world."

Tears flowed unnoticed down her cheeks as she rose from the chair and flung herself into his outstretched arms, sobbing and babbling incoherently. As he gathered her close, he felt his heart swell, his eyes brimming with both tenderness and passion. At last he untangled her arms and gently pushed her back into her chair. She watched, fascinated, as he knelt on one knee, all the while holding her hands in his.

His voice was husky with emotion as he spoke the words. "Katherine Maguire Radcliffe, I love you more than life itself. I have searched long for you and now, having found you once more, will never let you go. Will you marry me, my one true love?" And once again, his words were lost in a flurry of arms and tears as his one true love declared that marrying him was what she had been created for.

Epilogue

Another season was unfolding as the carriage turned onto a broad tree-lined avenue in the rapidly growing city of New York. Katherine and the children peered excitedly from the window as they eagerly watched for the brownstone that was now their home.

Katherine, recalling Henry Percival's reaction that she could bear no more children, had been reluctant to tell Jonathan but knew she must before they spoke their vows and so, one evening when they were strolling about her small garden, she invited him to sit beside her on a bench. Hesitantly, she told him of her pregnancy and the fact that both midwives agreed she would bear no other babies. His eyes were deep and contemplative as he listened to her tale, and when she had finished, he gathered her into his arms and held her closely.

"My own sweet love, we already have two beautiful children. I will always regret so many things—such as not being by your side for your ordeal, and I will never regain those lost years of our babies' first words and first steps, but Katherine, we have each other and, God willing, we will have many more years together. If there are no more babies, I will never have to worry about you and the risks of childbirth." With those words, she nestled into his welcoming arms, content to bask in his love.

It was some weeks later that Maggie wrote from Somerset Cottage trumpeting her and Jamie's joy that at last they were going to be blessed with a wee bairn. Her happiness rang through the pages and Katherine rejoiced with her friend, already planning to invite them to visit her and her family in the city.

As she sat at her tiny writing desk, a warm glow flowed through her. She felt an overwhelming surge of love and peace within her being, exulting in her happiness and feeling more alive than she ever had before. No more would there be dragons of happenstance because she at last had found her place, in the arms of the man she loved.

CPSIA information can be obtained at www.ICGtesting.com
Printed in the USA
267367BV00001B/10/P